THE A...
1ST PERSON
A NARRATIVE

George Register (signature)

GEORGE A REGISTER

outskirtspress
DENVER, COLORADO

This is a work of fiction. The events and characters described herein are imaginary and are not intended to refer to specific places or living persons. The opinions expressed in this manuscript are solely the opinions of the author and do not represent the opinions or thoughts of the publisher. The author has represented and warranted full ownership and/or legal right to publish all the materials in this book.

THE APOSTLES 1ST PERSON A NARRATIVE
All Rights Reserved.
Copyright © 2016 GEORGE A REGISTER
v1.0

Cover Photo © 2016 thinkstockphotos.com. All rights reserved - used with permission.

This book may not be reproduced, transmitted, or stored in whole or in part by any means, including graphic, electronic, or mechanical without the express written consent of the publisher except in the case of brief quotations embodied in critical articles and reviews.

Outskirts Press, Inc.
http://www.outskirtspress.com

ISBN: 978-1-4787-7335-1

Library of Congress Control Number: 2016905797

Outskirts Press and the "OP" logo are trademarks belonging to Outskirts Press, Inc.

PRINTED IN THE UNITED STATES OF AMERICA

A Note from the Author

HI, FOLKS!

I think it will take you only a few minutes to figure out that I'm not an accomplished writer. I've never tried to write before, but a nudge from our Lord said this was to be written. We are not to ask why or try and change His mind. So here we go.

Almost three years ago I was hit in the head by a spiritual hammer, telling me to write about His chosen apostles. For a year I fought the idea, but Jesus wouldn't leave me alone. So I gave in and started researching each one, and you would never believe the material that is out there.

I have had so much fun writing this. I've learned so much from studying about the different apostles and the details of their lives.

This book will not have "chapters" in it. The reason, in my feeble brain, is that we are going to be looking at an apostle through the eyes of that apostle. You will be able to see this right from the start. You know what is different about this book also is you do not have to read it from cover to cover. If you want to read about John, you can start there and then go to Peter. Each individual apostle has his own story.

I have used the Bible as much as possible; but if you look closely, a lot of times, several years will have passed between journeys. It is in these times when I have used many traditional resources, sources other than the Bible, to fill in the blank spots in their missionary journeys.

You will also find that most of the apostles were killed in various fashions. The Bible only records two of the apostle's deaths. A lot of accepted deaths are just traditional. For example, Peter being crucified upside down is from traditional sources; the Bible does not say this. But there are reliable sources that say that is the way He died, so that is how I had him die in this book. I have been faithful in keeping to the Scriptures when and where possible. But please be assured this is not designed, nor meant to be Biblically correct. This is designed to be, what I feel is, the way the apostle felt, the joy, bewilderment, pain, and suffering each one went through. I also tried to capture their distinct personalities. Each one of them reacted to Jesus in different ways. Some were convinced of Who He was right away, and some took a little more time. One thing is for sure; they all came to the same conclusion that Jesus was the Messiah.

Try putting yourself in the apostles' shoes as you are reading. Feel each one's personality, habits, and manners. Read along enjoying the weather and the dusty roads right along with each of them. Once again, I have had a blast putting this together, so I hope you have just as much fun reading it.

Table of Contents

APOSTLE SIMON PETER 1
APOSTLE ANDREW 19
APOSTLE JAMES (SON OF ZEBEDEE) 40
APOSTLE JOHN (SON OF ZEBEDEE) 57
APOSTLE PHILIP 82
APOSTLE BARTHOLOMEW 98
APOSTLE THOMAS 112
APOSTLE MATTHEW 125
APOSTLE JAMES ALPHAEUS 140
APOSTLE THADDEUS 153
APOSTLE SIMON 165
APOSTLE JUDAS ISCARIOT 178
APOSTLE MATTHIAS 193
APOSTLE PAUL 213

APOSTLE
SIMON PETER

"HEY, YOU, IF you going to hang around then get your (BLEEP) over here. I'm going to shove off here in a little bit. I don't like (BLEEP) people that don't work, so get ahold of that net and help or get the (BLEEP) out of here. Once we are out to sea I'll talk with you. Don't you forget who is in charge of this (BLEEP) boat. It's me, Simon . . . I'm sorry, I will try to watch my language.

"I have a few minutes here, but if something comes up, I'll have to leave you, okay? As I said, my name is Simon. My father was named Jon. I was born in Bethsaida. That is on the western coast on the Sea of Galilee. I don't remember anything about living there because my dad moved to Capernaum to work with Mr. Zebedee. Soon afterward, my father passed away from some disease. So my brother Andrew and I came to live with Zebedee and Salome his wife. They have two boys; their names are James and John. They are the same age as my brother and me. Boy, did we have fun; trouble was always around us. But since we have grown up, I have bought my own boat and have joined up with James and John, along with Andrew and Mr. Zebedee. I guess you could say this is a family business. Living with Zebedee is the reason I became a fisherman.

"Since we are out on the sea most of the time, I don't have any formal education. Zebedee tried his best to teach us all about the laws, but I didn't listen too well. I did learn how to speak Greek though. It kind of has an accent to it, because my natural language is Galilean.

"I must go help with the nets; it is time to bring them in. You go down the other side of the boat and help haul the nets in. As soon as we get the nets in and dock, you're free to go."

It seems to me that the fishing in this lake is getting harder and harder by the day. The weather has been great, in the upper 80s. We haven't had that many storms lately, and the ones we have haven't been very strong. I tell you, we have had some strong ones in the past, sometimes the waves can get to 15-20 feet tall. The wind sort of blows over the top of the lake because it lays over 700 feet below sea level. I was at the other end of the lake when one came up. I really didn't think I would be able to get to shore. I waited it out and as soon as it calmed down, I shoved off and tried to make it back home. The lake is 33 miles long and a little over 8 miles wide so it took a while to reach home. As soon as I got home my wife helped with drying the fish. It didn't take too long, like I said, the fishing isn't very good.

Oh, what a beautiful morning! I had my breakfast fixed by my family and have my nets all laid out and mended. My boat is washed and the deck is clean. The wind is blowing a little and that is a sure sign a storm will brew up this afternoon, so I feel I deserve to have a day off. My brother has been listening to a man called John

THE APOSTLES 1ST PERSON A NARRATIVE

preaching about a Messiah that is coming. I have heard of this Man but can't say I know very much about Him. I value what my brother has to say and he says the Man makes a lot of sense. I believe I'll go down the street and hear what He is preaching.

This is kind of fun; I haven't taken a day off for quite some time. As I stroll down the street I look around at all the people running here and there. I wonder where they all are going. I didn't know that there was a new shop on this side of town. Whoa, I just about got run over by a man and his camel; I guess I had better pay a little better attention to where I'm going. Looks like the city has removed a lot of the big stones from the middle of the road. It's about time. I'm starting to get into the housing part of town. Most all the homes are the same, one or two rooms, lots of the people sleep up on the roof, where it is a lot cooler. I am surprised that there aren't more people in town.

I have made it to the river. I now know why the town was almost empty, everyone is down here at the river. Oh, look over there; my brother is talking to some people. I don't think this John guy has started speaking yet. Good, I hate to miss parts of a speech. You never get the whole story when you miss parts. Almost as if on cue, I think I hear John speaking now. Wow, he sure is passionate about his message. He is saying "I am the voice of one crying out in the wilderness." Some people are talking with him. I wish they would leave him alone; I would like to hear what he is preaching. I think I recognize some of them; I've seen them running around with the Pharisees. John must have said something they didn't like, because all of them have turned around and have started to leave. Wait a minute . . . John is getting very excited about something. There is a Man coming from the north. Listen to the crowd. I can't seem to hear what it is all about, something about the Messiah. All right, I see what it is now; it is the One they call Jesus. Boy, He sure has a big following. You know what? If this John thinks Jesus is the Messiah, then I do too. Everyone is starting to get quiet. This Jesus is speaking, something about God's love for all people. When He gets done speaking, I'm going to go up and introduce myself to Him and John too.

I got to meet with Jesus and John the other day. I believe I'll follow along with John for a while, there isn't much going on with the fishing business. Mr. Zebedee, Salome, and my wife, along with the other helpers, should be able to take care of everything. John is preaching his heart out, all about Jesus. I have been able to get some very good knowledge from both men. John is teaching about the Messiah, and Jesus is teaching about God's love for all. I think they are getting tired of me asking so many questions. I don't care though; I need to learn all this. Besides, I like watching Jesus heal a lot of sick folks. I just can't keep my eyes off Him.

I guess this old lake is about to be empty of fish. I have been out fishing all night and have caught very little. I'm so tired now. The nets have been cleaned, and I am ready to go home and get some sleep. I hear some commotion going on just up the bank. What do you know? It's Jesus and a lot of people following Him. He is coming to my place on the beach. Jesus, a loving, and kind teacher, wants to use my boat to speak to all those people. What a privilege. I am pretty good at public speaking, but when Jesus speaks everyone listens. We all get into my boat and cast off just a little ways; what a smart idea. The water makes your voice louder so all can hear.

THE APOSTLES 1ST PERSON A NARRATIVE

When Jesus is finished I'll tell my men to go towards the house. Jesus and I talked about how we were out all night and the pickins were slim. He turned to me and told me to go out a little ways. So I went out to about the middle of the lake. He told me to now throw my nets over the side. Well, I had just cleaned those nets and really didn't want to get them dirty again, but Jesus insisted I do it. I admire Him so much and have seen him do some great things, so overboard they went. Just a few minutes later He said bring them back up. I was busy talking with Jesus and hadn't noticed, but the men were all hollering and laughing excited about something; so I excused myself from Jesus and went over to see about the commotion. I couldn't believe it! The nets were so full they were about to break. I hurried to the front of the boat and started waving to the others on shore to come help me. My nets are so full they are breaking, and men start filling the boats up with fish. My eyes are tearing up; never in 30-some-odd years has this happened. It could only be the work of Jesus. As soon as I get this boat back to the dock, I'm going to leave it all behind. I will follow Jesus wherever He goes.

Wow, what a group of people out here! Everyone is listening to every word Jesus is saying. As I walk along side of Jesus I hear him shout to some more of my kinfolk to join us. There are so many people that a large dust cloud is being made. No one is complaining though; I really don't think they have noticed it. We have reached the center of Capernaum and are headed for the synagogue. I think Jesus is going to teach in there; I hope so as it is the Sabbath. Like I said, I am pretty good at speaking to people, but I can't hold people's attention the way Jesus does. I am so absorbed in the message . . . wait a minute . . . what is all that commotion in the back? There is some nut case in the back babbling something about knowing who Jesus is. Of course he knows who Jesus is; there is something strange about this guy. Oh no, he is going to be in trouble now; yeah, he interrupted Jesus, and now Jesus is going back there to talk to him. I can't tell whether Jesus is mad or if He is giving a command. The man is shouting wondering if Jesus has come to destroy them. How can Jesus destroy "them" when it is just one guy? The man's nuts! Jesus just told him to shut up; then He said something strange. He said "Be silent and come out of him." Man, you ought to hear all the commotion! That guy is having convulsions, flopping all over the ground, and making the strangest noises. Finally, the man is relaxing. Jesus just commanded the unclean spirits to leave and they obeyed. I stand amazed at the things this Man can do. He is truly the Messiah. Jesus then told us we needed to leave the synagogue. So we went out and Jesus said that we should go to my house.

As soon as I entered the house, my two cousins came running up to me, they said my mother-in-law is very ill with fever. That kind of made me feel bad; I have been so busy with Jesus I haven't even thought of my family. Jesus overheard us talking and went upstairs to see my mother-in-law. He is coming back now. What is this? My mother-in-law just came bouncing down the stairs right behind Him.

Oh, what a glorious morning. The sun is shining and a cool breeze is blowing. Jesus is teaching, and everything is great. We are going through some of the prettiest country here. The soil is very rich and the flowers are beautiful. Jesus is teaching here in Gennesaret. A crowd is beginning to form, and Jesus is healing a lot of sick people. But now He says we need to go onto the next town. So now we are on our way to Magdala. More people, more healing. I'm getting tired, but Jesus is as fresh as He was this morning.

I've been watching as Jesus heals these people. I think my favorite is when He cast out the demons. I don't know how those poor people can go through all of that. The demons fight tooth and toenail; but they have got to do what Jesus tells them, and that is to get out. The poor victims thrash around on the floor and vomit. The cool thing though is the demons can't say anything because Jesus told them to be still. Glory to God.

Well, we have been out on the road now for several days. We went to a lot of towns healing; I should say, Jesus is healing numerous people and casting demons out. I am back home in Capernaum now. I think we are going to stay home for a couple of days. Whatever we do, we need to rest; or I guess I should say, I need to rest.

On our trip the other day, the opposition got so bad that we had to sneak out of towns. We had to sleep in hiding places just so we could get some rest. We even had to sneak into town, the crowds were getting so big. Oh no, someone must have seen us coming back home to rest, because here comes a big crowd. But Jesus doesn't seem to mind. I am seeing people I have seen in some of the other towns; they are coming from all over. Jesus just raised His hands and everyone got quiet. There are so many people in my house you can't stir them with a stick. Jesus begins to lecture on the love of God. What in the world? There are some people on my roof, and they are ripping a big hole in my roof. Now they are handing down a man on a cot. It looks like he may be a paralytic. Ah, Jesus has seen him; after all, they just got dust, hay, and dirt all over Him. No surprise, Jesus decides to heal him.

GEORGE A REGISTER

I am getting a little tired right now. Jesus and a few of us have been out spreading the gospel here in Capernaum; I thought we would stop at my house to rest since it is evening. But Jesus seems to have a certain destination in mind, so I guess we have a little more work today. Wait a minute, He is heading towards that bunch of thieves, publicans, and tax collectors. If there is a group of people that can get my dander up, it is them. Surely He knows they don't hear anything but "cha-ching, cha-ching", the sound of money going into their pockets. He is going straight up to one of the biggest thieves of all. I think his name is Levi. I have had to deal with him a bunch. He will suck the blood out of a turnip. This is so weird. Jesus is just standing there, staring at that bum. He hasn't said a word to him. Haha, I can see now. Levi is getting mad because Jesus won't talk. Hey, maybe this will be more fun than I thought it would be. Wait, wait, wait. Levi is getting up. Oh bummer, He is following Jesus now too. That piece of trash is coming with us. Jesus, oh Jesus, please tell me this nut isn't coming with us, please. We are going to do what? No, no, I'm not going to go to his house. This man is unclean, and his house is unclean. Okay, I know I was lost, and now I'm found. I guess if you can go into his house I can too, but I am going to stay clear of him.

We are traveling from town to town. Jesus is spreading the Gospel to everyone. As we travel, He is teaching a few of us some in-depth study on how we, as His followers, are to teach and act. There is a lot of learning to do. Also there is a lot of people that just follow us everywhere. What is kind of irritating to me is those snoops for the Pharisee priest. Even at times, the Pharisees themselves come to bother us. Jesus has answered all questions they ask, but Jesus has also lowered the hammer on them. I have noticed though they seem to be getting a lot more irritable each time. Jesus has been speaking in what we would call "parables," so a couple of other disciples and me were alone with Jesus and felt like it was time to ask Him about why He spoke that way. Jesus said, "So they may see but not perceive; they may hear, but not understand." I think I understand what Jesus is saying, but it all still makes me scratch my head. But, if Jesus said it, so be it.

Well, I've had a couple of days off so I'm feeling refreshed, but Jesus has sent a messenger to me. He wants to meet all of us today. So off I go again. All right, there is Jesus now with the other ones that He has chosen. The twelve of us are very blessed to be so close to Jesus. There's so much to learn. You know what He just told us? We are to split up and go to different places on our own. Not only that, but we can't take any bread, money, or even a change of clothes.

For the first time I have all this pressure on my head. I am responsible for the lives of those that will listen. I am so afraid I am going to mess up, but I remember what Jesus said, "Just pray." Some people have come up to me and asked to be healed. Well, let's try it. I opened my heart up to Jesus and prayed for these people to be healed. Oh my, they are healed. Glory be to God. I am going to try again; I prayed with an open heart. Yes, prayer has worked again! Oh boy, here is one that's different. The man came forward to me demon possessed. But I remembered what Jesus taught us. So I just told him, "In the name of Jesus, get out of this man!" I thought I had killed him. He started to shake, twist, and roll; but with a big scream, that demon came out and left in a hurry. Jesus is with me no matter where He is or I am. My heart is so full of love for Jesus, our Master. Here comes someone I know; He doesn't look too happy. He tells me John the Baptist has been beheaded. I am so weak right now. Why would someone do that to a very mild man? I bet Jesus is sorrowful right now. I think I'll go to Rome and help retrieve John's body. This is such a sad time. "Oh Jesus, give us direction to go in."

Well, all of us have come back to be with Jesus. I guess the stress of all that has happened is showing on our faces, because He told us to go up on the mountain and rest. We haven't had a day off in a long time, and I think Jesus is a little tired himself.

I have been walking for some time now, as Jesus said we were going to Caesarea Philippi. He has been teaching a lot lately. All of a sudden, Jesus turned to us and asked us who we thought He was. Of course I said He was the Christ. And then, strangest thing, He told us not to say anything about that to anyone. But I know Jesus has His plan for us worked out, so I won't say anything. But I wonder, because Jesus is talking out of His mind. He is saying people are going to cause him harm. "Jesus, Jesus, excuse me, but there isn't anyone who is going to hurt you. I will protect you. What did you say, did you say Satan is in me?" Oh, I thought He knew how much I loved Him.

It's been almost a week since we were in Caesarea; we are walking along when Jesus asks James, John, and me to follow Him. He then told the others to stay behind. So the four of us went up the side of the mountain. We are all kind of just sitting around when all of a sudden Jesus began to glow. Yes, you heard me right, He began to glow. Jesus is talking to people; I think He said Elijah and Moses. I am sitting here completely amazed. Wait a minute, Jesus is glowing even more, then God speaks to us; He says that Jesus is His Son. I bow down and worship Jesus, but when I look up it is only Jesus standing there. So we start to walk down the mountain when Jesus tells us not to say anything about this. I just don't understand.

We are walking towards Jerusalem; several people are following us, but from the way Jesus is talking many of them are afraid. Jesus is telling the others to step back a little; He wants to talk to His chosen twelve. Okay, we have sent the others back; now Jesus is talking about His upcoming problems He is going to face. I'm not going to say anything; you know, I don't want Jesus mad at me again. Jesus is calling two more of His disciples to Him. He just told them to go get a donkey from town. What's He going to do now?

Wow, what an entrance to Jerusalem! People are lying palm branches down in front of Him; they are bowing down worshiping Him and calling Him the Messiah. They are following us straight to the temple. Jesus is bringing a great message. Oh great, here come the Pharisees; when they are near, they cause all kinds of headaches. Those guys bother me, but Jesus knows how to handle them.

Jesus has made arrangements for us twelve to have supper with Him. I think He is going to tell us something important, as He has never done this before. I know it is Passover time. My, oh my, Jesus says that one of us will betray him. No way! I think all of us love Him and if allowed will protect Him. I just can't believe this!

Then Jesus takes a portion of bread and breaks it; then He says it represents His body. Now He takes a cup of wine; He says it represents His blood of the covenant. Once again I don't understand.

I had a great meal, even after Jesus telling us some of the things that will go on shortly. I love these little walks I take with Jesus. I just love Him so much. Ah, we have come to a garden and have stopped for a rest. Jesus turns to us and says that we all will turn away from Him. This is my chance. "Oh, Jesus, may I have a word with You, please? I just want to tell You that I will never forsake You. I will never turn away from You. My love for You is too deep."

Jesus looks at me with them deep penetrating eyes. "Truly, I tell you, this very night, before the rooster crows twice, you will deny me three times."

"If it means I must die, I will not deny You, and all the others say the same thing." Wait a minute; someone is missing, I think. Let me count. Yes, someone is missing. It's Judas. Don't know where he is but Jesus is wanting to pray. Here he comes now, what a crowd he has following him. Don't look like much praying will be done now with all this bunch. This isn't a typical crowd; that is a lot of soldiers and a lot of those cursed priest. What is going on? Judas is walking up to Jesus. He says something, and I hear Jesus telling him to do what he has to do. About this time soldiers come up and grab Jesus. Well, that's not going to happen; I don't carry this knife for nothing. Aha! There! I get that soldiers ear; I think I cut it plum off. I'm getting ready to do it again when I hear Jesus tell everyone to stop. Jesus then bends down and picks up the ear and puts it back on. A riot is about to happen, so I am going to step back aways; after all, Jesus said to back off. The soldiers are taking Jesus away; I'll follow to see where they are taking Him. All the people that used to follow Him are now wanting to kill Him; what a fickle bunch.

I have followed this group inside where there is a fire to warm myself. I can see all those priest hanging around; what's this woman saying? "What did you say? No, I'm not one of His followers."

A guy can't even come into the courtyard and warm himself without being bothered. I think I will go out to the gate. That rooster is crowing at a weird time. Oh well, this has been a wacky night. There is that women who accused me in the courtyard. She just won't leave me alone. I keep telling her I am not a follower. But she keeps on and on. I have had enough of her. "I am bringing down a curse on me, and I (BLEEP) wish you would leave me alone." There goes that stupid rooster again; oh, no . . . Jesus said I would deny him three times before the night was over. Oh God, what have I done? I get on my knees and pray and pray. Please forgive me Jesus. I don't know how long I've been praying, but I hear they have taken Jesus to be crucified.

I've been walking back and forth on the streets; I am at a loss as to what to do. My stubbornness and lack of attention to what Jesus was saying to the twelve of us . . . if only I had stayed and fought the soldiers more . . . no, no, Jesus told me to back off when I started to fight, so I can't blame myself for that. I'm just going in circles. Maybe we all should get together and figure out what to do; yes, that is what we should do.

"Brothers, we need a direction to go in; do you have any suggestions?" The ladies have gone to prepare the body; it was gracious of Mr. Joseph to supply us with a tomb. "What are those women hollering about out there? Slow down, we can't understand you. You say Jesus is gone? That He has risen from the grave? Out of my way. I'm going to go see."

I am looking in the tomb, Jesus is gone. I am beginning to remember now. Jesus told us He would be crucified but would rise again on the third day. I want to believe this, but that is so far out there. You know? It's hard to comprehend. Let's all go back to the room and lock the doors. The Jews will be looking for us; they will say we stole the body.

"How did you get in, Sir? The doors are locked, besides this is a private meeting. OH, MY GOD, IT'S JESUS! He is alive! MY JESUS IS ALIVE! YAHOO!"

After Jesus left, the eleven of us, with my persuasion, decided to appoint a replacement for the one who betrayed us. We have decided on Matthias.

All of us have been busy ever since Jesus came back and left to go home to heaven. He has given us great power to heal and cast out demons. But all of us have been just speaking to small crowds of people. It is time to have a public lecture. The others have told me that it should be me who gives this sermon. I don't mind. I did it many times when I was a fisherman. So I'll pray and let it rip.

"Men of Judea and surrounding areas, give ear." That sounded good even if I did say so myself. I have no idea about the words coming out of my mouth. I just open my mouth and the words just keep coming. I don't know how long I've been speaking, but the people are crying and bowing down to Jesus.

We must have a baptism. We will go to the river. I have never seen so many people coming to be baptized. I would say there is over 3,000 people. People are coming up to me and just touching my robe, and then they are healed.

Jesus said there would be trouble, and sure enough here comes some soldiers. They said I was under arrest. What did I do to be arrested? Oh yes, I remember. Those Sadducees were getting rather annoyed at me when I was speaking. The council is telling me not to preach. Ha, like that is going to happen. When they said this, both

THE APOSTLES 1ST PERSON A NARRATIVE

John and I started bombarding them with Scripture and common knowledge. I don't know how long we have been at it, but the council stopped us and let us go.

I am so pleased with the way the church has been growing. But I have a feeling things are about to change. Sure enough, here comes the Sadducees. They say I am under arrest again. They throw me in prison, with no ease. As a follower of Jesus, we expect this from time to time.

Well, it's early morning. Something is going on; my thoughts are a little cloudy. I raise my head and I am standing outside; something that looks like it could be an angel tells me to go preach in the temple. I am looking around and not only me, but all the apostles were standing there. "So, let's go, men."

As I was preaching, them stinking Sadducees came and took us before the council again; boy, were them bobbleheads angry. I swear, they want to kill us. One of the Pharisees stands up. He is sending us outside; what this is about I don't know. "Come back in," they say.

"You going to release us? Let go of me!" Ouch! Oh, Jesus, let this be over soon. How many licks am I going to get? I can hear the others being whipped too. I guess it's over; they are telling us to get out and don't preach in His name anymore. Like I said before, that's not going to happen.

As we stand outside, we all have the biggest grins on our faces. I tell the others that we have been persecuted for Jesus; what a privilege we have been given.

GEORGE A REGISTER

I have been in Jerusalem several years now and can see the followers growing by leaps and bounds. But I got some disturbing news yesterday about our brothers in Sebaste, Samaria. Seems like the Holy Spirit was not given as of yet. They have been baptized in Jesus but have not received the Spirit. So I have spoken with the brothers here, and John and I are going there.

We have arrived, and it is time to lay hands on our brothers. You can feel the Holy Spirit coming through the bodies of my brothers.

We are traveling back to Jerusalem, but I think we should stop in this little town. I think they call it Lydda; many years ago it was called Lod. First rattle out of the box, we come upon a man who has been paralyzed for eight years. I looked at the man and said, "In the name of Jesus rise up and take your bed home." Bam! He got up, and all the people who saw what happened became believers of Jesus.

John and I are ready now to go on to Jerusalem; my wife and I along with John had just stepped onto the road when a disciple from Joppa caught up with us. He asked if I would come back with him. I figured it would be okay; it isn't very far over there. I told John to go on to Jerusalem, and I would catch up later.

I guess my friend Tabitha passed on, because the people all around are wailing and carrying on. I hear she was a faithful servant of the Lord Jesus. I need to go upstairs to see her. "All these people need to leave; please remove them, so I can concentrate." I am going to lay my hands on her, and pray. "Tabitha, rise up." Her eyes are open now. "Take my hand and get up." This is going to shock a few people when I open this door. A few months ago this would have surprised me, but I'm getting used to Jesus controlling things through me. I think I will stay here a few days. I have a friend here that is a tanner I can stay with.

THE APOSTLES 1ST PERSON A NARRATIVE

"People, will you excuse me for a few minutes?" You see, I just heard that John's brother, James, has been beheaded. I also heard that the tyrant King Agrippa was out to get me, because there are a lot of the Jews liking what he has done. I can't get out, so I might as well just wait for them to come get me.

Well, that didn't take long. "No need to push; I'm going, man. Give me time to get back up; you pushed me down." Thank goodness we got to the jail. My knees and elbows are bleeding a little from scraping the ground.

I hear the believers are gathering at John Mark's house, I sure wish I could be with them. I guess they really think I am some kind of a monster, because they have put me in chains. They have two, get this, two soldiers beside me, and two sentries by the door. They are making sure I'm not going anywhere. I am kind of sleepy, so I'm going to try to at least take a nap. Something just poked me in the side; what's going on? This voice is telling me to get up and put my clothes on, because we are leaving. Like how? I'm bound, or am I? I'm lose! I get up, walk right past the guards, and right out of the prison. Jesus is at work in this I know.

I'll go to meet up with some of the disciples at Mark's place. Boy, are they surprised! We all hug and I tell them it isn't safe for me to be there. I ask them to please tell James I want him to take over leadership of the church. We all then say our goodbyes for now.

I have been in Corinth now for quite some time. It is time to go on to Rome; I am getting a little older now, and my wife and I can only travel so far. I think this will be my last journey. I think I will write to my beloved disciples; I have so many. I'll wait till I get to Rome.

I am back in prison again, I swear this old body can't take a whole lot more of this abuse. I have heard that Paul has been put in prison also. I don't know this for a fact but wouldn't be surprised. I think the worst part about this is that my lovely wife has been put in prison also. She has been so faithful to Jesus, and to tend to my needs also. Everyone seems to be mad about our preaching about Jesus. But we have been able to reach people, like the guards, that we weren't able to before. I have been taken out and beaten so many times now that I don't feel anything much now. Here comes some new guards. I don't think I like the looks of this.

"Where are you taking me? Ah, come on guys. I'll go; just stop pushing me down. Ouch! Why the whip? Ouch! What's this? You're going to crucify me?! Please, I'm not worthy to die like my Lord and Savior. Can't you let me walk? Dragging me won't do anything. Wait a minute. Isn't that my wife they're dragging off? Where are they going? Oh no, you're feeding her to the lions? Oh, honey, I love you. Ouch! You hit me again; I'm laying down. Grant me one favor please; put me upside down." This hurts so badly, but I'm keeping my heart and eyes on the fact that I am going to be with my Savior in just a little while. I can feel the blood rushing to my head. "Jesus . . . my . . . Savior . . ."

APOSTLE
ANDREW

"MY NAME IS Andrew. My father's name is Jon, and my mother's name is Jonna. I have a brother whose name is Simon. I was born in a town called Bethsaida; it is a place along the shore of the Sea of Galilee. It is an old city, dating back to around the tenth century BCE. The city was founded on a mound and was divided into two sections. The upper part was called an acropolis and was on the northeastern side. This part of the city had a massive wall that surrounded it. That wall, they say, was around six meters thick. Where the gates were, around eight meters thick. Inside the walls was a plaza which led up to a palace for the kings. It was called The Palace of Bethsaida, imagine that. Did I mention this was all done by the Aramean people? I think the king's name was King of Geshur. If that sounds familiar, King David married a women named Ma'acha, King Geshur's daughter.

"The lower side of the city actually covered most of the mound. I believe this is where most of the inhabitants lived, the workforce you might say. The city was destroyed by an Assyrian King Tiglath Pileser III. If I remember dad's schooling me, that was around 734 BCE. Not to many people have lived here since the city was destroyed, but here in the last few years the little town now has grown to a small but active place. My father came here to practice his profession, which is fishing, commercially. My brother Simon and I have grown up learning the trade. This is a hard life to live. You work from sunup to sundown, and sometimes a little longer. My dad is calling me, so I need to go see what He is wanting.

"Hi, Pops, what you need? I see, I knew things was getting kind of rough, but I didn't know it was that bad. When do you think we need to leave? Tomorrow?! Wow, that soon, you say? Does Simon know this yet? He is on his way, okay. Where are we going? Capernaum, to our uncle's place? I guess we are going to go to work for him, that right? Sir, Mom isn't feeling very good, you know. Will she make the trip okay?

"Hey, James, John, what's up? Good to see you all. Hi, Mr. Zebedee, how are you? I do want to thank you for giving us these jobs. I promise we will work hard and long for you. Mom isn't doing too good; thanks for asking. That trip didn't help her any. See you bright and early tomorrow morning." James just came by then and whispered something in Mr. Z's ear. He is coming over here; he sure don't look very happy. "Mr. Z, something wrong? Mom passed away a few minutes ago? I knew she wasn't feeling good, but I didn't think it was that bad. I need to find Simon, and we need to go have a grieving time together with Dad. Would you all excuse us, please?"

Things have started to get into a good rhythm down here at the shoreline; Simon and I have been given a boat with a crew. We make quite the spectacle when the Zebedee fleet leaves the port. My father and Mr. Z stay on shore and takes care of the previous days leftovers and oversee the cleanup. They do seem to get along good, not like my brother and me. Simon is a rough, gruff type of kid; I'm sort of a laid back type. Everybody says I shouldn't let

THE APOSTLES 1ST PERSON A NARRATIVE

Simon bully me around. I'm not about to get into a fist fight with him; he is muscular and would beat the tar out of me. Besides if we got into a fight we would get kicked out.

Well, we are back in port, but my dad and Mr. Z aren't anywhere around; I guess we will have to unload everything ourselves. Although Simon and I are young, we have done this for awhile; we know what to do. Oh, here comes Mr. Z; he don't look very happy. He is motioning Simon and me to come over there; I sure hope he isn't going to fire us. I don't remember doing anything to warrant that. "Mr. Z, something wrong? Dad died? He was standing there one minute; then the next he was dead? Just fell where he was standing? Simon, what are we going to do? Do what, Mr.Z? You saying we can stay with you? Oh, thank you, sir. We are too young to try and live by ourselves. Yes, sir, we will keep our noses clean. No fighting among us. May Simon and I take a day or two to grieve for Dad? Thank you, sir.

"Simon, it is just you and me brother; we need to lean on each other for strength. I know we don't agree on a lot of things, you know, like how to take care of a problem or what kind of discipline to hand out to our crew; but I have you to back me and you have me to help you. Love you, brother."

My brother and I have been at this fishing business for several years now. Mr. Z has been very good to us, and he even gave us this boat and made us partners with him. Things have gotten so slow that Simon and I have been able to take some time off. Simon has got himself married now. We all still live in Mr. Z's house. Simon and I didn't have the opportunity to be schooled by the priests, but Mrs. Z would teach us how to read and speak two languages, Greek and Aramaic. I have picked up a little Hebrew also. I understand that there is a man that is preaching something about the coming of the Messiah. They say he travels from one place to another, and he actually lived in the desert. I have heard about this Messiah before, but I would like to find out a little more about Him. I hear he is in my old hometown right now. "Simon, I'm going to take a little trip, okay?"

All right, I made it to Bethsaida, and over there is the man I have been hearing about. I think they call him John. The way he is sounding right now he is all wound up. The message is on the Messiah coming and that the Messiah is greater than him. We all need to repent of our sins. After he gets through with his preaching, I'm going to ask him a lot of questions. Sure is a lot of people listening to him. I'm not real sure, but it might be awhile before I can talk with him. What's he doing now? He is headed to the shoreline. He went into the water. Oh, I see, he is baptizing them. Seems like the whole town is out here watching.

Well, it has been a couple of hours of him baptizing people, but I think he is finished. "Hey, Mr. John, may I speak with you for a moment?" I thought I would ask him some questions but as soon as he reached me he began telling me about this Messiah. He told me I needed to repent of my sins, and then I needed to get baptized. He told me we all had sinned and the only way out was to accept the Messiah. "Sorry, Mr. John, but I have a long ways to go to get back home. Where you going to be tomorrow?"

I got back home and began to tell John Zebedee about what John the Baptist had said and that he was going to be just down the road tomorrow. "You want to go with me? I would like to hear more. I have to tell Simon about this too." Simon is a workaholic, so I don't think he will come along though.

I'm afraid I went a little too far to make it back home tonight. John and I decided to follow John the Baptist a few days; I am sure we can learn a lot. Wow, I don't know if I can keep up with J.B. He doesn't dilly-dally around any. We have been out on the road now for several days, and J.B. gave us some good news today. He said that he would be going to Capernaum in the next day or two. That is great news for us; I'm sure Simon is wondering about us.

J.B. is preaching away today. I don't know how many people are here on the banks with us. It seems to me that JB is exceptionally high-keyed and excited about something. What's happening now? J.B. has stopped talking and asked John and I to separate the crowd to form a path down the middle. And then in a voice that shook the ground around us, he said, "Behold, the Messiah has come!" I am looking down the road and there was Jesus walking towards us. Jesus walked right up to J.B. and asked him to baptize Him. J.B. told Him that he couldn't do that, because Jesus should be baptizing him. But Jesus insisted on being baptized by him. I think I can understand what J.B. has been preaching about how we needed to follow Jesus, not him. It all is making sense; I have to go get Simon. "John, you stay here, and I'll be right back."

"Simon, Simon, you need to come with me; I have met the Messiah. Come on. Stop fixing that net and come on. You can work on that later. You won't believe this, but J.B. said that this is the One he has been preaching about.

"Isn't it wonderful, Simon, Jesus wants us to follow Him and wants us to help Him with His ministry. I know we have to work but when He is around close we can help Him. All these people around and Jesus chose us. I would say that is a big blessing. Jesus is going to call us His disciples. We need to share this with James."

GEORGE A REGISTER

This has been a very fast-paced year between working on the boats and helping Jesus when He was around or close by. Even Simon has been helping with the ministry chores. I heard that Jesus was going to be in town in a few days, but to tell the truth, I think we are going to have to stay on the boats. Our work is so far behind.

Oh my, I see Jesus coming now. I can't tell how many people is following Him, but it is a bunch. Here He comes over to us now. He is walking up to Simon and talking to him; Simon is white as a sheet. I don't know whether I should go see the problem or just wait here. Simon is getting up now. Jesus is raising His hands and looking at us. Jesus said, "Come follow me and I will make you fishers of men." Jesus wants us to come with Him full-time. Simon has already walked off the boat. I can't help myself; I have to follow. I am looking around and James and John are getting off the boat too. Jesus is preaching and teaching every day. As His disciples, we get to teach smaller crowds. We are headed out to the country, and then we will go to the next town and then the next.

We are back in C-town, but we aren't going to stay very long. Simon has gathered his wife and children up and is going to bring them along with us. Mr. Z has said he is going too. What an undertaking, getting the whole family ready; I'm glad that I'm not married. I just have myself to worry about. I don't have anything against marriage, but it is just not for me. Before we leave again Jesus wants to talk with a few of us out on the hill.

Jesus is telling us about our ministries and what we are going to be expected to do. Me and about eleven more of us are on our knees praying about the message and it being accepted. Jesus is telling us to look at Him, look in His eyes. Oh my, Jesus is saying that we are going to become His apostles. We are going to be taking over some of the preaching duties. Jesus will give the main course, and we will continue in smaller groups explaining the Gospel further. Jesus is laying His hands on us and giving us more power to expel the demons and to heal people. This is becoming a tight-knit organization, well put together. We have brothers that are great orators, such as my brother Simon; when he speaks, loud and full of fever, you listen. Then you have people like Jude and James with the greater, softer voices that demand your full attention. We have a banker (treasurer) and tax collectors that can handle the money and other items received. Then there are people like me that are good at administration. Some are even good at planning our trips, and others are able to organize the trips. Whatever our gift is, we all must engage the people. The main focus though is to learn what is important to Jesus and to gather around and listen to instructions and explanations of some of the parables that Jesus uses throughout the day. Every day that goes by, the more intense Jesus' preaching gets.

We have all been invited to have supper with Jesus at a room in the city of Jerusalem. In the last few months a lot of our ministry has been done here in Jerusalem. Most of the time if Jesus wants to talk with us He will send a disciple to give us the message. But this time Jesus came by and invited us personally. He didn't look very happy, almost distraught, like something heavy was on His mind. I believe the invite wasn't optional as to whether we wanted to go or not, sort of mandatory.

Wow, what a feast set out in front of us! Lamb and other meats are laid out in front of us. 'Course, I don't remember if I told you or not, but I am a vegetarian. It is still a beautiful table though. There's all kinds of fruit and veggies, so I won't be going hungry. Jesus has blessed the food and everyone has dug in. Being one to observe others and their attitudes, I noticed Jesus was being quiet, and that is highly unusual.

The meal is almost over now and Jesus is getting up to speak. He says that we are to love all as though they were our own but that His time on this earth is almost over. I don't know why He would say this. He isn't but around thirty, so He should have a lot of years left. He has taken a loaf of bread and pulled it apart and given each one of us a piece. Then He told us to eat this bread as it is a symbol of His body and to do so as a remembrance of Him. What now? He has taken a cup of wine. He says to drink a sip as though it was His blood that has been spilled out. Jesus just lowered His head, and I think I see tears in His eyes. He raises His head and says that there is one among us that will betray Him. "Not among us, Jesus. No way! You can't mean that." He isn't laughing; He is dead serious. It made Judas Iscariot so ill he had to leave. Jesus says we need to go pray now.

Normally, we would go out to a town somewhere to preach, but Jesus said that we should go up on the hill to pray some more. Thought that was a little different, but this whole evening has been different. I hate seeing Jesus so sad. His shoulders are drooping; His head is down, and there's no pep in His walking. He has called Simon, who He nicknamed Peter, James, John, and me to the side. He told James, John, and Peter to follow Him. I was to do my normal thing of keeping the other apostles focused on events at hand.

Jesus, my brother, James, and John have been up the hill for some time now. Oh look, here comes Judas Iscariot. He must be feeling better. Look at all those people following Him; I hate to tell Him, but I really think Jesus wanted to have quiet time with just us. What in the world? Those are soldiers with him! I think I smell a rat. Just in time, Jesus and the others have come down off the hill. Jesus went right up to Judas. I heard Him say, "Do what you have to do. A fight just broke out and Simon has his knife out. Jesus told us all to settle down. Now aren't we the brave ones? We all have hidden in the bushes and in the trees. We left Jesus out there alone, except for

Judas; and now the soldiers are taking Jesus away. Maybe this is why Jesus has been so down; He knew this was going to happen.

Most all of us have come home now. Peter (that is what we have started calling Simon) has really been down in the dumps since they took Jesus away. Peter, decided to go up to Jerusalem to see what is happening. But John is going to stay with Aunt Mary, Jesus' mother. Someone needs to look after her. Peter travels back and forth to let us know the latest news. Salome, who is Mary's sister, and John have rented a cottage until this whole thing blows over. All of us are going to go to Jerusalem tomorrow and try to help out. Peter came back last night and said that they had crucified Jesus, and He is dead now. I am a pretty good judge of character, so I don't think I was wrong in believing who Jesus was.

I don't know how but all the apostles are here in this little cottage. I have heard that the Pharisees are out on a man hunt for us, but I think we all agree that this is where we should be. John tells me that a gentlemen came forth and took Jesus' body to a grave that was meant for him. That was very kind of him. One of the last things Jesus said was for John is to take care of His mother. So it is his responsibility, but there isn't a one of us that isn't going to help him.

The women have gone out to prepare Jesus' body. My brother, Simon Peter, said that we need to all pray for some kind of guidance. He is asking Judas if he would do the honors. Judas is standing, not saying anything, but his eyes are full of tears. Poor guy, he just asked us if we would not call him Judas anymore. He said that name has a curse on it, and would like us to call him Thaddeus. That is his middle name I guess. I can't blame him for wanting that.

I hear a big commotion outside. The women are running fast

down the path flailing their arms wildly. Something is wrong. "Okay, let them in. (We have the door locked, and we keep guard). Slow down, ladies, we can't understand you. What do you mean Jesus is missing? The soldiers put a large boulder in front of the tomb. No one could have moved it, especially with two guards in front of it." Whoa, the front door just opened up and Peter and a couple of others started running to the tomb. The ladies said that Jesus spoke with them. They said that they didn't recognize Him at first. He told them to go tell the others that He is going to ascend to heaven.

The ladies are still wound up. Were they seeing an illusion? Like their minds playing tricks on them? You know women have a history of making things up. Wait a minute. Somebody just entered the room. Impossible. The door is shut and locked, and no one opened it. Oh my! It's Jesus! I need to get on my knees and worship Him. What a ruckus in here! Jesus showed us His hands and spoke peace on us.

Jesus has been revealing Himself to people for a few days now. But He said it is time for Him to go meet His Father. But He said that He would be back to establish His kingdom. We are standing listening to what Jesus has to say. I don't really know how many there are here, maybe five hundred or so. All of a sudden Jesus starts to rise up towards heaven. Everyone is standing in amazement at the sight of Jesus in His white robe and a glow around Him.

Things are still pretty much in disarray around here. But since we were filled with what Jesus called the Holy Spirit when we were in the upper part of the house, I feel, and I think the rest of us feel, a strength inside of us, to go out and continue preaching the Gospel. And we have a lot of help. I would say there were at least one hundred twenty other people in the room with us. These are disciples who can follow us and help explain our teaching in the small groups.

Peter is trying to get us all together, for we need to start going out to the world and spreading the Gospel to the ends of the earth. This is where I come in. I'm so proud of my brother; he is keeping everything together which isn't a small undertaking. As I told you before, I am sort of the administrator. I am going to cast lots as to where each one of us is going; no need to have everyone going to the same place. Peter and John will stay around Jerusalem most of the time; both will be planting churches. James, the brother of Jesus, was in charge of the Jerusalem congregation, but the Pharisees have got the people all stirred up again and they stoned James to death. Our missions are definitely dangerous, but we have to have our heads held high and be strong for the Lord.

Today I start out on my first real missionary journey. I am going to take a few of the disciples with me so I can spread the Gospel better. I am first going to the Samaritans in Gaza. The people are of Greek descent and are very wicked and mean, but God loves them anyway. I'm not planning on spending a whole lot of time there, but if I find some interest, I will have one of the disciples stay behind and nurture the new believers. If I thought Jerusalem was bad, these people take the cake.

I am going to slip through Jerusalem and head on out to Lydda, maybe spend one two days there. The people are a little more receptive to the Gospel, so I'm leaving a couple of the disciples here. Now that we have established a contact for these people to go to, I am going to go on to Ankara. I hear they have heard the Gospel before.

I think we may be in trouble though, here comes the pesky priests again. Let us go ahead and leave as they have asked us to. The only reason is because Thaddeus is just down the road from here in Edessa.

"Hello, Thaddeus, how're things going? That is good to hear. You think you are going to start a church here? Wonderful! You converted the governor? Wow, that is so great! I can see we aren't needed too much here, so I'm going to go on. Keep up the good work, brother."

I am here at Byzantium; this city is close to the Black Sea. It's big, so I will spend a few days extra here. I never seen so many different idols. They haven't heard much about the Gospel, so I'm having to start from scratch here. To be so wicked, they are pretty receptive. I am going to have a couple believers remain here to spread the Gospel, but I need to continue on.

We have been on the road for several days now, and I haven't stayed long at any place. Since we left Byzantium a few hours ago, we have been to a lot of little towns. We have preached in Bithynia and Cappadocia. We have come all the way up to the Greek Pontus. We've had limited success but still the Gospel has been given. I really think that I need to take our group towards home now. So I am going to go through Georgia to Armenia and then to Jerusalem.

Okay, people, it is time to go on another journey. I think we will start by going to and checking on some of our brothers that we left behind in a few of the cities. My first stop I am going to Antioch. That isn't too far from here.

My brother has really been busy here; I have met several new brothers in Christ. I'm not needed that bad here, so I will go ahead to Ephesus and meet up with John. I haven't seen him in a long time. It would be nice to see Mary again too. I am going to take a boat up to Ephesus; it will be a lot faster.

This boat is going to have to stop in Cyprus; we need to take on a new water supply. I'm not planning on going ashore. This would be a good time to rest and get ready to meet up with John. I am hearing a lot of shouting going on. Wonder what the problem is? The crew of this ship don't look too happy. "Do what? They won't give you any water? They are having a drought and the water supply is very low? Okay, okay, let's not panic. I will go ashore and see what I can do to help. All my disciples, gather around and get on your knees. I am going to pray for some water for us. Lord, please help us with the problem of not having enough water and allow these people to see Your greatness. You, disciples, stay on your knees praying. But if you will look at that rock over there, you will see water coming forth. As long as you are praying the water will be flowing ... You have plenty now? Then let's get aboard and continue on our journey."

Well, we have arrived in Ephesus now, and it is good to see John. He has started a few little churches around town; the Gospel is reaching out over the countryside also. John has allowed me to speak at a couple of the house churches. I feel the Holy Spirit telling me to spend a lot of time here in Ephesus. Most of these people on this side are barbaric in nature to the point of being cannibalistic. The people are amused at the teachings we are presenting, a lot of them even laugh out loud at us. My guys and I have to be very careful because some of these pagan priests want to sacrifice us to their gods. Our God is more powerful, and He is watching our backs. Now I need to have my group head back to Antioch and then start up to Nicea.

GEORGE A REGISTER

We have had a lot of success here in Nicea. But after nearly a year here, my guys and I need to continue on. I need to go back to Pontus and address a couple of issues. Then we will go on through Georgia, then on down to Parthia, and then drop on down to the desert of Gedrosia. While travelling, we haven't been bothered by any road bandits or robbers, just another sign God is with us. Heaven knows there is a lot of them on these trade routes.

It sure does feel good to have my feet in the sea. After traveling all this way down through all the "stan" countries, you know, Uzbekistan, Kyrgyzstan, Tajikistan, Afghanistan, Balochistan, it makes me tired just thinking about them; every one of them were barbaric to the max. What in the world is the matter now? All my disciples are running towards me. "Oh my! Run for your lives! Get in the boats! We can push off far enough to keep out of those monsters' reach. Hurry! I've never seen anything so hideous in my life; they look like rabid dogs in the face. Oh, Jesus, what have we got into? We can escape by sea to another part of the desert. What is that smell? It is the sweet smell that God sends down to us when we are supposed to teach people the Gospel. Guys, God is telling us we have to go back. I am sure God has seen them. We are about to land back on shore; we will have to rely on God to take care of us. I know! I will preach from the boat, you know, like Jesus did."

I believe these people are listening to what I am saying. The fearsome display of violence doesn't seem to be there. I'm going to go ashore amongst them, after all God is still here. They are offering us food and drink. The head person, I don't know what to call him, king, governor, or whatever, said they would like to hear more. As we are eating, the king is telling me why they look like they do. As soon as the baby is born, they start reshaping their heads, the more they do this the better for the baby. When people try to invade them, they come running after them just like they did us. They are actually very calm, sensitive people who wouldn't hurt a fly. Now we have shown them that with our God, He will keep them safe as long as they worship Him and Him alone. I am going to leave several disciples here to help them get started. I need to backtrack a little and then head back to Jerusalem. This has been a very rewarding journey so far.

Oh, how good it feels to be back in Jerusalem. That last journey was quite lengthy, but it was very rewarding. Many people, from peasants, to governors, to kings, have come to know the Lord. I wonder how some of the others are doing? I have talked to several of the disciples, and they are bubbling with excitement over how the Gospel is being preached everywhere. Here comes one of the disciples now. Looks like he has bad news of some sort. "Hello, brother. Someone needs to go help him. Yes, I know I just got back, but Matthias is in trouble. So I will go after him. No, I will go by myself, with the Lord of course. I'm not going to preach, just to rescue Matthias."

Matthias has been down in the Tanzania area, and a group of people called the Anthropophagi have captured him. We all have been put in prison at some time or another, but this is different. These people eat humans. I went through a lot of barbarians who sacrificed humans and ate parts, but these people eat humans on a daily basis.

I think it would be wise to take a boat to Tanzania; I can catch one of them from the ports in Yemen. This will take a while for it is close to 2,000 miles from here. I have asked the Lord to keep me safe and to allow me to rescue Matthias. There are a lot of ships that go this route; it is a big trade route from the Arab countries. I will get off at the Cape of Delgado. I understand Matthias is somewhere around that area. "Dear Jesus, please guide me to my brother's side and have Your name glorified to these people. Amen."

We have arrived and the good Lord has been guiding us along to Matthias. I can feel the demonic presence around this area, so I feel we are close. The air is thick with the stench of death. Bones are everywhere, human bones. "Satan, you must be gone from us, in the name of Jesus! Oh, thank You, Jesus!" As I look up ahead, I see Matthias. He is still alive, but it looks like he is on the menu for tonight. He is being heavily guarded but standing beside me is my Redeemer.

"You, standing by my brother, loosen those chains from him. Do this or forever burn in hell." This is such an amazing site; the ground is beginning to shake. Look, the chains have come loose! "Come stand with me, Matthias. Let us depart from here. Who is this that stands in my way? Give me your name. Amayal? I stand in front of you and tell you to leave this place, in the name of Jesus. Oh, yes, I see, you're bringing in the reinforcements, huh? There is no way for you to defeat us, no matter how many you bring in. I ask You, dear Lord, would you please bring me some help? I cannot defeat this demon by myself. Thank you. Who said that? I must see who just spoke to me. Oh, Jesus, You sent me the best, Michael. Yes, sir, Michael let's clean house. Where did they all go? It was almost like in a blink of an eye. Poof, and they're gone! Thank You, Lord. I must say though, I am wore out; but we have Matthias and can go home now. Do what, Matthias? You're staying? Well, yes, these people have seen and are believing in the Gospel. Yes, they need to be nurtured. Okay, let's pray then, and I will be on my way."

THE APOSTLES 1ST PERSON A NARRATIVE

I have been praying a lot lately because I feel like I need to go on another journey. I am getting a lot older now and these journeys are very hard on me. But as long as the Lord wants me to go, I will. I am having the urge to head back to visit some of the disciples that have been left along the way. My first visit will be back at Pontus. It has been many years since I have seen them there.

"Look at the progress that has gone on here. So many are staying within the teachings. Yes, some of you, as I have, been thrown into prison for preaching the Gospel, but that hasn't deterred you from spreading the Word. So many of the apostles have been crucified for their faith, yet the Gospel is still being spread. Praise the Lord. I must continue on now, my brothers. I am going to travel around the Black Sea, through Georgia, on up to the Caucasus, and then into the Sea of Azov in Russia. I'll cross over to the Crimea which is a little island.

I have found this little island a very friendly place. A lot of Greeks from Sebastopol and from Cherson are living on the island. What is nice is, they are very interested in hearing the Gospel. I will be leaving a few disciples to take care of the new believers. "Okay, you folks, pack your things and let's start back on the road. We are going to go to Valaam, which is up by Lake Ladoga. We won't be too far from the Baltic Sea.

"Brothers, we have arrived at our destination. There seems to be a lot of tension in the air. We have been ministering here for about three days now, and the people are very skeptical about the Gospel. I have encountered a lot of hostilities even. I am getting tired and I don't have the strength I used to have. I must rely on you to get the message to the people. Here comes more trouble. Why do you want to throw us in jail? I am sorry, but we must present the Gospel to the people. If you put us in jail, we will just preach to the prisoners and the guards, so you won't be stopping us

"I have been drug across the ground, then I was flogged, spit upon, and beaten. It is not just me, but you, my brothers, are undergoing the same things. I think we should start our journey back towards home. What do you think? Sebastopol would be a great place to revisit. I know the brothers there could use the help. I am going to go with you until the city of Dervent." I am so wore out, I am getting too old for all this. I could not take another beating like we had back in Lake Ladoga. I am not giving up; I am merely going to work out of one place. I believe the good Lord is okay with this decision.

"Okay, brothers, I will meet up with you in Romania. You have a great journey. Don't worry about me, for I have the blessing of the Lord. Please preach the Gospel in all instances for this is our mission. Thank you for being so loyal . . .

"I am so glad to see you once again, brothers; I have heard good things about you and the ministry. I believe that this is the place for me to rest. I am going to plant a church here and nurture it myself. Most of you are free to go back to Jerusalem. They need a lot of help there also. I have heard that most of the apostles have been martyred one way or the other. The only one left would be John, and I'm not sure of him. One of the disciples that came through told me John had been banished to some island. I would like to ask that a couple of you stay with me until I get settled in . . ."

I have purchased a cave here. I know, that doesn't sound like much, but a lot of people live in caves around here. The cliffs are full of caverns and people have made their homes out of them. I was fortunate to find one that was on the bottom of the cliff; I know it was by the hand of God. I don't think I could have climbed up the side very easy. The people in this area are very receptive to the Gospel, and most all of them are vegetarians just like me. Another thing nice about the people is they have no slaves. Each family serves themselves. They are very friendly towards me; they even brought me some food over to help me get settled. As soon as I get rested up, I will go out to the surrounding country. The good Lord has allowed me to stay in a very warm, accommodating place.

I think I will go to a place called Moldavia for a few days. It's not that far, and I have been resting a lot. I feel refreshed and also feel the Lord telling me I need to go there. I understand the people there are just like those here in Dervent, only they eat meat.

This is such a beautiful walk. The Danube is on the right over there. I could take a boat there, but I want to experience the countryside. The shores around the waters are full of rocks. But there is a thin strip right at the edge that makes for a great place to rest; I will take advantage of this along the way.

In my prayers as of late, God has been telling me to make one more journey, and that would be to Greece. I know that the Lord will not ask us to do anything that we can't do. I have been around these people here in Romania for a little over twenty years now. I am over eighty-five years of age but have been blessed with good health, other than "old person syndromes." Haha. I must gather my disciples around me and pray for them to continue the good works they have been doing. This is going to be hard; I love them so much.

GEORGE A REGISTER

The good Lord knew what was happening; these people in the northern part of Greece were starving for the Gospel. I should have brought more disciples with me. Most of them are grasping at every word I say. I pray that this whole journey will be this way. I don't keep count of how many I baptize, but the lines are long, and they keep getting longer. What is nice is it is the rich and the poor being baptized together.

I feel like I need to go towards the town of Patras. I have been going through Greece now for a little over two years; it has been a very blessed time. Once I get to Patras, I can catch a boat headed towards Jerusalem. I understand there are a few disciples in Patras already. They just need to get organized.

My brothers are sure taking good care of me here. Their faith is strong. "Excuse me, someone is here to see me. It is the pro consul's wife; she has left her husband and wants to be a follower of Christ, which her husband is totally against. What she asks of me I cannot condone, but neither can I tell her not to follow Christ. I have been snatched by a couple of soldiers, and they are taking me to see Aegeates, the proconsul. Yes, that is Maximillia's husband.

That didn't go so good; he has thrown me in prison. I have until tomorrow to convince his wife to return to him, or he is going to crucify me. I am but a humble man that tries to stay out of marriage problems. Yet here am I, a single person, being threatened by death because of marriage. Go figure.

THE APOSTLES 1ST PERSON A NARRATIVE

I hear that a lot of people have stormed the palace and are demanding my release. These people have a lot of spunk. I also have heard that Aegeates refuses to, so as I am being carried out to the X-shaped cross. People are storming the palace again. I have found a new way to spread the Gospel, by standing firm in my beliefs. Here comes the soldiers; they say Pro Consul Aegeates has agreed to let me down if I tell Maximillia to go home. Here comes the crowd, demanding my release. "Stand back! Do not touch me. I am an old man, but my faith is great. And this is my way of showing how strong it is. My brothers, as long as I have a breath left in my body, I will preach. I ask that those of you who have become followers of Jesus be strong also."

Many people have come to know Christ in the last three days that I have been on this cross. But I am getting weak, and there's not much time before I go home to see Jesus. "Believe people. Jesus is the Lor . . ."

APOSTLE JAMES (SON OF ZEBEDEE)

"**I SEE YOU** people aren't going to leave me alone. What is your game? I am not the easiest person to get along with, and once more I have no intention of changing that, not now for you guys, and not for anybody else. Now get back and stay out of my way! I have to get on that boat over there and go out fishing. Simon and Andrew, and that pipsqueak brother of mine, and dad are going to be on the boat over there. Where do you think you're going? Pay attention to me, I said that boat over there. I can tell already I'm going to be sorry for agreeing to this. John, you knucklehead, I told you that net was broke. Don't you go sassing me, Squirt. I don't care if Dad is the boss. You're going to do what I say, or I'm going to beat the tar out of you. John is my younger brother, and if I hear any of you guys talking disrespectful to him, I will personally pick you up and throw you overboard. You got that?! Now get on!"

THE APOSTLES 1ST PERSON A NARRATIVE

"You want to know about our boats? My father, whom you will call Mr. Zebedee, has owned these boats for most of my life. What you want to know? How many hands does my father have? I really don't know how many hands Dad has, but we have three or four boats. I'm always on the same boat is the reason I don't know the number of hands. How big are they? These boats are around twenty-five feet long and I guess about ten feet wide. They are very stable in rough weather, which comes in handy when we get caught out in the middle of the lake and a big storm comes upon us. By the way, if this should happen, you all get in some corner of the boat and stay out of our way.

"All of our nets are handmade. Every time we go ashore, we spend hours working on the nets. They have to be in good repair or all the fish will break through. It takes three people to cast the net. You never want it to be tangled up. When we have a good haul, it takes several people to bring it in. We cast the nets in the front side of the boat; then right behind it we throw another. We do the same thing on the other side. We don't just sit around waiting on the fish to fill the nets, we are always fixing or making other nets. We also make sure we have sharp knives to help get nets untangled.

"What kind of man is my father? Well, Dad grew up with nothing, but he worked hard all his life. He hasn't had a whole lot of education. He isn't amongst those snobs that gather around and gossip about everybody, but He has acquired enough money to be able to buy out just about anybody He wants. Dad is a very honest man; I guess that is why He has instilled this kind of life in us. He is also level-headed; I can't say that too much about John and me. We fuss and fight all the time, but we admire each other down deep. Don't you go telling him I said that.

"We have lived around Capernaum and Bethsaida all our lives, and I don't figure I will be going anywhere else. We have made a few trips to see my aunt. She lives in Nazareth, which is a forty-mile hike, so we didn't go too often. But we had a blast when we did go. My aunt has two kids, one is named Jesus, and another has my name, James. We would play hide and seek sometimes. I'll tell you something, Jesus could hide so good we would hunt for . . . let's see . . . well, it seemed like ever, and then all of a sudden, there He was. You know, we would do things to try and get Him mad, but He never did. We ended up getting in trouble ourselves. He was strong. I guess He must have gotten that strength from lifting all those carpentry projects around. He could run like a cheetah; none of us could catch him. His brother James wasn't as good an athlete as Jesus, but he was fun too. As we all got older, our trips to see Aunt Mary were few and far between. I heard that Jesus was doing a lot of carpenter work now. That is what Joseph, my uncle, does for a living. I really don't know what James is doing. Well, I have goofed off long enough, I have to get to work."

I have been looking into some of the goings on with another relative of mine, John, called the Baptist. He is preaching about a Man coming that is called the Messiah. Now John has been out in the wilderness for some time, but the last time I saw him, he still was making a lot of sense. John has a large booming voice that will get your attention. He is so passionate about what he is preaching, so much so that you can't help but pay attention to what he is saying. He has come to Capernaum several times. He likes to baptize people in the River Jordan.

In the last few days John the Baptist (I have to say it that way so you won't think I am speaking about my brother) has really been excited. I mean the intensity of his preaching has been taken up a bunch of notches. He keeps saying the Messiah is on His way here.

THE APOSTLES 1ST PERSON A NARRATIVE

"Come on, John. I don't think you are going to help your cause by preaching something you can't back up." A lot of people are buying it though. There is a whole line just waiting to be baptized. I just came down here to see what all the commotion is all about.

"You must repent and be baptized!!!" J.B. just kept repeating this over and over him and that great big voice of his. Just that voice would make you start to tremble. But there is something different about this preaching today. I mean, J.B. is showing more enthusiasm in his message, and he is a lot louder than before. I can hear him clear over here on the lakeside at our boat. Can't make it out but man is he getting with it.

As if that group of people at the river wasn't enough, here comes another bunch following another Man. They are a ways off yet but seems to be a pretty big group, because I can see a big dust cloud around them. "Hey, I can see that guy now! It's my cousin, you know, the one I was telling you about earlier. He's close enough now I think I will holler at Him. Hey, Jesus! What's up, cousin?" He saw me because He is waving at me. I have heard through the grapevine that He is making quite a name for Himself. Seems like He has healed a few people.

Wow, I have been paying so much attention to Jesus approaching that I haven't noticed J.B.'s group of people are all standing around looking towards Jesus. J.B. isn't preaching. He just said something; I couldn't hardly make it out. But it seemed to be, "Here comes the Messiah."

"Well, you guys have been goofing off long enough, let's get to work. I'm sure Jesus will come over and say hi to us."

GEORGE A REGISTER

Man, oh man, I'm dead tired, Simon, Andrew, John, and I, along with a few other hands, have been out all night long trying to catch fish. One of the worst nights of the season. Simon thinks the lake is about fished out. I almost agree. Of course, whether we catch fish or not, we have to clean these nets. Look up on the ledge, here comes a crowd of people. Just what I need. Yep, there is Jesus, I knew it had to be Him. Crowds are following Him everywhere; I can't blame them. He has been healing people and causing havoc to some of them demons in people. I can say I am proud of the fact that He is related to me. With that said though, I am too tired to deal with all those people. Oh good, Simon is going to talk to Jesus. What's this? Jesus just walked right on by Simon. I don't know who He thinks He is. He just got on Simon's and my boat; He didn't even ask if it was okay. Oh, now He is talking to Simon. What does Simon want now? He is waving for us to come over. "Do what? I'm too tired to go out. I don't care if it is just a little ways. Okay, okay, I'll help you. Come on, John; you might as well help too."

Jesus has been teaching for some time now; I'm glad, because this has given us a little time to rest. Looks like Jesus is done preaching for now, so I guess we will go back in and start to work. What is He saying? Go out and cast our nets? I guess I can't blame Him. You see Jesus is, or was, a carpenter not a fisherman. This is the worst time of the day to go out fishing, but I guess we will. This is Simon's boat, and it is okay with him. Here goes nothing. I guess we can get a little more rest. "What is those guys over there yelling about? Let's go see. Oh my (BLEEP BLEEP)! The nets are full; they're so full they are about to break! Not just one, all of them are full! Call the other boats out so we don't lose none of them! There is only one answer to this miracle, and that is Jesus. Let us go up front and say thanks to Jesus." What in the world is going on with Simon? He is on his belly praising Jesus; and look, Simon is crying. I believe we had better get down also and worship Him. Only the True One could have did this for us. Simon is asking what Jesus wants Him to do. Jesus told Simon to get up; now Jesus is looking at all of us. Looking back and forth, He told us not be afraid and from now on we will be fishers of men. I can't help myself; I am being drawn to Jesus now. Simon, John, and me are stepping off this boat for the last time. All these fish will make a lot of money for my dad. Mom and he will be able to live okay.

I have been completely surprised at how strong of a message Jesus is preaching and teaching. As matter of fact, even my mother Salome has been following us. My wife and daughters are also coming along. They are helping with the cooking and cleaning. All this makes for quite the group of people. Then you add all the people that is just following Jesus. Seems like the people just want to hear what Jesus is teaching.

We don't get a lot of time to just sit down and rest. You know, get off of our feet but we do every once in awhile and when we do Jesus confides in us about how bad it felt when His own people, from His own town, would not accept Him. A lot of people don't believe in Him but His own people, including even some of His relatives, that is what hurts the most.

Well, we have been on the road again, but now we are back in C-town. The bunch of us that have been following and helping Jesus are ready once again for some downtime, but Jesus is still fresh as he was this morning. I can't believe this; Jesus is going over to pay some taxes. Wait a minute, He is preaching to the tax collectors. Like they will listen. Hold on, this guy is getting up. I sure hope He isn't going to try and hit Jesus, I swear if he does I'll plow his chariot for him. No, no, he is following Jesus over here to us. I think this tax collector's name is Levi, mean as a snake, and just as crooked. He is getting close enough I can see his eyes now. It looks like he is crying, or at least there is water coming from his eyes. "What did you say, Jesus?! No! I say no! That weasel isn't going with us!!! He is nothing but trash! John, let's beat the crap out of this guy and send him packing. Jesus, you can't be serious. Yes, I know I have not been the best but not as bad as that hunk of dung. Okay. I said okay, but the first false move he makes I'll . . . well . . . . I'll make him pay. John, where you at? Get back here. If I have to stay, you do too."

We have been everywhere, preaching and teaching. We even went out on the boat and Jesus preached there, because the crowds are getting so big. On the banks of the rivers and the lakes, the sound echoes better around the waters.

Jesus has healed so many. The best times though is when He makes the demons come out of people. The demons just go to twisting and shaking and making all kinds of weird noises, but eventually they disappear. I fully expect one of these days Jesus is going to command the demons to get out and that Levi guy will fall down writhing from the demons in him. I think Jesus is calling us, so I had better go over and see what He wants. Jesus is calling for a few men to follow Him up on the mountain, sounds like He has something He wants us to hear.

"Wow! Just wow! Oh, my God, I've been blessed beyond words! What do you mean my eyes are red, looks like I have been crying? Well, I have been. Jesus has chosen twelve of the disciples to be His apostles. I was one of the chosen ones. Jesus has given us miraculous powers like casting demons out of people. No, I'm not going to try it out on Levi, because Levi is one of the chosen also. What a privilege to be able to help Jesus carry out some of His ministries."

THE APOSTLES 1ST PERSON A NARRATIVE

Jesus has been preaching in the temple for almost two hours now. People are gathering big time to listen. I knew the calm wouldn't last very long; here comes one of the rulers of the synagogue. I bet he is going to throw Jesus out. What's this? The ruler is falling to his knees saying something to Jesus. He is standing back up now and Jesus is motioning us to come over. He said that He was going to the ruler's house and that Simon, John, and me were to follow them. The rest of the apostles were to take care of the crowd. It sure does feel funny going into an upper class government person's home. All these people around here are crying, I see. Someone just told me the ruler's daughter has died. Typical Jesus, He told them she was just sleeping. Jesus ran everyone out of the house except for the mom and dad, and us three. We went upstairs, and there lay the young girl. She looked dead to me. But Jesus sat down on the side of the bed, took the girl's hand, told her to get up, and she did. Jesus told the parents to get her something to eat. Jesus also told us to say nothing about this to anyone.

Once again Jesus is calling us together. He is saying that we need to go out and spread the Gospel all around us. We aren't to take anything with us, not even a change of clothing. Most of us are going out to various locations in Galilee. We are so used to having a bucket full of people hanging around us, it seems strange to be just the two of us. I don't know who is going with me just yet, but there will be two of us.

GEORGE A REGISTER

Ever since we have come back from our little mission trip, Jesus has been talking about dying. He keeps telling us people are going to turn against Him. Jesus has taken Simon, John, and me aside a lot in the last few days; Jesus has opened our eyes to His teachings. Since Him opening our eyes, He has bestowed upon us the duty to help teach the others. This is a big task, but with the blessings that Jesus has given us we have been able to perform our new duties. Just a few minutes ago, Jesus said that we had been working day and night, so we needed to go up on the mountain and take a rest. I do believe He is correct; I know I am tired to the bone.

Jesus is calling Simon, John, and me to follow Him up the mountain a little farther; it would be great to get away from all the rest of the crowd. Now that we are here, I think I have found me a good place to lay my head down. I'm so tired; I see Simon and John have found themselves a place too. Jesus said He was going to find a place to pray. Well, I watched Jesus go up a little further all alone. My eyes are about to shut. Wait a minute. Jesus was alone up there, but I hear people talking. Oh, well, I'm too tired to worry about it.

Wow, I don't know how long I was asleep, but I sure do feel a lot more rested. Must be noon, 'cause things are sure bright around here. John and Simon are waking up too. I wonder where Jesus is. "Oh, my God! Jesus, what has happened to you?! Your face and those clothes You have on! You're shining as bright as the sun! And who are those other people with you? Oh, Jesus, You are scaring me! Who're these guys? Oh my! That is Moses, isn't it?! The other one is Elijah?! We must build an altar here and put up tents for each of you. Where they going? Now what?!" There is a cloud above us; I've never seen one so dense. Oh my, it's totally on the ground. Jesus is motioning us to come with Him into that cloud. I don't know about this; I think the other two are just as afraid as I am. But I trust Jesus, so I'm going to follow Him. "John, Simon, are you all coming? I can't see the end of my nose in here."

A booming voice came out of nowhere, it sounds like it is coming from far above us. There is a great rumbling and the voice is saying, "This is my Son, my Chosen One, listen to Him." I am so scared I am on my knees with my head and eyes buried in the dirt.

Nothing is happening right now. Do I dare to look? Okay, I will take it slow, turn my head just a little bit, and open my eyes. Hey, that cloud is gone. I'll look around a little farther. There is Jesus; He is all alone now. Do I dare get up? I think it is okay. As I stood, along with the other two, Simon and John, Jesus told us it is time to come down off of the mountain. Jesus also told us not to say a word about what had just happened. That is okay with me; I don't think anyone would believe us anyway. "By the way, Jesus, what do you mean about rising from the dead?"

We have been on the road for several days now; Jesus has been gathering us together a lot lately. He has been teaching us a lot about the times coming up when He will be crucified. I remember what the voice on the mountain had said. It is so hard to believe that with all the power that Jesus has that somebody, the Romans, will be able to put Him on the cross. I know what Jesus is saying, but it is still hard to accept. We are crossing Samaria. Most Jew will not come here, because they think they are better than the Samaritans. I can see why they think this, but Jesus said the Gospel must be preached to everyone.

We are here in a village; it is small, but the people are very agitated because of our teaching. Here comes a group of them now; they look like they are going to cause trouble. "There is no need for you Samaritans to be so upset. We are just trying to show you some goodwill and love from God. Now, now, no need in being abusive. You don't have to cuss at us.

"Okay, Jesus, can we use some of this power You gave us? John and I will call down fire from heaven and flat destroy these ungrateful people. Oh, come on, Jesus. Please? Yes, I know You don't need our help on this, but I want to teach these guys a thing or two. Okay, I'll get my stuff and leave with You. Man, that would have been so awesome. We still going to Jerusalem?

"You ought to see our caravan of people. I really don't have any idea as to how many there is, but it's a bunch. Hey, all of you, hush for a minute; Jesus is trying to say something. Jesus is calling out a lot of names; none of them is us apostles though. Did you hear that? Jesus has given those disciples power to throw out demons and heal the sick, just like us. My goodness, I bet there is over seventy of these people. Jesus is going to send out all these into towns just up ahead of us. This way they will be prepared to welcome Jesus. These guys are going to be just like we were. They can't take anything with them. They are instructed to just go in and see if they are receptive to the Gospel or not."

It doesn't seem possible but several days have gone by now. Jesus has been teaching in parables and been healing so many. He has allowed us to help in the healing department and the casting out of demons; there seems to be so many. I think Jesus has taught us how to conquer just about any situation that might arise. Over there it is all those disciples Jesus had sent out ahead of us are coming back. Looks like they all have smiles on their faces. They are dancing and carrying on, and Jesus is smiling also. Jesus is holding up His arms to try and get them to settle down. Jesus told them not to rejoice over the demons, but rejoice over the fact that their names are written in heaven. We have so many new people; some haven't known the truths that Jesus taught us before they came. One of the disciples just asked Jesus how they were to pray. So Jesus took time out to teach them. Jesus is so loving. Well, Jesus said it is time to hit the road, so I guess we will be going to the next town.

THE APOSTLES 1ST PERSON A NARRATIVE

Jesus doesn't waste any time; even when traveling from town to town, He has us apostle up close around Him. He has been speaking in parables once again. I don't get it all, but I think I get more than some of the others. Every once in awhile, He will stop and start teaching to all the disciples about things that are about to happen. Of course, they didn't understand, because most of us don't understand it. But our eyes have been opened to a lot of prophecies.

We have traveled a long ways, but we are getting closer to Jerusalem. We are in a little town called Bethany; Jesus said we should go up on Mt. Olivet and pray.

Jesus told a couple of the apostles to go get a colt, so He could ride into Jerusalem. I haven't known Jesus to ride anywhere. He keeps telling us that is what was prophesied. So here comes the two apostles with a little colt. Some of us put our cloaks on the colt and a couple helped Jesus on. As we have started to go people are putting their cloaks on the ground for Jesus to ride over. They are even putting palm branches down. What a noise they are making.

I see that big beautiful town now; I glanced over at Jesus and see He is crying. I thought something was hurting Him, but He said He was crying because this beautiful town was going to be destroyed. After we get into town, Jesus started telling us many parables. Jesus was also answering a lot of questions from the crowd that is gathering around us. Every night Jesus takes us up on Mt. Olivet to rest after the busy day.

We have been praying now for several hours, all but Judas, the Galilean. Today is Passover, and Jesus just said that Simon and my brother John are to go into town and find a place to have the meal.

This is a great meal we have before us. We are having a great time talking about some of the things that we have done and making some plans for later. Jesus is a little down it looks like. "Jesus, what is wrong?" Jesus ducked His head and said someone in this room was going to betray Him. Well, now that put a damper on the evening. Made Judas so ill, He left the room. Jesus said He wanted us to go pray with Him on Mt. Olivet. I guess we will spend the night there. Seems like something strange is in the air. Can't get my mind around it but something is wrong. Looking around I see everyone is here. Wait a minute. Judas isn't here. Maybe he is still feeling ill. I'm going to close my eyes for a minute, and then I'll start to pray.

Hey, someone just kicked me. "Oh, hi, Jesus. I'm sorry. My eyes were so heavy; I couldn't help myself. Hey, look, Judas is coming. Why is he bringing all the soldiers with him? Judas, what's going on?" I guess he didn't hear me. He is going right up to Jesus, I hear something that soldier is saying. Now the soldiers are grabbing Jesus. Oh, no, Simon has his knife out. Oh my, he just cut that soldiers ear off. "Go, Simon, go!" Jesus is telling us to stop. He is reaching down, picking up the ear and putting it back on. As I look around I see that all the apostles are hiding some place.

I haven't went to see what they are doing to my Jesus. I don't think I would be able to look upon Him. I understand they are beating Him unmercifully. I ran into one of the disciples, and he said that the priests wanted Jesus crucified. I remember Jesus trying to tell us that this was about to happen. I just couldn't believe those hypocrite Pharisees would go this far. I'm glad that it was just us apostles that was up on the mountain. I would have hated for the flock, His disciples, to see how cowardly we have acted in the last few days. Here comes another disciple. "Hey, what's up? They're taking Jesus where? You mean them knuckleheads finally got what they were wanting? I hadn't heard. I have been trying to take care of my wife and kids. We've come back to C-town. You said Simon wants us to gather up and have a prayer session? Okay, I'm going to leave everyone at home and go back to Jerusalem to see what he wants."

Everyone is in a somber mood. Can't say as I blame them; I myself am in a down mood. I must say though the ladies have fixed a good-looking meal for us, although I don't think anyone is hungry. Jesus has appointed Simon as the leader for now, and he is getting ready to speak. His face is all shriveled up; you can tell He hasn't had much sleep. As he is speaking, his head is hanging down. He said that he was so ashamed of the way He had denied Jesus when the people revolted. There isn't any reason to be ashamed, because all of us ran and hid. "We all would like to call you, Peter, if you would allow us to. I believe that is what Jesus had called you. Please tell us what we are to do. Oh, yes, I remember Him telling us to stay here until some time when He was going to send another to help us. Oh my! Look! It's Jesus!" I need to get on my knees and bow to Him. Now there is a cloud coming down on us. I remember something like this when the four of us, Simon, John, and me were with Jesus on the mountain, and Moses and Elijah showed up. I can feel something entering my body, it must be the one Jesus said he would send. I now know what we are to do. We can go into all nations and preach the Gospel, no matter what language they speak. Simon, excuse me, I mean Peter, has given us our assignments, so I guess I need to gather my family and a few disciples and head on out. Sounds like we are all scattering from here to there. I am being led towards the Iberian Peninsula. If I had to go by land it would be over 3,000 miles. We can cut a lot of this off by going by boat.

GEORGE A REGISTER

This is pretty country, mountains in the distance, lakes galore, wildlife in abundance. And unlike the area around Jerusalem, it's not overpopulated. It will be a great place to raise my family.

Teaching God's Word to the people here in this country has been great. Many little congregations have been started. I have been blessed with disciples full of the Holy Spirit who are staying behind to nurture these new brothers. Some of these new brothers are following us and preaching to other towns. It is so good to see this going on.

It is now time for us to go back to Jerusalem and report our activity. I had a little meeting with my brothers. Many want to stay here instead of going back; so we prayed about it, and I found peace in doing so. I hate leaving them, but I must get back. My family and I are on the stern of the boat looking at all my brothers as they wave goodbye to us.

We are getting close to home; we have been sailing for days now. The good Lord has blessed us with great weather all the way back. Looks like we are going to land in Capernaum. That's good, the family can visit relatives there while I go to meet the others in J-town.

Man, things have sure changed in Jerusalem since I have been gone. The town has grown so much, not just in people, but also in hatred towards Christians. Jesus' brother James has his hands full. The Pharisees are harassing us and throwing us in jail for no good reason other than that we are Christians. Ever since they crucified Jesus, the government, in particular Herod Agrippa, has seen how it found favor in the Jewish community, and this makes things a whole lot easier to govern. He has one bully that is very fond of persecuting us; his name is Saul. You see him coming, you had better run and hide. They tell me he has a list of people who has become believers and that is what he uses to hunt you down.

THE APOSTLES 1ST PERSON A NARRATIVE

There is a big commotion going on down the street. Oh, my Lord, they are dragging a disciple down the road! Oh my, it's Stephen! Stephen is one of the kindest people you will ever meet. Unlike me, he can keep his cool in all circumstances. He is all bloody from being dragged. That monster, yeah, it's Saul, sitting up on his horse laughing at Stephen. "Oh, Jesus, they are going to stone him, so please take the pain away." People are throwing rocks at him, and he is still proclaiming the Gospel. Things have got quiet now. Oh, my Lord, Jesus had said there would be times like this. It only makes my faith, and the faith of my brothers in Christ stronger. I sure do miss my brother John although I would never admit it. He and Peter are out taking care of the congregations that has been formed. I don't know how much more my brothers here in Jerusalem can stand. So many are being thrown in prison and then beaten. I'm glad my family is still in C-town. I am going to go to the synagogue and preach this morning. James is teaching right now, and then I'm going to teach. James has matured so much since Jesus' death. Our understanding of events has opened our eyes.

I hear some scuttlebutt going on. I don't believe it, but one of the brothers said that Saul has been won over to Christ. I just don't see that happening with him, but I have seen things like that happen before. Take that brother who was a tax collector. His name was Levi, but Jesus said his name would be Matthew. I actually have grown to like Matt, and I know he loves Jesus. But Saul? That's another story. Some of us apostles are together trying to get our minds around this development. "What's all the commotion outside? I'll go look. Everyone better go hide for a little bit. I think it is that Saul guy. Just in case what we have heard isn't true, only one of us will be captured. I volunteer, okay?

"Hi, Barnabas, who's your friend there?" I'm playing it cool here; I know good and well who that is. "You say this is Paul, formerly known by all as Saul? I have heard that you have been presenting the Gospel to people. Is that true? Please, come on in. It is okay, brothers. Come on out. This is Paul, and what a story he has to tell!"

"I, a believer in the Lord Jesus Christ, come to you this morning to tell you of His grace and mercy! Please open your hearts and know the peace of Jesus. Please listen, I can't tell you all about this if you aren't a little bit quieter. Well, sir, you may not want to hear this, but there are others who might want to. You know you aren't supposed to be up here with me. Get your hands off me! Ouch, that hurt! Where are you taking me? You have no reason to treat me like this or to put me in jail. You think this is going to stop me from preaching the Gospel? You got another think coming. You'll never stop me! Go ahead. Take me to Herod; I'll preach to him and his whole court. Hey, guard, you ever hear of Jesus? Man, you got to hear about Him; He will give you hope and peace. You like that, huh?"

Well, things didn't go so well with Bozo Herod. He said I was a nuisance to society and that I was talking against the government, so he has sentenced me death. But I still will teach about Jesus till my last breath. I think that is going to be sooner than I care for. I don't know what I would do if I didn't know my Savior. Peace is in me, and I can smile as they lead me away. Matter of fact, here they come now. Oh, look, a new guard and the one who has been watching over me. The one that I know is looking peaked. "What is the matter, friend? Oh, I see, time for me to meet Jesus, huh? Sir, you have been kind to me, but I wish you would accept Jesus and have this peace that I have." I will walk out with my head held high . . . Well, look at this, Herod is going to do this himself. "Friend, what you doing on your knees? You are accepting Jesus as your Saviour? Oh, thank You, Lord Jesus, for my new br . . ."

APOSTLE
JOHN
(SON OF ZEBEDEE)

"I'M TELLING YOU, James, if you don't get off my back, I'm going to thump you good. I know you are older than me, but I am stronger than you. You want to try me? Come on. I'm ready. Yes, sir, I understand, dad. I'll get to work. I'm the only one around here that does any of the work. I work, and they play. My dad owns this company. Have you met him? We have several boats, and we have a lot of people that we have hired. Some of them are slaves we have bought. It hasn't always been this way.

"My brother James and I was actually born in a town called Bethsaida. Dad, his name is Jon Zebedee, didn't have a dime to his name but was able to save and buy his first boat. After that, the business begin to grow. We met up with the problem of not a big enough port to grow anymore, so Dad moved us to Capernaum. We now have several boats.

"My fondest memories though are of James and I back in Bethsaida. Dad and Mom would take us on long walks. We would go down by the beach and play in the sand, go swimming, and collect shells of all kinds. Sometimes Dad and Mom would take us over to my aunt's house. She lived in Nazareth. Aunt Mary and Uncle Joseph have two kids also. We had so much fun. James, not my brother, but Aunt Mary's kid, was a little on the shy side, but once he got use to us being there he was a lot of fun. Now the other kid, his name was Jesus; He would jump right in the middle of us. I liked him a lot. I have heard my mother talking about how Jesus was conceived and the problems that followed them. Jesus was good with His hands and able to figure things out. The toys that he would make! Wow, I wish I had that much talent! But if what they say about Him is true, no wonder He can do these things. He is pleasant to be around. I have to admit though, my brother and I would do a lot of teasing, trying to get Him mad, but He always stayed cool. Before it was all over though, we would get in trouble. But it was fun. A lot of times the whole family would sit around an open fire, and Uncle J would tell us all about their travels into Egypt Jesus was always talking about God. He wouldn't even eat a stick of candy or bread without blessing it with prayer; the prayers wasn't short ones either. I remember falling down and scraping my knee while playing one day, and He prayed over that. Being we were pretty young at the time, it was kind of weird. But you know what? It did make it feel better. I really didn't understand what Jesus was talking about, but His demeanor made it seem right. Oh, well, I need to get to work."

I have been thinking a lot about the Torah. The only education I have is through our dad. And although he is a very smart person, everything has been taught about the fishing business. Mom taught us to read and write, but my reading isn't the best. I just couldn't sit still long enough. But I have read a lot of the Torah. Seemed so boring at first, but 1 am enjoying it now. Andrew has been going over to listen to a man called John the Baptist. Said that this man was telling about someone they called the Messiah. Andy sure likes him. I think I will go with him the next time, you know, check him out. Maybe he can answer some questions I have. I would go to the Pharisees and ask but they don't want to be bothered with such "trivial" questions. "Andy, are you going over to listen to this John guy anytime soon? You don't say. Well, that is good timing. Would you mind if I tagged along? Thank you." I guess I had better get permission from Dad. If we miss work, he gets pretty mad. When Dad gets mad, you know you're fixing to scrub a deck.

Dad said it was okay, not a lot of work going on, because the fish are going too deep for our nets. I like hanging around with Andy, because he is a vegetarian just like me. I really don't see how people can put meat in their mouths. And they have the nerve to make fun of me. Hope they choke on it.

My goodness, look at all these people. This guy must have them hypnotized or something. A person could go along and pick everyone's pockets, because they are so engrossed into what he is saying. Hundreds are in this crowd. You know, as big as this crowd is, I can still hear every word that this John is saying. I have a loud, deep voice, but it isn't anything like his. I wonder who this Messiah is. Now I see why they call him John the Baptist. He is in the river, baptizing any and every one that wants to be. If this guy gets as big a crowd everywhere he goes, he must be one tired puppy at the end of the day. "Hey, stop pushing me! I got a right to this spot. You keep pushing, and I'm going to thump you on the head. People. They don't care about anyone else but themselves. Ouch, Andy, let go of my shoulder; you're going to get it. Hey, this is a good spot. Thank you; sorry I snapped at you. We can sit here on this rock and see and hear everything. What is this "repent" thing he is talking about? I thought he only talked about this Messiah?" I am feeling drawn to him. It's like someone has a hold of my shoulder pulling me to him, and it isn't Andy this time. "No, no I don't want to leave yet. You go on ahead to the house; I'm going to stay a little longer." I can't believe the power this man is having on me. I sure hope I get to talk with him.

Well, I talked with him, and he said that he was not the Messiah, nor would he ever be, but that the Messiah would be coming soon. I ask him if I could follow him around for awhile; he said it would be okay, but I needed to be baptized. So, even though he had been working all day, preaching his message, he took me down to the water and baptized me.

My dad has been very generous to me by allowing me to spend my time with J.B. John is going to be leaving town soon, like tomorrow, and I think I'm going to go with him. I am going to ask Dad first though. I know, I am old enough to do what I want to do, but I might want to come back someday you know. Andy would like to go too, but he feels like he should stay and help Dad. Besides, I think J.B. will be coming back here several more times.

J.B. and I have been on the road now for a few weeks. We got back into Capernaum yesterday evening. While J.B. started preaching, I ran over to see the family. It sure did feel good to see them. Dad is telling me all about what has been happening out on the lake. He even asked me if I would like to go out with him on his next trip. I sort of miss this so I think I will. J.B. has enough help at the moment. Here comes Andy. "Hi, bro. How you doing? Okay, I'll go over with you; I'll even introduce you to J.B. Mom, you doing okay? Smells like you are fixing something good for supper. I don't know, Mom, but I'll ask J.B. if he would like to eat with us. How is the rest of the family? Yes, Mom, I'll tell you all about our adventures, but for right now Andrew wants to go listen to J.B.

"Andy, I believed that this John the Baptist was the Messiah, but he was real fast about telling me that he wasn't. He said that the Messiah would be coming soon. Well, you have been with him almost as much as me. You think that if he said he wasn't, then he wasn't? You are a better thinker than I am, so I guess I had better believe him. You know James and me, when we get something stuck in our head we have a hard time changing it. I just wonder who this Messiah is going to be. I think that is a good idea. Go get Simon, and let him hear this J.B. I don't think he will come either. Maybe someday..."

Today J.B. is acting a little strange. He seems to be anticipating something. The crowds are starting to gather; they seem to get bigger every time we start to baptize people. I haven't figured it out yet. Are the people here to listen to J.B., or are they here to see what kind of questions the Pharisees have for him? J.B. doesn't pay much attention to them though. He has one mission to do, and that is what he sticks to.

I bet he has baptized fifty people already today and more are coming down. I would say one hundred more or so. J.B. doesn't seem to get tired of baptizing people. "Hi, Andy, you see all the people. Do you see something in the eyes of John? He is acting like a cat on a hot roof. Hey, he has stopped baptizing; what is he doing? Look, he is separating the crowd. He has made like a pathway, reminds me of a story I read about Moses parting the River Jordan, only John is parting people. Listen, John is about to speak. Andy, did he say what I think he said? He called that person walking towards us the Messiah. Look, Andy! It is Jesus! John the Baptist just called Jesus the 'Messiah.' Everybody is looking at John and then back at Jesus and then back at John again. From what I have been reading and hearing about the Messiah, Jesus does fit the bill. Think about it, Andy; we have known the Messiah for all His earthly life. Our eyes were blind to it, but now we can see. Remember the stories we were told by our parents? You know, the ones about how Jesus was conceived? How Aunt Mary and Uncle Joseph had to go to Egypt? It all makes sense now. I bet J.B. knew this all along. By the way, J.B. is motioning us over to him. He and Jesus is talking something over.

"Hi, Jesus, haven't seen you for some time. I heard you were going about the Lord's work. I guess the last time we saw you was at the wedding. Is it true you made that water into wine? I thought they were joking, but I see now it is true. Do what J.B.? I can't do that; I'm loyal to you. I can't just up and leave you. Yes, I know you always said there would be One greater than you. I have learned so much from you, sir. Yes, sir, I'll stop arguing with you; if you want me to follow Jesus, then I will follow Jesus. I guess You are stuck with us, Jesus. Yes, I know You will teach us many wonderful things. You want to stay here in Capernaum a few days? Well, that is good; this way I can get all my affairs organized. Oh, this is going to be good. I am getting excited, and I haven't even left yet."

Jesus and I left for Jerusalem this morning. It is going to be a little walk ... one hundred twenty-one miles to be exact. So we will be on the road for about three to four days; it will depend on how many times we stop so Jesus can preach. I have found out one thing already, when walking with Jesus; he doesn't dilly-dally around. He walks fast, but if someone wants to talk, He stops. This walking time isn't wasted time either; Jesus is always teaching us different points from the Torah. I say "us" because there are several people that are following Jesus. Some of those Pharisees are even following us. I thought J.B. was good at answering them, but Jesus is a hundred times better than J.B. was, or should say, is. There is a couple of people writing everything that Jesus does down. That is good; I write a few things down, but I write after we settle down for the night. These guys write all day. Kind of funny, a couple of times they fell, or stumbled down, because they wasn't paying attention as to where they were going. It is even funnier to see the Pharisees, with their noses stuck up in the air, trip and fall, they get them pretty white robes of theirs dirty. If one of us falls, Jesus will wait till we get up, but if one of those Pharisees falls, He just keeps on walking. It isn't that He doesn't care about them, because He cares about everyone. But he can't wait on them to brush off their pretty white robes or listen to them grumble.

Look, it is Jerusalem, we have made it. With Jesus teaching and talking all the time, it makes the day go by so fast. It is getting close to Passover time. So the city is getting full of travelers. I figured Jesus would stop on the outskirts of town and preach, but no, he just marches right on in. With His eyes fixed straight ahead, with nothing deterring Him, it looks like He is going dead ahead for the temple. Makes sense. He wants to preach. Look at His face. He looks angry; I have never seen Him angry. What is He up to now? He is making something; He has a bunch of string; it could be small rope thread. I can't see too much; I am standing back a ways from Him. He has made a whip; now why would he make a whip? Wow, listen to that whip snap! I think Jesus is headed for the temple. Snap! Snap! Snap! Snap! Man is He swinging that whip around! All those vendors are starting to run for their lives. Jesus hasn't hit anyone with that whip, but they think He is. Jesus is on a rampage in the temple. Look, He is at the money changers tables. Oh my! He is going down the line and is turning every table over, money is scattering everywhere. The strange thing is the temple guards are just standing around; they must be too stunned to react. Snap! Snap! Snap! Jesus is wielding the whip again. This time it is the vendors with the pigeons that are running for their lives. He has blasted out with a voice of venom; He told them to stop defiling God's House. Some of the vendors, mostly the money guys, wanted to know with whose authority He did this. Jesus said that if they would destroy the temple, he would raise it back up in three days. They all laughed at him, and basically they said it took over forty-six years to build. Then Jesus laughed at them and walked off. As a follower of Jesus, we know it wasn't a literal temple he was talking about.

Things are starting to calm down somewhat now; it has been a few days since Jesus cleaned house at the temple. Even the Pharisees have slowed down with the questions. Actually, one of them is listening with a good ear. They ought to, Jesus is doing one miracle after another. I can't count how many He has healed. Jesus even lets me help sometimes. But for now, we are going to rest for the evening. It is getting late; the sun is down. Everyone is tired, and Jesus is in praying.

What is that noise? It seems to be coming from over there. Man, it's one of those Pharisees, not just anyone, but an upper Pharisee. Wait, it is that one that was listening today. I think his name is Nicodemus; he wants to talk to Jesus. He has actually acknowledged that Jesus must have come from the Lord. He wants to know what to do. Jesus told him he must be born again. That about blew his mind. "How can that be," he asked? Jesus didn't mess around with words. He told the man that he was a teacher, but didn't know what he taught, something like that anyway. Nicodemus went away scratching his head. I believe he would like to accept Jesus but is afraid of man.

Jesus came around and told us it was time to travel again. We were going to go through Samaria, at least that is the short route.

THE APOSTLES 1ST PERSON A NARRATIVE

We have been hoofing it for several hours now. Jesus said we could get to Sychar and rest. I am glad we are going pretty fast through here. These are half breeds you know. I hate to be around them even. If Jesus heard me saying that, he would have my hide. Jesus loves everyone, and He expects all of us to do the same. They don't even go to the same temple to worship. I don't think they are going to listen to Jesus if He tries to preach to them.

All right, we have reached the well. Oh, just great, there is a women there. Maybe she will leave, and then our women can gather us some water. "Do what, Jesus? You mean, go into town and buy from these folks? But Sir, You do know they are Samaritans, right? Sorry, Sir, we will go get some food and supplies from town; but can You get rid of that woman, so we can get a drink? Yes, Sir, we'll get a drink when we get back." Boy, the things I'll do to follow Jesus. These people better not try anything, or I'll thump them on the head. You know what? I just remembered, that well back there is called Jacob's Well. God provided that water for our ancestors. I think when we get back to the caravan I will have it out with Jesus over this. Why should I have to wait? Oh my, we are in town, and I feel like a sheep in the pen with a hungry wolf. Is it just me, or does it look like it bothers any of the others? Maybe I'm overreacting a bit.

Isn't that the women from the well? Jesus must have told her to scat and don't come back. Look at her run. Look close. She is smiling; no, she is laughing. She isn't just running either; she is dancing around. What is she doing talking to us? "Hello, and have a good day." The nerve of her! That is the reason I don't have anything to do with those people; they have no respect for their superiors.

How did Jesus get all that water up? Probably waved His little pinky and filled the buckets. "Jesus, You didn't have to do all that work filling the water jugs. What do You mean that woman did it all? She has confessed all her sins and is a believer now? Is that why she looked so happy when she ran past us?

"Everybody, get your swords out, and get ready to fight. Here comes the whole town down to destroy us. But Jesus, we need to be ready. Yes, Sir, I'll put my sword up."

Why are they stopping at the edge of camp? They are sitting down, chanting, "Jesus, Jesus, Jesus." I guess I need to get the whole story before I go flying off the handle. These people were nothing but kind to us. Not only that, but are my brothers and sisters in Christ now. Praise be to God. Jesus said we will be staying here a couple of days. I'm actually glad.

I am so sorry. I have been so concerned with myself that I have been taking credit for a lot of things that I have been involved in but not including others that have helped. There are twelve of us that have been appointed as, what Jesus calls, apostles. We take care of organizing the missions we go on. I have acted like I did all this, but I haven't. A lot of my family, like Simon, Jesus calls him Peter, my own brother James, and even Andrew, has followed us to help. Of all things, we even have a tax collector. His name was Levi, but Jesus calls him Matthew. Hundreds of people in various areas help us; Jesus calls them disciples. A lot of them have traveled with us; one is real young, and I think they call him Timothy. He's one smart fellow. Another one is a guy name John. No, I'm not tooting my own horn again; this guy's last name is Mark, I believe. He is the one that keeps writing everything down. Of course, we do have people that are following us just to cause trouble too.

THE APOSTLES 1ST PERSON A NARRATIVE

We have been on the road now for a long time; we have re-entered the Galilean country. Nice and hilly here with lots of trees and valleys. I guess someone must have told the people we were coming; this has to be the biggest crowd yet. Jesus is sitting on top of the hill, preaching as always. He has been at it all day, and it is getting later. So we suggested He let the people go and He could start all over again tomorrow. But instead, Jesus told Judas Iscariot to give money to buy enough food for everyone. Phil told Jesus there wasn't enough money in the world to buy food for everyone. Jesus wanted to know if there was any food among the people. Andy piped up and said a boy had a couple of fish and some bread, but that was all there was. Don't think that will feed all five thousand or so people, and that is just the men. Jesus said to get the baskets out, and put the fish in one and the bread in the other. He said to start feeding everyone; the others went from one person to the other, and the baskets never ran out. I wish I had more faith.

Jesus said it was time to leave Bethsaida and head for Jerusalem. So once again, as has happened so many times before, we start off on another journey. We are now about two miles away from Jerusalem, when a woman comes running up to Jesus. I recognize her now, and her name is Mary. She is crying, so something is wrong. I got a little closer. I guess one of our good friends, Lazarus, this woman's brother, had died. I guess he died four days ago. So Jesus went to the outskirts of the city of Bethany and approached the cave where Lazarus had been buried. I don't think I have ever seen Jesus crying before, but He was crying with Mary. And then, Jesus took His arm from around Mary, walked up to the front of the tomb, and started to pray. Then He told some of the men to roll the stone from in front of the cave. I think I will stand back a ways, after all Lazarus has been dead for four days, more than likely he is smelling pretty bad right now. Without any warning or anything, Jesus raised His arms toward the heavens, and with a voice so loud and deep, told

Lazarus to come out. That voice, I never have heard Jesus use that deep of a voice before, it was so different than normal. I turned to look into the cave, and there stood Lazarus, still wrapped up in the burial cloth. Talk about a happy time; let's have a party! What a miracle! Everybody was smiling, laughing, and dancing in the streets. I looked at the Pharisees to see what they might be thinking; they weren't even smiling; let alone rejoicing for the miracle.

Word about Lazarus spread all over the country; I say this because the crowds have grown tremendously. I can't even begin to count how many there is. Jesus is doing miraculous works right and left, healing people and casting out demons. As one of the apostles, I have been given the ability to perform some of these miracles. You take and multiply this by the work of all the apostles, and you have a lot of work being done.

We finally were able to get some rest last night. But we are up early because Jesus said He was going to go to Jerusalem today. That's not a big deal because we are only less than two miles from Jerusalem. Jesus has sent a couple of His disciples into town ahead of us to get a small donkey. Don't understand why, but He wants one. We have several animals that go with us, you know, to carry supplies and so forth. He said it needed one that hadn't been ridden or carried anything, which would leave ours out. Here comes the boys. That is the prettiest little donkey I have ever seen. "Woah, Jesus, you can't just jump on that donkey. He hasn't ever been ridden before, and he will buck you off in a heartbeat. Well, I'll be! Jesus just jumped on, and the donkey just stood there."

Looks like we are on our way to Jerusalem. People are standing alongside the road waving and shouting, "Hosanna!" This is quite the welcoming committee. People are laying their cloaks down on the road so Jesus can ride on them. Now look at them, they are laying palm branches down. They are treating Him as a king. The closer we get to town the louder the disciples are getting. Look over there; in the row, it is the Pharisees. They are getting more and more agitated. Here comes some of them now. They just told Jesus to make His disciples be quieter. I like this, Jesus told them if He was to do that, the rocks would start singing in our place. Man, did they stomp away mad.

We have entered into Jerusalem now, so I think Jesus is going straight to the temple. As we walk through town, the crowds keep getting bigger. Oh, no, those vendors are there again, and Jesus is headed straight for them. There He goes again; He is chasing the vendors out once again. Most of them have seen what Jesus can do to them, so they are gathering their goods up before Jesus gets to them and scatters everything all over the floor.

Jesus has been teaching in the temple for several days now. That guy never gets tired. He teaches in the day, and then in the evenings He teaches us outside of the city. Jesus' messages are being taught with more and more urgency. He keeps talking about someone is going to betray Him. I can't see that happening; we all love Him so much, me particularly. Peter was raising such a stink about it that Jesus said Peter would deny Him three times. That didn't set with Peter too well. Jesus is calling us over, Peter and I that is. Besides me, Peter is another one of Jesus' favorite apostles. "Do what? You want Peter and me to go into town and secure a large room so we can have supper? You want Peter and me to cook the dinner? That is our duty as of now?" Jesus said that a man carrying a jug of water would give us a room upstairs. "Okay, let's go; we have a lot of work to do."

Once again, Jesus was correct about the man with a jug of water; He gave us the upper room, completely furnished. It is a good thing Peter and I have a few disciples with us as I don't think what I cook would taste too good. We have the table all set up. I, of course, have reserved a seat right next to Jesus.

It is a good thing we finished, because here comes the rest of the apostles and Jesus. Everyone needs to take their sandals off before they come in. Jesus is getting a bucket of water over there. What is He going to use that for? Now He has a towel; I see, He is going to wipe His feet. I guess He is going to wash His feet instead of wiping them. He is bending down in front of Peter. Wait, Jesus is going to wash Peter's feet? Peter is arguing with Jesus about how he should be washing Jesus' feet. Jesus wouldn't hear of it. Jesus is washing everyone's feet. I don't know what it is, but Jesus is looking a little pale. Something is wrong. I can't believe what Jesus just said. One of us, His apostles, is going to betray Him. No, No, that can't be true, but that is what Jesus said. I am so upset, I don't think I can eat this meal. Peter wants me to ask Jesus which one of us is it, so I ask Him. Jesus said it would be the one he hands a morsel of bread to. No sooner had I heard this Jesus dipped some bread in the wine and handed it to Judas Iscariot. Then He told him to go do what he had to do. Afterwards Jesus told us He wanted to have the Passover meal with us before He had to suffer. Of course, Peter started to argue again that no one, especially not him, was going to leave Jesus. Jesus told Peter he would deny Him three times. Poor ol' Peter, just can't seem to stop arguing with Jesus; but I must say, he seems to be the most devoted to Him. Jesus is telling us that we need to go pray on the hill.

It is just the apostles that have come up to pray. Jesus wanted to be alone with us, and He may want to teach us something tonight. We all gathered together while Jesus went up farther to pray by Himself. There is something in the air that doesn't feel right. I can't seem to be able to put my finger on it, but something is definitely amiss. Oh, man, here comes Judas, and he has a bunch of people with him. I guess he didn't get the memo we wanted to be alone. That isn't people; that is soldiers. What are they up to? Judas went up and kissed Jesus and the soldiers went to arrest Jesus. Good ol' Peter came to the rescue and cut off a soldier's ear; Jesus told him to stand back. Jesus reached down and put the ear back on the soldier. Most of the apostles have scattered. It was all I could stand to see them dragging Jesus off. Peter and I, along with another apostle, followed behind not too far away.

The trial, if you could call it that, was swift and without any reasoning. They have taken Jesus from the High Priest to the government leaders. Without proof they have condemned Jesus to die on the cross. I have been waiting outside; I haven't been able to see Jesus or know what was happening to Him. I heard they were going to take Him up on Golgotha and hang Him on a cross. Jesus kept telling us this was going to happen. Here He comes now. Oh, my goodness, is that Jesus? He has been beaten to within an inch of His life. Parts of His beard has been pulled out. His back is nothing but one big whelp. There is big clumps of hair missing. The gashes in his legs are clear to the bone. I don't see how He is standing up let alone trying to carry that timber. Oh, He just fell. I can't get to him; too many people standing around. These aren't the same people that was following Jesus out on the road. I didn't know so many people hated Jesus. I don't think it is so much that they hate Jesus, as it is the Pharisees have whipped up so much animosity against Him. Of course, the soldiers get to have their time with Him. They love to beat people, especially Jews.

With some help from a bystander, Jesus arrived on Golgotha. They are driving the nails through His hands and feet. Now they have Him raised up; He is just hanging there. I think by them beating Him so badly He has become numb to the nails. Look, there is Mary, His mother, and a couple of other ladies standing as close as they are allowed to. Maybe I can get up next to them. "Mary, lean on me if you want. I don't know how you can stand up to this pressure. It is good that Jesus can still recognize you." Jesus looked at His mother and told her to look at Him. Then to my surprise, He looked at me and asked me to take care of His mother. I will take care of her just like she was my own mother.

As I prepare Mary to go home with me, I turn to Jesus one more time, just to be able to look upon His body. "Oh, Jesus, You have went home already. Your lifeless body now is of no use to You, but I know You are alive in Spirit."

GEORGE A REGISTER

―‹‹‹●›››―

I was so privileged to be one who was close to Jesus. My brother James and I, plus Peter were able to spend a lot of one-on-one time with Jesus. Many times He would call us over to the side and show us and teach us some of the finer points of His teachings. I wasn't always such a good pupal. My strong-willed self, hot temper, and know-it-all attitude got in the way a lot of times. But Jesus always calmed me down and told me He saw goodness deep within me. He had asked Peter and me to lead His people in the correct ways. I can feel His presence in me; this hatred I have always had has completely disappeared, and I only feel love for all people. This could only be a gift from Jesus. My beliefs, and all the other apostles as well, was made firm by Jesus appearing to us and a lot of the other disciples after His death. The most glorious moment was when He arose up into the clouds disappearing in body, but ever present in Spirit. Enough of this looking back, I have a lot of work to do. Peter and I must gather all the apostles up and have a meeting as to how we must proceed.

"Okay, we need to find Philip; he is real good at planning activities. Jesus had said that we needed to spread the Gospel all over, so Philip can give us an idea where to even start. Timothy, would you go find Bartholomew for us? He is good at organizing everything. John Mark, would you take a few of the brothers and go find the rest of the apostles? Then Peter and I need to have you write down our proceedings. Thank you.

"Peter, do you think we need to replace the traitor? I believe Jesus chose twelve for a reason, kind of like the twelve tribes maybe? As soon as we get the people together we can run this by them. Peter, are you going to be the one to address the meetings and do the preaching in the temples? Whatever you need, I will be your assistant if that is okay with you. We need to have a budget meeting with Matthew too. He has been keeping the books, and I guess he will be the treasurer now also."

Hey, you know this "loving people" thing is all right. I feel so much better about myself. It is so much better being pleasant; I should have done it earlier in life.

Peter is about to address the group now so it needs to be quiet for a bit. It is very understandable that everyone is a little scared right now. The Romans, especially a soldier named Saul, are waging war on the disciples, taking them to prison and beating them. That man Saul is meaner than a rabid dog. As Peter is bringing up, this is what Jesus said would happen. We have to take up the cross.

Peter just brought up the subject of replacing the traitor. Everyone is in agreement that we should. But who should it be? We are all going to pray over this. Everyone is in agreement that the one to replace the fallen one must have been with and followed Jesus while on earth. There was two that everyone thought was right, and that was John Mark and Timothy. But both was really new to Christianity and very young. Two more names came up; they were Barsabbas and Matthias. Both of these men are more than qualified to serve. Let us pray to seek Jesus' will on this matter. We will cast lots on it to see who becomes the replacement. It has been settled, Matthias has been chosen. Now we can get back to the business at hand.

We all have gathered together again; we need to give out instructions. "Is it storming outside? Tim, would you check it out, please? Strange, I see out of the window and not a cloud is in the sky, but the wind is getting stronger and stronger. Look! Fire coming out of nowhere, not just one, but tongues of fire is resting on every one of the apostles shoulders." Peter is telling us that Jesus predicted this also. Remember, He said He would send another. Well, it is the Holy Spirit that has descended down upon us. People outside must have seen it because they think we are drunk or something. You see, we are speaking in a language everybody can understand. People from all over are here for it is Pentecost time. This ought to be good, Peter is about to give a message. When people hear Peter, they hear him in their own language. They just don't understand, but Peter is giving it to them with both barrels. Thank You, Jesus, hundreds are accepting Jesus as their Savior. Like I said, some hard-headed ones think we are drunk. It is their loss. For the most part though, people keep coming and coming. Peter has been teaching now for several hours, and he said as long as they are coming, he will teach. Look, he isn't even tired yet; kind of reminds me of Jesus and His long teachings.

Peter and I have sent the apostles out to various places. We are staying around Jerusalem so that things can get established. There are plenty of people who haven't heard the message as of yet, and people from other parts of the world come in every day. So the work is never done.

Peter and I are headed for Solomon's portico this day. Peter will be preaching from the steps there. That is such a pretty place, the whole interior is of cedar, from top to bottom. It is on the east side of the temple and is about fifty cubits long and thirty cubits wide, so it holds lots of people. As we are entering the gate, Peter sees a man setting there begging for money. Ever since the Holy Spirit has come upon us we have been full of compassion. Today is no different. We stopped and ask the man how long he has been begging; he said all his life, because he was born unable to walk. Peter looked at me and I looked at him, and we both smiled real big. Peter told him we haven't got any money but have something better. Peter to him to look him in the eyes, get up from there, and walk in the name of Jesus Christ. That man was able to leap straight up, and he began praising the Lord and dancing all over. Everybody around that place knew this man, and they were all in awe. The door was wide open for Peter to preach. And before it was all over, as many as I would say five thousand, came to know the Lord. What a day.

I guess we must have struck a nerve or something because some temple guards came and arrested Peter and me. We had to spend the night in jail, but that was okay. We got to witness to the guards all night. Here comes the Saducees now. They ordered the guards to take us up to the council chambers. Oh, look, there is the man Jesus healed yesterday. He's standing with us, praise Jesus. Those Saducees want to know who gave us authority to do the miracles yesterday. Well, Peter, who was full up to the top of his head with the Holy Spirit let it all out. They were glad to get rid of us; Peter was making them look bad.

The priests of the Saducees must have went up and told the high priest what was going on. They say he got beet red. Here we go again; all of us have been arrested. As we were all in the jail, we started to sing and praise the Lord. All of a sudden the jail doors all swung open and all of us were released. The angel told us to go preach from the temple, so we are headed back there now. You should have seen those guards; they were all too scared to move.

We have been preaching for a while now; I have been expecting to see more guards. Speaking of the devils, here they come. They are being very polite for some reason. Peter says they are afraid of the people, makes sense to me. The high priest is standing now, demanding we stop preaching about Jesus. With a unison of voices, we all said, "We must obey God rather than man." Oh, boy, that high priest went ballistic; I don't think anyone has ever told him no. He is ready to give the command to kill us all. The high priest waved his hand and the soldiers all come running in. Ouch, they are grabbing the back of my neck. "You just threw me down. Is that a whip?" Oh, I will not yell out in pain. "Oh . . . Thank you for . . . oh . . . being my

... oh ... Savior ... oh ... Lord Jesus. You're grabbing my neck. I'll walk; you don't have to drag me. Ouch, you just threw me down the stairs. Hi, everybody, you all okay? We have been persecuted for the sake of Jesus. I feel so blessed."

Peter said that Bartholomew has laid out some plans as to where we needed to send people. The plans is very ingenious; he has apostles crisscrossing from one spot to the next, that way we can keep in touch and spread the word as to how everyone is doing. Peter and I will stay in Jerusalem for a while to take care of local business. It sure is going to get lonely without the brothers around.

I'm so proud of how the disciples have stood firm in their new faith. Even Barsabbas who was a contender for the role of apostle. I believe it is going to get rough in the next few weeks; I heard the Sadducees are so mad that they have called in that Saul guy to help eliminate us. They have already laid their hands on one of the disciples and took him into high court. Oh, boy, I think I just saw that wicked man Saul going in. Here comes the Sadducees dragging Stephen by rope. They're taking him outside of the city. "Oh, Jesus, help Stephen."

Here comes hotshot Saul on his horse. He is egging the people on, "Stone him! Stone him!" I heard Stephen say to Jesus, not to judge them, for they know not what they do. I think he has went to sleep; Jesus didn't let him suffer too long.

As advertised, Saul is going through the whole town, house to house, dragging people off to prison, but most all of the disciples have scattered all over the country. Saul don't care, "act and ask questions later" is his motto. Despite all of this, all of us that are apostles have stayed in town for now.

THE APOSTLES 1ST PERSON A NARRATIVE

"Peter and I have been on the road now for quite a long time. We have been visiting many of the churches that have been started. It is amazing to see how far the Gospel has been taught. Now that Saul is gone . . . Oh, you haven't heard? Saul has converted over to Christianity. No, I'm not kidding. Jesus blinded him and then gave him his sight back. Now He is preaching the Gospel everywhere. Jesus even gave him the title of apostle, just like us. I tell you what, when he was brought to us the first time, I was sure we were goners; but his attitude was of a man under complete convection. His ministries are mostly with the Gentiles. That is good for we know that Jesus said He loved the whole world, not just the Jews.

"I just received some bad news; I understand my brother James has been executed for his faith. I know he has went to be with Jesus, but as a human I still feel sad. Mom and Dad are beside themselves, but to the glory of God they are standing fast. All of this just strengthens my faith for Jesus Who foretold all of this beforehand. Hey, I have to get going before Peter leaves me. I think we are going over to Corinth and then Thessalonica and then back to Jerusalem."

Wow, things are sure in a big mess in Jerusalem. I can't keep up with the Roman chain of command. They have had four different rulers in one year. I have heard that a man named Vespasian is now in charge. If that is true he would be the first one not in the Augustin line. Oh, is he wreaking havoc on Jerusalem. Thousands and thousands of Jews have been sent into slavery. I have heard also that all the town is being burned to the ground. This guy is a madman.

Paul, that is the name that Jesus started to call Saul when he converted to Christianity, and I are in Ephesus. Paul had started a church here on one of his journeys. Nice place. I have been ask if I would stay here and take care of the church's needs. I am more than glad to because, (don't tell anybody) I'm getting older. The efforts to stop us from preaching the Word are getting stronger every day.

I must have company, a knock on the door is more like a pounding on the door. Do I answer, or do I hide? I know it is a bunch of soldiers. What am I saying? Of course, I'll answer. "Yes, may I help you? Who wants to talk to me? He is coming here? Oh, I have to go there, to Rome? Oh, boy, I guess you know that is over 1,000 miles from here. Okay, let's go see the emperor."

Goodness, that was a long trip for an old man. The boats that the soldiers use are not made for any accommodations by passengers. I was thrown into the belly of the boat; all the sounds made on the boat, and the water being sliced through, all echoed so loudly that if any sleep was to be had, you would have to cover your ears. Also the stench was strong. The food was bread, stale bread I might add, a cup of water maybe, I say twice a day. But Jesus put His hands around me, protected me, and kept me nourished.

The soldiers didn't waste any time taking me to see Emperor Domitian. I don't think they want me to have a chance to witness to anyone in Rome. Looking around this palace, I see gold, silver, and precious gems all laid out in roll after roll, leading straight up to the throne. All this and people out in the city starving, typical government. It is about time, here comes the emperor now. I've been waiting for over an hour to see him. All this time, as you can see, I have been on my knees, not an easy task for me.

"You say you want me to stop spreading this Gospel to the people? I am sorry, sir, but I will not stop preaching until the heavenly Father tells me to. I obey God before I obey you. Sir, you have sentenced me to death? But I must ask you, would you allow me to tell you about my Jesus? Ouch, I just wanted to ask you; no need in getting bent out of shape.

"Well, guys, looks like this may be the end of the road; thank you for listening to me. I have had the privilege to witness to these prisoners, and if it wasn't for my jail time, these people wouldn't have heard about Jesus. Okay, here they come to execute me. Let's pray and rejoice in the Lord. Oh my, what is in that big hole; whatever it is it's hot? Wait, you're going to boil me to death?! Oh, Lord Jesus, please allow the pain to be fast." They have tied my hands above me with a long rope. They have pulled me up in the air; now they are swinging me over that hot oil. I am being lowered into the oil. What in the world?! It feels cool. "Oh, thank You, Jesus." I'm submerged completely now, but I don't feel a thing. I have no idea how long I have been in here, but they are pulling me back out. "Can you see their faces? Complete shock, their jaws dropped to the ground. Hi, Polycarp, what do you think of our Savior now, friend? Not a drop of oil on me." I guess it's back to see the emperor.

"I tried to tell you, Emperor Domitian, my Savior is the best. You need to let me tell you about Him. Yes, sir, I'll listen but I won't be stilled. You going to send me back to Ephesus? Then off to an island called Patmos? I will still preach to the heavens if necessary."

Once again, this was a very long trip back to Ephesus; but it did feel good to be back, if only for a few days. I guess I don't even have a few days because here comes the soldiers to take me to Patmos; at least it isn't a long trip, about fifty miles. After that trip to Rome, this was a piece of cake. My friend Polycarp is going to help keep the church going while I am away. There is around 1,000 true believers here in Ephesus; Polycarp will be busy.

Isn't it just wonderful? The emperor put me on this island for punishment, but God put me here to witness to these outcasts of society. God is good. I am going to miss my friends, but I am going to enjoy working with these people. I have already been able to speak to some of them.

I have the strangest feeling right now. I feel like I want to go to sleep, but I'm not sleepy. I need to go sit down; maybe I should go lay down. I have a place to rest my head; nobody ever bothers me while I sleep. If they did everyone involved would go away empty-handed. Man, this feeling is getting stronger and stronger. "Excuse me while I sit down; I think I'll take a nap.

"I seem to be floating through the air. What a beautiful place. Oh, look, there is someone coming. You all bow down; it is my Lord Jesus. Oh, Lord, have I come home to heaven? I see, I am having a vision that You have arranged? This looks so real; it is like I could reach out and touch that white horse. Look over there; it is seven of the churches I have visited. Oh my, they aren't following Your laws, are they? What is that one by itself? Ephesus, they are doing what is right? That's my people, thank God. Over there, look, there is a battle going on; I thought I heard trumpets a blowing. Destruction everywhere. Yikes, there is Lucifer; his time is short, very short. Now things seem to settle down. Jesus, tell me about your love for all mankind. All a person has to do is open that door that You are knocking on? If they let you in their hearts You will bring them to be with You? Praises, I shout out praises to You, dear Lord.

"Hello, I seem to be wide awake now. I had the strangest vision, but I remember every word and every action of that vision. I need to write this down; I might be able to share it with my friend Polycarp someday. I wonder how he is doing. Dear Jesus, would you let Polycarp know guy."

THE APOSTLES 1ST PERSON A NARRATIVE

It sure is good to be back in Ephesus, and to see my friend again. I'm going to have to take some time off to catch up on what has been happening. "Polycarp, you old scraggy piece of dirt, how great to see you! How are you? How is my, or I guess I should say, your congregation? Can't wait till the next meeting.

"My friend, I need your help; I have written down a vision from our Lord Jesus. But I have also been taking down notes from the time I started to follow Jesus until now. Would you help me transpose them into one paper? Be sure to show the love that Jesus gave to all. While you are doing this, I am going to write some letters to the churches. We must show love to one another; don't you agree, friend?"

"My friend, I am not feeling too good; I haven't any energy left. I think my time has come to go home with Jesus. I know, friend, but I am so tired; and Jesus is waiting on me. I love you, my friend. Please keep the brothers facing the true Messiah. Make sure all get my letters. I am going to go to sleep now, friend, and I will wake in heaven. Goodbye."

APOSTLE PHILIP

"**WELCOME TO MY** home; we call this Bethsaida. It is in the Jordan Valley. My hometown is a very old town. In school they taught us the town was first built around the 10th century BC. It has been destroyed several times but is still such a beautiful place that people want to live here. The mountains are on the north and east of us. We were the capital city of Geshur until being destroyed the first time. Our beautiful town lies on the shore of the Sea of Galilee. It is interesting to note that the lake was formed hundreds of years ago due to earthquakes in the mountains. A river ran down the sides of the mountain until the earthquake, but when this happened a lot of rocks and boulders plugged the mouth of the river and formed a lake. When the lake got full, it overflowed and brought water rushing down the sides which then caused deep gorges to form in the sides of the mountain. This happened, I think scholars said, three times. When the waters rushed down the mountain a lot of silt washed down with it and settled in the valley. That is why the Jordan Valley is so rich.

"People grow a variety of products in the valley. Wheat is a major crop while barley is another prominent crop, but some of the people also grow olive trees and fig trees. Other people raise domestic animals, such as cows, sheep, goats, and (now don't faint) pigs. Yes, I said pigs. Not everyone here is a Jew, okay? Also in the countryside running wild is fallow deer, wolves, and wild boar.

"Another occupation is fishing. Comes naturally, don't you think? That is what my father is, a fisherman. You ought to see my father; he is a deep thinker. He can figure things out that no one else would even try to. He never has made a snap decision. Always thinks it out. Not me. I can't even imagine what is going to happen the next hour. I'm just not wired that way. I sort of take after my mother in that department. I am good at organizing things though; I am also good at mathematics. I am pretty good at athletics; I can run for long distances or sprint for short distances. I have a best friend that I run around with. His name is Bart; well, it's really Bartholomew; but I call him Bart. He is so smart; did you know he can understand and speak every language that is used around here? I on the other hand can't speak but a couple of tongues, but I can put all of those papers that Bart uses in an order that you can go straight to what you need. I am also good at managing money or food staples. Bart can't do that. He can understand it, but He can't put it in order. I think that is why we get along so good. He knows what it is, and I can put it in order.

"Things are changing now though because I am about to get married, and Bart is moving to Capernaum. I'll miss him, but we are grown now. I have to work and Bart is going to study at the temples. I am going to help my father in the fishing business. I won't do much of the fishing partl; I will keep records of all the nets we have, how many are needing major work, and how many only need a little work. Also, I will go and try to sell the fish we catch for the best price and take care of salaries for the workers. I have a lot of responsibility for a guy that is only twenty-seven years old. What makes it even better is I get to work with my dad. I also have time to go run and exercise which I love to do. A lot of times I can go listen to the priest give their sermons; I learn a lot by listening to them."

I went down to the temple yesterday. I heard about some preacher-type person becoming a problem to some of the Pharisees. Seems as though he was proclaiming that the Messiah was coming soon. He also was telling people that they needed to be baptized and repent of their sins. Some of those priest was saying that his name was John. They also was saying that John was on his way here. I would kind of like to hear what this guy was saying to get the Pharisees so worked up. I don't like just taking what someone says, I want to hear it straight from the horse's mouth, so to speak. Enough of this daydreaming, I need to get back to work, so I can take off when John does arrive.

I finally met up with the man called John. He sure isn't what I was expecting. You know what they say though, don't judge a scroll by the way it is rolled; so I need to hear what he has to say. As he starts to proclaim his message, his voice is like a booming bass resounding with a clarity I have never heard before. If you were about to go to sleep, you got woke up with a start. His message was exactly what I had heard it was going to be. Repent from your sins, and the Messiah is coming soon.

John is a rough looking character; I am going over and speak with him. "John . . . sir . . . John, I need to speak with you. I need a moment of your time, please, sir. Why are you wearing that ridiculous looking coat? Isn't that camel hair? That has to be hot . . . You're kidding me, you aren't? Wow! You want to look like Elijah?! That is what Elijah wore when He was taken away? Well, you know my next question.

Are you saying that you are Elijah? You're not? Okay, then what is your purpose in traveling around preaching? You say that God has set you apart, giving you the challenge to spread all over the country about this Messiah and His coming soon? I must say that is a big undertaking. But I like your message and the way you have presented it. You are very intelligent, and I can see the Spirit of the Lord working in you. I see you have some people that are close to you. May I follow you? Maybe even help you in your ministry? I will have to first tell my father and my wife I am going to assist you and that I will be back later. Thank you so much. I think I have so much to learn. I'll be back in a minute."

So many people are coming to John to hear his message and to be baptized. They are flocking here by the hundreds. I can't see how John is standing up to all this work. He is going day and night, but I have never heard him complain about anything or any condition. He won't sleep in a house on a bed, always under the stars. The only food he has eaten is honey and locusts. Must be something in the food that gives him energy. John always gives God the glory. He has also made it clear that he is not the Messiah or Elijah.

John never goes into a town; he stays out by the river and the people always come to him. I guess that way he can preach and baptize at the same time; I say that is good use of His time.

John is a little more excited today than usual; I didn't think He could get that way but he seems to have a bit more bounce in his step. I think I'll go over and ask him about it. "John, oh, John! What's with you today? You don't say! Is this the One you have been preaching to us about? Oh, glory to God! When is he going to be here? Sorry, I ask too many questions, don't I?"

GEORGE A REGISTER

Man, oh, man, look at all these people! They are all lined up to get baptized. I bet there are three hundred or so in this line. "What is going on, Andrew? John is taking a little more time with this guy. Who did you say it was, Simon? I'm going to get a little closer to see." John has his head down in a very humbling position talking with this Man. I can hear him now. He just told this other Man that He should be baptizing him. I never thought I would hear that. Oh, boy, am I going to unload with the questions tonight. John has told the other people to go home for today; he is through with his preaching and baptizing for now. There is never a dull moment around John. Something is happening all the time. I found out this other guy's name is Jesus.

This is the One John has been preaching about? I might get to meet Him if things go right. Looks like Jesus is asking John about something. John is pointing his finger at one of us, probably Peter or Andrew. Did you know that those two came from my hometown? They have been touring with Jesus so I should have known who that guy was. Looks like Jesus is coming up here to speak with his disciples. Look at that crowd just a gawking at the disciples and Jesus. Man, you can feel a sense of greatness in Jesus, and He isn't even by us yet. The others, Peter, Andrew, James, and John Zebedee, have sort of stepped off to one side. I guess they think Jesus wants to talk to them in private. But Jesus isn't going over to the disciples; He is coming my way. That is good; I would like to talk to Him anyway, you know, pick His brain type of thing. Jesus is getting closer and closer to me. There is static in the air. It feels like I am being drawn into Him. John has told me that He was the Son of God Himself. I can believe it.

Oh my, I can't help myself; I'm being sucked in like a whirlpool.

THE APOSTLES 1ST PERSON A NARRATIVE

The things I have learned from the Torah are all racing through my mind. I feel like I am about to explode. I open my eyes and standing right in front of me is Jesus. Then out of the clear blue, Jesus says, "Follow Me." Jesus wants me to follow Him. I couldn't say no if I wanted to. Jesus is the Messiah that has been promised, and He wants me to follow Him. Unbelievable, flat out unbelievable. I have to go home and tell the good news from Jesus and the promise He has made to mankind.

My dad says he has heard of this Man; and since I believe in Him, he will too. Oh, glory, my whole family is accepting Jesus. My wife is wanting to go with me to help in any way she can. This makes me so happy. I'm sure Jesus won't mind. He has several women helping with the daily chores.

John has taken off to some other place now and Jesus is working His way to Capernaum. That is good for me because my good friend Bart is there. "Hey, Jesus, You mind if I run ahead of You to go see my friend? Thank You." I know Bart is going to accept this guy. After all, he knows the Torah frontward and backward. There won't be any of this trying to slip something in on him. That is what the Pharisees try to do to all the inhabitants of the country. I have seen some of these guy's change rules so as to make people go to the temple to cleanse themselves. That then gives more money to the Pharisees to line their pockets with. They are a bunch of thieves.

Wow, I'm getting mighty hot and sweaty; I haven't run this far in a while. I hope I can find Bart before too long; I need to get back to Jesus and my wife. "Did you hear that?" Sounded like someone called my name, but no one knows me here, except Bart. Hang on, let me look around. There, up by that fig tree that looks like it's Bart. It is! My prayer has been answered!

"Bart, Bart, thank God I found you. I have someone I want you to meet. His name is Jesus. Bart, He is the Messiah. He has come in our time. What do you mean you don't believe He is? Bart, you know I don't hang out with just anybody. Please, just come with me and listen to Him."

I can't believe my good friend is rejecting Jesus. My heart is so broken. "Please help me, Lord, I need my friend to see the light." I will go meet up with Jesus across town. I must say all the starch has been let out of my sails. I hear someone holler at me. It's Bart. He is waving at me, but I can't go to him now. It hurts too much knowing he is losing out on the best thing that could happen to him. He is walking towards me; I guess I will have to meet up with him. "Hi, Bart, I haven't got much time because Jesus is already in town, and I have a duty to fulfill. I sure would like to have you just come and hear what Jesus has to say. You will? Oh, Bart, you don't know how much this means to me."

I will give Bart this, he is listening to Jesus, so that means he is keeping an open mind. I think I will bring Him over to meet Jesus. If Jesus just thinks I ask a lot of questions, wait till Bart starts. Haha!

It does feel good to be out and about with Jesus going from here to there. My friend Bart is soaking up a lot of knowledge; and I am as well. I didn't realize how much I didn't know. We have been traveling to many towns and cities. The crowds have been growing bigger everyday. My wife is busy all the time with teaching the Gospel. One of my sisters, Marianne, has come to join us. It has been good to see her again. She gave me a good report on the family, that they were spreading the gospel in and around our hometown.

Jesus has gathered a group of us together. Jesus is telling us that the crowds are getting so large that He wants to choose a few of us to kind of take care of the business end of things, so to speak. Each one of His chosen disciples will be called "apostle." They are to follow close by Him while Jesus travels because, He want to teach them some of the more tedious subjects, while the rest of us disciples do the baptizing and explaining the gospel to people. Wouldn't it be great to be in that small group? Personalized study by the Son of God Himself. Wow. Jesus is telling each one their duties. He is coming over to me; surely He isn't going to choose me. I'm a bit on the sinner side; I'm not as knowledgeable as, say, my friend, Bart. And then it happened, He looked me straight in the eyes and said I was one of the chosen ones.

Me. Imagine that! Jesus is going to teach me some inner teachings. The only thing that makes it better is He also chose my friend Bart. I feel like getting up and dancing around the room. I'll call it the Happy Dance. "Yahoo! Sorry, Jesus, I'm interrupting, sorry." Jesus told me, after I settled down, that He wanted me to take care of the food distribution and organize the crowds. "I can do that. I have done this all my life, you know, with my father. You tell me what you have planned, and I will organize it." I guess this meeting is over now, Jesus said it is time to go out and minister to these people.

Man, oh man, this crowd is big; we have been walking all day and the crowd has been growing. It sort of reminds me of a storm that is brewing. Starts off small, and then keeps building until the sky is dark from clouds. Well, the fields are dark with people all over the hillside. One of the apostles hollered at me that Jesus wanted to talk to me. I sure hope I haven't done something wrong. "I'm coming, Jesus . . .

"You want to know how much food we have. To be honest, Lord, we don't have much. You want to feed all these people! Sir, we don't have enough in the treasury even to feed a small group of people. Maybe we could dismiss the crowd and have them come back tomorrow. Peter, you can see all these people. Andrew, where are you going? You say there is a boy out there that has a fish and some bread? Oh, come on, Andrew, surely you're not going to take that poor little boy's food from him. That little one can't stand up to you all. What did you say, Jesus? Put the food in a basket?" Okay, I can't believe Jesus took that poor kids food; I might have to give this a second thought. What's going on? That basket is full of food. Andrew is putting more food into another basket. Everybody is taking food out but the baskets just keep being full.

Every person here has received some food, there has to be over 5,000 men here. I believe I have just witnessed a miracle. I feel so stupid; I ought to have known Jesus could feed everyone. I think He was testing me, and I failed. Jesus is looking at me with those penetrating eyes, but they are eyes of forgiveness and understanding. I hope I do better the next time He gives me an assignment.

It has come to the Passover time in Jerusalem. We have been having a grand ol' time listening to what Jesus has been trying to teach us. I really don't mind telling you most of this is going over my head, but I also think I'm not alone. Wow, Jerusalem is sure crowded. Everyone is here. Jesus told us we were to go out and witness to these people. I can do a lot of things but I'm not good at talking to people one-on-one. Put me in front of a crowd and I can talk all day. Maybe I can get one of the Jameses to help me. Oh, boy, here comes some Greek brothers. They're coming right at me. "Hi, guys. How are you? Well, I don't know; let me see. Okay. Hey, Andrew, these guys want to speak with Jesus. Will you help me take them to Him? Thank you."

I have noticed the Pharisees have been getting agitated a lot more here lately. I even heard of them plotting to kill Jesus. Here comes one of the disciples. He says that Jesus wants to gather all the apostles up in a room, and he will take us there.

Looks like we are going to have supper. What is this? Jesus is washing everyone's feet. If anything, we should be washing His, but He insists on it. Jesus looks like He has a burden on His shoulders right now. He is about to speak. What?! No this can't be right; no one in this room would betray Him! We have been faithful to Him. Now Jesus is taking a loaf of bread and telling us that this is His body. Now He is pouring wine, which this represents His blood, in a cup and telling us to take a drink. With all this, I have to ask, "Jesus, can you show us the Father?" Boy, was that ever a mistake; I should have known better. He has been telling us all this time that He and the Father are one. I sometimes just can't get things to stick in my head. Jesus just told us that we need to go pray on the hill. I never have seen Jesus in such a serious mood.

We have come up to Mount Olivet. Jesus has told all but a couple of the apostles to stay below Him while He goes to pray. We are to pray also, but we have had a long day and I don't know if I can keep my eyes open. "Ouch, who kicked me? Oh, it's You, Jesus. Oh my, I went to sleep. Jesus, who are all these people coming up the side of the mount? I guess they know the great message You have for them, because Judas is leading them." Hey, those guys are soldiers. What is going on? Judas is kissing Jesus on the cheek. Look out, the soldiers have come over and grabbed Jesus and are trying to take off with Him. Now Peter is going to fight back. Ouch! He just cut the ear off of that man. There's more commotion going on than you can shake a stick at. I'm going to hide over here; they haven't seen me yet. Maybe I can get some help down below.

I can tell here in town I'm not going to get any help. I don't know what happened to all that followed Jesus, but everyone is hollering to kill Him. I better get out of town before they turn on me. I may go back up home and think this through. I feel sorry for the brothers and sisters who cannot leave. Of course, silly me, they are hiding just like I am. I don't understand, Jesus is so sweet in nature and yet the Pharisees want to kill Him. I know, I know, Jesus is taking their people away from them. Well, I'm going to go try and disappear for a while. This noise is so loud. Look at all that hate built up in their eyes.

They actually put Jesus on the cross and killed Him. What were they thinking? It's been a few days now; I haven't seen any of the apostles since Jesus' death. I would imagine they have scattered over all the country. I know I did. I'm not going to tell you where I went; I might have to go back and hide again. Oh, look, I recognize that man over there. He is a follower, or I should say, was a follower of Jesus. He sees me. He is coming my way; maybe He can tell me a little bit of what is going on. "Hi, brother. What did you say? The apostles are gathering together? They want me to meet them? Where? Okay, I'll be there. You be careful; don't get too close to them Pharisees." I can't believe we are still going to meet. I guess we have to discuss what we are going to do with the meager assets we have.

"Hi, Peter, James, John, good to see you all. What has been going on? You've got to be kidding me! Did you all have too much too drink or what? You say the grave is empty? Someone steal the body or what? You say you have seen Jesus? He is the One that wanted us to meet. I want to hear what Peter is going to say. Wait a minute, who is this other person in the room? Oh, my God, it is Jesus!" There's a lot of confusion going on . . . What did He say? He wants us to stay in Jerusalem until He sends the Holy Spirit. I don't think that is going to be a very good idea; the priests are still stirred up about Jesus' teachings and all of us that followed Him. I do remember a lot of what Jesus was trying to teach us before He died. I have to admit I didn't understand a lot of it.

Peter is going to be the leader now; after all, Jesus said He was the Rock. James is going to be over the Jerusalem group, and the rest of us are going out on our proposed journeys. My assignment is going to the city of Samaria.

I have traveled to Sebaste; some people call it Samaria. It is about thirty-five miles from Jerusalem. These people are eager to hear the Gospel. The Samaritan people aren't use to receiving good news. There are so many coming that I am spending hours on end baptizing these Gentiles. My heart is pounding so fast. I feel plum giddy. I am singing out as loud as I can. (That is the funny noise you are hearing, haha.) I've got to get ahold of myself, but I can't help it. Oh, thank you, Jesus, thank you. I have sent one of the disciples back to Jerusalem to tell about the Good News. As you know, I'm not very good at thinking up new or different ways of getting people to come to the Lord. But I haven't had any problems in getting this message out. Praise God.

I am trying to stay up with all the things happening. Every time I speak, more people accept Jesus in their heart. I need to take some time out here to pray for God's guiding way. What's going on outside? The disciples are cheering and laughing and making a big commotion. I'll go out and see what is happening before I pray. "Hi, guys, what's up?"

I see them now; no wonder they are excited. I see Peter and John coming down the road. There goes my heart doing flips again. "Oh, man, it's great seeing you two. I hope you have come to help with this bunch. You want me to gather them all up? The new believers, you mean, right?"

Peter and John both are speaking to the new brothers in Christ. They sound so much better than me. What are Peter and John doing now? There is a great gusting of wind. Oh, my Lord. I remember this back in the upper room; the Holy Spirit is descending upon the Gentiles. Peter told me God accepts the Gentile as well as the Jew. Jesus had said that God loves all.

I feel so good now, but I need to get back to my mission. I have so much work to do here. I doubt I will be able to get it all done in my lifetime. Goodness, I just got a chill on the back of my neck, not possible. It is 80-some-odd degrees. Oh, well, off I go. There it goes again; it's like someone is blowing on my neck. Maybe if I close my eyes the feeling will go away. "Where did you come from? Do you all see this?" It looks like an angel, and it's coming closer. "Yes, I see, you are from Jesus . . . Are you sure I'm supposed to go south on the road from Jerusalem to Gaza? I haven't finished here yet. No, sir, I'm not going to argue. If you say go, I'll go."

I'm sort of glad I am to go south; I haven't been able to run for a long time. I hope I don't tire out too quick. I've made my way through Jerusalem, and now I am running along the Gaza road. Man, this place is such a desert. I would hate to live around here. Not a whole lot of traffic along the road. Here comes some rich dude, in what looks like a mighty fancy chariot. Looks as though he might be an official of some sort. He is educated for sure; I know this because

THE APOSTLES 1ST PERSON A NARRATIVE

he is reading something. I won't bother Him; I'm just a commoner, and he is royalty. "Hi, Angel, what do you want now? Okay, I'll go over there. Hello, sir, how are you? What're you reading? Do you understand what you are reading? I see it is from Isaiah. Well, thank you, I will join you; maybe I can help you. So you are from Ethiopia? You are a long ways from home. The treasury secretary? That's a mighty important job. Let us talk about Isaiah . . .

"I am so glad that I was able to meet you, sir, but I am even happier that you have accepted Christ. What did you say? Yes, that is water over there; I don't see any reason why we can't stop and baptize you now. Oh, how wonderful this is. I now baptize you, my brother, buried is the old, raised to wa . . ."

"Hey, what happened? Where am I? Where did the eunuch go? He was here, and then he was gone. Sir, sir, can you tell me where I'm at? I think I might have passed out or something. This is the town Azotus?! Wow, I need to get back on the road again; but it seems like I need to go to Caesarea, so I guess that is where I will go." I am going to tell people about Jesus all the way up to Caesarea. There are a lot of small towns between here and there.

Well, Bart has caught back up with me, and he says that my sister, Marianne, isn't too far behind us. Man, has she ever been a trooper. Just like Bart and myself, she has been ridiculed and put in prison and even stoned at one time. I love my sister; she is calling for me to come over to see her.

GEORGE A REGISTER

Well, I knew this was going to happen. My sister is going to go off in another direction, but I know she will do a great work for Jesus. I still have my family with me and my best friend. Let's get started; we have a lot of territory to cover. I did convince Marianne to come with us a little while longer.

We have arrived in Hierapolis, a great big town. People are running around everywhere. "Sir! Yes, you, sir. Have you ever heard of a great man named Jesus? I would like to tell you about Him. What did you say? You worship a snake? Where is this snake? I'm sorry, I mean serpent. Thank you. Hey, Bart, I think we have our work cut out for us. Let's go over and see this snake, okay? Well, now, that idol doesn't look so strong, now does it? Bart, do what you say? Sounds good to me. We will pray that piece of junk out of here. You go first Bart, and I'll go second.

Hahahaha! Bart, you shouldn't have prayed so hard. You prayed that thing out of existence before I got a chance. That was fun. Oops, I think that group of . . . uhh, looks like some kind of priests, have got mad at us. They are over there talking to a bunch of soldiers. Here they come. "Yes, we are the ones who made your "god" disappear. If your god was so powerful, why didn't he stop us? Ouch, what you getting so worked up about? You don't have to drag me; if you would just let me get on my feet, I'll go with you. Bart, I think these guys are out of their minds mad at us." Ouch! That hurt. Why you hitting me, and where are you taking me? "Hey, Bart! If I don't see you here, I'll see you up there, you know, heaven. Thanks, bud. I don't see my family around, so hopefully they have managed to escape.

"What kind of trial was that? There wasn't even a judge, it was the priests only. I know, we're not in Jerusalem. What you going to do with us? Crucify us? When? You all don't waste time, do you?" Oh my, ouch, dear Jesus, these people are being blinded by Satan. Forgive them; be with my friend, and take the pain from him. I'm about to lose consciousness . . . "Sir, Jesus is a loving God, and He forgives you. Would you let me tell you more about Him?" Oh, that was hard, I think he broke my jaw. How many times is he going to strike me with that whip? Ah, they are cutting me down. What's this? They are putting me on a cross. I'm being crucified. I'm so thankful to my Lord for taking the pain away. "Sir, I can't talk too good right now. You broke my jaw, but I need to tell you about Jesus. No, sir, I will not stop talking about Him." I can't see now; I think the blood is rushing to my head. I'm not sure, but I think I caught a glimpse of Bart over on the other cross. I'm losing my thoughts now. What is this? Either I'm starting to shake or the ground is. It must be the earth. I am so weak, "Oh, God, I ask forgiveness. My sins have been washed . . ."

APOSTLE
BARTHOLOMEW

"I'M SO GLAD you came by. I don't receive very many people. I'm sort of a stick in the mud, you might say. I really don't understand it when a person who likes to read and to study is made to feel that something is wrong with them. I also like playing games outdoors. Just the other day I was hanging out with a few friends and we were playing tag. I hate to brag, but I could out run everyone who played. It kind of embarrassed them, but I guess they will get over it. I have my good times, but I would rather spend time studying the Torah. I believe that people think it is odd because I am a teenager, but I have had to work most of my life. My family has a vineyard and we all work it. Even though my father is of royal blood, he works as hard as the rest of us.

"The countryside of Cana is gorgeous, especially when all the vineyards are in bloom. Also there are olive and fig trees; when they all bloom, it is a sight to see. The country is small rolling hills, but they get bigger as you go toward the Sea of Galilee. I have sat under those trees many times studying or sometimes daydreaming.

"I am very fortunate that a group of men from my home country moved to Capernaum because of the better location for their fishing business. I have been working for them, oh, I don't know, for a while I guess.

THE APOSTLES 1ST PERSON A NARRATIVE

"But here as of late, most of them have been going around following some guy; I think His name is Jesus. Even my best friend is following Him. I don't have time for all of that nonsense. I moved down here to Capernaum because of the temples here and the teachings by the Pharisees. You know, they are the supreme priests who are smarter than all of us put together. And many work around here.

"I haven't seen so much activity in town for quite some time. It is becoming so crowded that we have a hard time docking the boats. We have our own docks, but the boat traffic is horrendous. I was steering the boat one day not too long ago, and as I was coming in, a boat went right in front of me. I probably didn't miss them by two feet. Scared me to death. Mr. Z wasn't too happy either. It's not only the boats but also the people are so many that as you walk down the street you can't tell if a shop is even open or not because of the clouds of dirt in the air. And the camels, donkeys, and their riders have no respect for others. I mean they race through the streets like maniacs. It's a wonder more people haven't been hurt. Maybe they should put some of those rocks back in the middle of the road, that would slow them down. Oh, well, no use worrying about it, nothing I can do about it.

"Maybe it will rain soon and that will settle the dust. It has been rather humid the last few days. The temp is running around eighty degrees right now. I think I'll go find me a tree to sit under. People don't believe this, but the shade of a tree cools the temperature, oh, I say, about fifteen degrees. Makes it nice there. Besides I need to study some more on the Torah. Not to brag on myself again, but I have most of the Torah memorized. I have studied it all of my life. I also can speak every language known. If there is a new one to come along I can learn it within a couple of weeks.

"I still miss my friend Philip though. He has been traveling with some guy, he was always making me laugh. I could talk with him and he wouldn't take me down or make fun of me.

"Well, we have made it outside of the city now. Let's get away from the road, so the dust won't be so bad. I don't know about you, but it might just be nap time. Look over there, a fig tree all by itself. While you're sleeping I'm going to go over the Torah in my mind . . .

"Who's that running, there? See him? Well, I'll be, it sure does look like my friend Philip coming. Hey Phil, over here! Oh, boy, it sure is good to see you! What have you been up to? What do you mean you have been traveling around with this Jesus character? I know you are a fairly smart guy, and I know also that you are persuaded pretty easily. Remember when those kids down by the pier told you there was a diamond down in the water? Someone had thrown it overboard. I think they said it was a woman's. They also said it was too deep for them to get but they knew you could. So you jumped in. You never found the diamond because it was never there. Then they wouldn't let you back up out of the water. I know, that was a long time ago. But Phil, didn't you tell me this Jesus was from Nazareth? You know good and well, nothing good ever comes out of Nazareth. Nothing. Look, you might be totally enamored by this man, but I'm not going to waste my time. Now, why don't you come sit down with us and take a rest? What do you mean, "we" don't have time for that? I told you, I'm not going with you.

"Well, it looks like I'm not going to get any studying done. So I might as well go with you. I'll listen to Him, but please do not expect me to pack up and follow. Okay? Slow down Phil, that guy's not going anywhere. Man, I haven't seen you so worked up about anybody in a long time."

THE APOSTLES 1ST PERSON A NARRATIVE

Is that the Man over there? He sure don't look like much. Where is His white robe and jewels around His neck? I have heard of this guy before. Yes, I remember now. My dad spoke of Him. If I remember correctly, there was a wedding party going on and the host hadn't bought enough wine. My dad tried to tell them, but no, no one would listen. So they ran out. But this Jesus guy took some water in the barrels, and it came out wine. Not just any wine, but the best tasting wine. My dad tried to get the recipe, but no one would cooperate.

I really didn't pay much attention to Him then, and more than likely I won't this time either. You say He has performed a lot of miracles? I've heard of some people doing that. Most of them were fake though. I'll tell you what, I will not allow myself to judge this Man until I listen to Him.

"I will say this, He has a smooth voice, easy to listen to, but still a voice that commands attention. What is He doing now? What are all those people surrounding Him for? Hey, I saw that man walking up to Him, dragging his leg, now he is running around hollering something. What is it? Oh, he says he has been healed. All those people are laughing and praising that guy you call Jesus. They have been cured of different types of illnesses. Nobody could pay off that many people, so there just might be something to this man. I listened to His message real close, and everything He said was correct. I might just have to follow Him a little more, that way I can better understand what His purpose is. Hey, Phil, have you actually ever met Jesus personally? I would kind of like to talk with Him one-on-one. What do you think, Phil? Phil, where are you?" Now why did he leave me out here by myself? I'm going to thump that guy's head if

I catch up with him. Oh, I see him. Hey, Phil is bringing Jesus over here, and I think I'm going to get to meet Him.

Jesus is walking right up to me. I don't understand; but being this close to Him, I haven't any words to describe Him. But He acts like He knows me. Wait a minute, He is saying something about me. Oh, my God. He said, "Behold, an Israelite indeed, in whom there is no deceit."

How did He know that? I'm going to ask Him. "Jesus, I enjoyed your message, but how did You know me? You saw Phil running to see me? Even before that? I have to say, Rabbi, You are the King of Israel. You say I will be able to see angels ascending and descending on the Son of God? Yes, I say, yes, to whatever You need me to do." Why did I say that? I couldn't seem to help myself.

I'm so happy Jesus has decided to go to Cana in Galilee where I come from. My parents still live there. I can't wait till my dad, Mr. Thalami, hears this message. I'm sure he will come join us. Jesus said we won't be spending too much time here but a little time is appreciated very much.

We have been traveling all through towns in Galilee. We first went to Gennesaret, then on to Magdala, Tiberias, and all the way to Nain. Then we took the western route back to Capernaum. As soon as we got back to C-town, a soldier wanted Jesus to heal his son. Guess what? He did. While we are here, He wants twelve of us to be what He calls "apostles." I am so honored He has chosen me to be one.

We have set out on another tour. This time we are going to Nain and then crossover to the Decapolis and travel to their ten cities. This is very interesting because all these people are Gentiles. This is so new to them; they, for the most part, are opening their hearts to Jesus' message.

Jesus is telling us it is time to go back to C-town. This has been a long, drawn out tour this time. But the Gospel message has been presented. I think the reason it seemed harder is because all twelve of us were incorporated into it. We were given the power to heal and to cast out demons. What a wonderful feeling that is. But it also was very tiring, but it didn't seem to bother Jesus. Anyway, we are headed back and are taking a boat which will give our feet a rest.

Jesus just sent His messenger to gather us up; we are going on another trip. "Okay, Jesus, we are here. Now what? Oh, boy, you mean we are going on our own? Where do you want us to go? Not like the last tour, right? No Gentiles? Preach only to the children of God? Got You. I guess I should go and pack my bags. What do you mean, no backpack, no food, and no shelter? We are to just go with what we have on our backs? I'll have You know, I wouldn't even consider doing this for anyone else. What're You going to do?"

I guess Jesus must be getting a little homesick. He says that He is going to Nazareth. That is where He considers home. I have heard Him speak of that place; He has already gone there once before.

Well, I have been spreading the Gospel all over Samaria and Galilee, but it is time to get back to C-town. I have met up with Jesus and the other apostles. He has told us to get in the boat, and we will find a quiet place near Bethsaida. Jesus says He needs to teach us some important things. But as soon as we got there, about 5,000 men met us. We did get to go up and have a little quiet time, but all those people stayed until we came back down. After feeding them and having a nice, beautiful message, we get back in the boat and start back without Jesus. He says He will catch up later. He didn't tell me how He would do it. He just walks right out to the boat; we are in the middle of the lake. I'm not going to get into what happens next. Jesus is teaching us many things that are beyond my ability to grasp. He keeps talking about being crucified, not only His being crucified, but that we all will abandon Him. I just don't think that's possible.

Jesus has given us quite the road tour. We have been to Syria-Phoenicia and then went back through the Decapolis. All along the way, people were being healed and the demons thrown out. We are heading back now to C-town. I think it is taking longer because His teachings are getting more, what can I say, personal. He is praying a lot more, and His messages to the people are stronger, almost pleading. "Be quiet; Jesus is saying something." As soon as we get back to C-town, we will leave for Jerusalem. That is about a two to three days journey. A lot of us were in Jerusalem the last time and almost didn't get out. But Jesus is determined to go back.

We have been traveling for a couple of days, and Jerusalem is up there on the hill; we can see it. We can also see a crowd of people coming to meet us. I don't know exactly when Jesus did it, but He sent some of our group to get a young donkey. Maybe Jesus' feet are tired. I then remembered reading about the Messiah riding into Jerusalem on a donkey. The crowd is going wild. They are putting palm fronds down on the road and Jesus is riding over them. What a beautiful sight.

We have all gathered together for a meal, but something is strange. You know, it feels different. What is Jesus doing now? He has a bowl of water and a towel. Oh, my gosh, Jesus is going to wash our feet. Did I hear Him say that one of us wasn't clean? That one of us is going to betray Him? He just broke a piece of bread and said

THE APOSTLES 1ST PERSON A NARRATIVE

that it is His body. Then He took a cup of wine and said that represented His blood. Then we ate and Jesus said we needed to go up on the other hill and do some serious praying for His time was short.

Once again it was proven that Jesus is a lot smarter than all of us put together. Remember I told you Jesus said His time was short? Well, I didn't even know just how short He meant. You see, Jesus was put to death a few days ago. That's why I haven't been around. All of us went and hid because we were scared to come out. I guess you could say we all let Jesus down. But glory be to God, He said that He would come back in three days, and He did!

The most beautiful thing I have ever seen was Jesus ascending up into the heavens. But before He left, He poured out the Holy Spirit upon us and told us to go to the world and preach.

Each one of us has now been given our duties. So I must go and prepare myself to leave. I remember Jesus telling us to go out without food, a change of clothing, or money. So that is what I'm going to do on this journey. I am going to go over and tell my best friend, Phil, goodbye. I have no Idea how long this is going to be. Great news. Philip was given the same assignment; this will make my journey a lot better.

Philip and I, along with Phil's sister Marianne, started our long journey up through Samaria. I can't pronounce half of the towns we have been in. I can say this, these people don't want to accept the Gospel. The precept in one of the small towns is getting pretty stirred up. A crowd of people is gathering around us. I really don't think they are wanting to hear the Gospel. Ouch, someone just threw a rock at me! Ouch, another one, we are being stoned! "Oh, Jesus, please get us out of this if it is Your will. Please, release me, sir. Why are you throwing us into jail? Yes, we will leave the area if you release us."

Jesus saw us through that situation, so we both went to the other little villages and preached the Gospel to them. "Hey, look over there. It's John. Boy, it's good to see you. How have you been doing? We kind of got ourselves thrown in jail and stoned. Sure, I think Phil will go with us to Hierapolis. I see, you are going to stay in Phrygia? That's okay, Phil and I have to go on. It has been good seeing you. Keep safe and spread the Word."

Wow, we have been on the road for several days now. But we have come to Hierapolis. This is a big place. I hear they have these big hot springs all around the city. I think I will find one and get in to soak. People from all over the world come here; these springs are called by their gods to flow. But I see another god over on the next street. I haven't really seen it but I have heard about it. It's a great big snake. Let's go over and look.

Look at all them; people are bowing down to that monster. Let's pray it out of existence ... That didn't take long. Praise Jesus!

There is a lot of sickness here and a lot of demon-possessed people. The more we pray over them and Jesus heals them, the more people come. Ah, there is a man that's blind. "Hi, sir, what's your name? Well, Mr. Stachys, how long have you been blind? Forty years? Wow, well, let us pray over you. Mr. Stachys, open your eyes and see the world that our Lord and Savior has allowed you to see now. Go and believe in the Lord Jesus."

THE APOSTLES 1ST PERSON A NARRATIVE

"Hey Phil, you remember that blind man? Well, he is here to get baptized. Not only him but hundreds of people. God is sure blessing us these days. What're all of those soldiers doing? Looks like they are coming over this way . . . Ouch, hey, what you doing? What do you mean we are under arrest? For what? Ouch, you don't have to be so rough. We are going straight to trial? Oh, man, you didn't have to kick me; I'm going with you. What do you mean we have been found guilty? Just because those bozos don't like us? Okay, okay, no need for all that cursing and kicking us. Hey, soldier, what're they going to do with us? What?! They going to crucify us!" Well, looks like my ministry is over, but it has been wonderful.

I guess I need to act like a man and walk with great confidence to the stake; I know my God is bigger than theirs. If He wants me to survive this He will protect me. Ouch, these ropes are mighty tight. "What're you doing now? Upside down? I ask for swift death my Jesus."

I've been here for some time now, the blood is rushing to my head, and I'm about to lose consciousness. My arms and legs don't have any feeling to them. "Oh, Jesus, please be with our new brothers. It isn't them causing my problems. Please bring someone to help them to get to know You. Help them have the faith to stand guard . . ."

Something is happening; the ground is shaking. I can barely open my eyes, but people are running everywhere. Oh my, someone is cutting me down. Bless you. I don't understand too much, but some of my new brothers are carrying me to safety. I'm starting to get some of my senses back. They told me that they couldn't save Philip, but I need to leave the area. Most of the priests and the city perfect have all been killed in this earthquake.

Upon leaving town, I ran into Marianne, she was still sad due to the death of her brother. She decided that she would go with me to Lycaonia. It is good to have someone to talk to on this journey. We both have been through a lot, but our Lord brought us through it.

"I guess this is going to be goodbye for now Marianne. I am sure that you will spread the Gospel all throughout the country. The people seem to be friendly and open to Jesus' Gospel."

These long and dusty roads have become lonely. Every once in awhile, I will run into some travelers; matter of fact, here comes some now. "Sir, may I ask if you have heard of the wondrous love of a man called Jesus?"

That sure did feel good. If everyone is like that in India I can be filled with joy. I had heard of the language of India before, so I brushed up on it and now can speak with the residents. I am feeling so good right now. I love these people. They are so ready to hear about Jesus. Oh, I have some of the writings that my brother in Christ, Matthew, wrote down before we left on our mission trips. I think I can translate them into their language. This will help spread the Gospel a lot faster. Thank You, Jesus, for allowing me to serve You.

There is so much country to cover; I need to go on up to Greater Armenia. You know, it's up between the Kura River and the Tigris and Euphrates Rivers. I can't afford to stay in one spot too long for I wouldn't be able to cover all.

God is blessing these people in abundance. I am able to perform miracles through the name of Jesus; a lot of demon-possessed people have been freed. I have been able to spread the Gospel now for, oh let's see, I guess around twenty-seven years. People are so hungry for hope.

Oh, no, I see a company of soldiers coming. I wasn't expecting this. I haven't even heard of any animosity towards the Gospel. All I can do is try and bring the Word to them to as they haul me off to jail. "Yes, I am the one you seek. I will go with you without any trouble. You're not taking me to jail? You want me to follow you to go see the king?"

"Yes, I am doing fine, Your Honor. Yes, thank you, I will accept a glass of water. Thank you again. Sir, may I tell you about this Man I know? His name is Jesus. Jesus is the most loving God; He has given hundreds, if not thousands, a reason for hope. He has given us a chance at everlasting life with Him in heaven. All we have to do is believe in Him. Give our all to Him and worship Him. Yes, sir, I have been able to heal people from demons that inflict pain and suffering on people. It is not I, but Jesus that does the healing. You say your daughter is ill? If you would allow me to see your daughter, I will pray over her. Thank you for trusting her with me; now I must pray. Demons, in the name of Jesus I command you to leave this child! King Polymios, because of the love of Jesus, I present to you, you're healed daughter. No, sir, don't thank me. Thank Jesus; He is the great healer. No, sir, I cannot accept any gifts from you or anyone else. The only thing I seek is for the salvation of souls of mankind."

GEORGE A REGISTER

I am here at the river. Hundreds of people who saw the king's daughter released from the bondage of demons are here to be baptized in acceptance of Jesus as their heavenly King. Oh look, here comes King Polymios, and he has brought all of his family. "Hi, sir, how is that daughter of yours doing? Ah, that's great. You say your whole family wants to be baptized? That is so wonderful, not only your family, but your household servants also? Glory be to Jesus. You all have become my brothers and sisters in Christ."

As bad as I hate to, I must go on to other towns. I think I'll be in Alban in a couple of days. I sure hope the people there are as open-hearted as they were back there in Greater Armenia. I am so full of joy right now, I could run and skip all the way. I have been running into people on the road who have heard of the daughter's healing; they are sure full of questions. I am trying to answer all that they ask. Many accept Jesus right there on the spot. Happiness is everywhere. God's glory is spreading like wildfire.

Well, I have arrived in Alden, a beautiful city. It reminds me of Jerusalem, all kinds of shops along the main road. People are scurrying along, one going one way, another going the opposite way. Some are on camels, others are on foot carrying baskets of all sizes on their heads, some with food, and others with laundry. Little children flitting around under porches and in the middle of the street. I understand that King Polymios's brother lives here. I hope to see him while I'm here. Oh, boy, here comes a large group of people. "Welcome, my friend. Yes, I am the one who is speaking to people about the one they call Jesus. So you have heard about the king's daughter? It is all true. Please, there is room for all in the house of the Lord."

THE APOSTLES 1ST PERSON A NARRATIVE

There is one more thing in town that reminds me of Jerusalem. Those, I think they are priests, over there, don't look to happy with me, just like the Pharisees back in Jerusalem. They are not concerned with the welfare of the citizens, only their pocket books. I will say, they are staying over there and not bothering us. But they look like they are cooking something up. I haven't got the time to worry about them. So many need to hear the Gospel.

Here comes a group of people; a lot of the priest are with them. I knew they were up to something the other day. "Hello, my friends, may I help you? So you are King Polymios's brother? I have been wanting to meet with you. Yes, I did convert your brother and his family to a life of Christianity. Please, sir, I am not trying to take anybody or anything from your kingdom. I only want to teach your people about Jesus. No, sir, the priests are wrong if they are telling you that I'm here to take the country. Why don't you ask your brother? Why don't you see the change in his life? See how happy he is. What do you mean, you don't have time to check with your brother? What have I done to you that makes you put me in jail? You say I won't be here long enough to even go to sleep? I will not stop speaking about Christ, no matter what you do to me. Your brother isn't going to like you doing this to me. Ouch, I can't believe this. You're going to crucify me upside down?! People, listen to me, Jesus is a God of kindness and love. Please, open your hearts and your minds to the Gospel . . .

"As long as I can breathe and have consciousness, I will preach. No, I will not stop. What're you doing with them knives?! Ouch! Oh, Jesus, help me. These men are starting to cut off my skin. Oh, that hurts! But I will as long as I can, tell you about . . . Jesus, do not blame them; they know not what they dooooooooooo . . ."

APOSTLE
THOMAS

"**I DO BELIEVE** that you need to shorten that beam. If you don't, the building is going to be out of square. I would say you need to cut at least a foot off of it. Yes, that would be a good idea, which is thinking outside the box. Good job.

"Hello, my name is Judas Thomas, but most people call me Thomas. There are so many guys named Judas that I don't mind going by my last name. I am a Galilean by birth; I was born in this little town called Pansada. My folks came from a very poor section of town. There were many times when we didn't have any food, so I would go out and fish a lot. I think that is why some people thought I was a fisherman but I'm not. I studied on my own and learned how to construct buildings or roads or anything else that could be built. I also studied the Torah from cover to cover; at one time, I thought I would like to be a member of the priesthood. My father said I couldn't because we didn't have the money to send me and pay for the education. I just think he didn't want me to go. Now that I am grown I am kind of glad I didn't pursue that way of life. I not only design the buildings, but I like to get in there and get my hands dirty. It is a pleasure to see something you have put on parchment come to life in the real world. It also keeps my body in good shape. I like getting into arm wrestling with the fellers. They think they can beat me, but you should see their faces when I put them down in less than a minute.

"I am working on a couple of buildings at this moment. They are right next door to each other. Maybe I should make a competitive adventure out of it between the two crews. Nah, when you do that, the quality of work goes down. The two buildings are right on the main road coming into town. I meet a lot of travelers, some coming from a long way, and others coming from just down the road at the next town. You hear all kinds of stories; they say there was a man claiming he has been sent from God. That was a new one on me. I knew about some prophet named John going around preaching about the Messiah coming and that we need to repent.

"This has been a warm but not too hot day, just right for working. A lot of buzz is going on in town; it seems as though that guy doing the preaching, not the one called John but the other one, is going to be pretty close to town here. What can one guy do? One of my workers says that a lot of people follow him all the time; sometimes there are hundreds especially when he starts to heal people. I don't know what to think about all of this; I hope he does come here.

"The rumor is getting stronger and stronger. You know, the one about this character coming here. If you hear it from one or two, it probably isn't true; but seems like a lot of folks are talking about it. I guess only time will tell. I don't see why he would come here as this town is so small it isn't even on the map. I guess if he was headed for someplace else he would come through here. You know what? I think I am worrying about this way too much. It is supper time, and I am hungry. Would you like to come eat with us, just my parents and me? They would enjoy some new company."

"Good morning, everyone; breakfast time is a great time. I would have slept longer but all that commotion that is going on outside woke me up. I guess it must have woken you all up too. I wonder what is going on. Mom, have you heard anything? You mean the rumors are true? That man is coming this way? I hope I can get some work in before he gets here. The guys get distracted easy anyways; this isn't going to help." Maybe I'll go out and see this for myself; you know, most of them healers like that bring along people who fake it; and people will give money hand over fist. He will meet his match with me here; I know everybody in town and all the little towns around here. He isn't going to fool me. Man, look at that cloud of dust out there on the road. If that is him, a lot of people are following him. They say that sometimes there will be hundreds in a group, all the better to fool you with. I'm sorry; I should give him a chance before I judge him. If he is who he says he is, I will bring my dad and see if He can heal him. There is a knoll just outside of town; it looks like he is going to set up shop there. Look at all those people; some look like they can hardly walk, and others are being carried on stretchers. I know one thing, this ought to be good for the economy. These people have to eat.

I have found myself a great spot to sit and listen to him. Man, I've never heard a voice like that before. If I were to go all around this group of people, I would still be able to hear Him, just as though I was standing next to him. I went ahead and gave the guys time off for as long as He is here. I wouldn't get any work done anyway. What is that He just said? He hasn't come to destroy the law but to fulfill the law? Now what does He mean by that? Now He is saying He is the Son of God. That, my friends, is a pretty bold statement. This is intriguing, I have to look all this up; it has been a long time since I have studied any of the Torah. Looks like He is done talking; now comes the real test. Here comes the first one, looks like he has a foot problem. This guy just put His hands on him, and he is healed.

THE APOSTLES 1ST PERSON A NARRATIVE

This is so fake. I don't know that guy, so he must be a plant. Wait a minute. I know this next one; yeah, that's my neighbor. He has been sick for years; he is so weak he can barely stand up. I think that is his wife who is helping him stand. I guess when this is over I should help her get him back home. Wait a minute . . . what just happened? Coburn is standing all alone; he is dancing and running around. My eyes must be deceiving me or I'm dreaming. That just can't be; I am going to go get Dad, and this will prove it one way or another. I have to admit I want this to be true.

"Come on, Dad, let's see if you can get better. Now, don't get your hopes up too much, but I have seen our neighbor, Mr. Coburn, get healed. Come on. Yes, it is scary; but it is worth a try. Help me, Mom; put him in the wagon." Oh rats, somebody got my good spot over there. That's okay because I want to try and get close to this guy. I don't even know His name, and here I am wanting Him to heal my dad. I should be ashamed of myself. "Hey, you. John, you know this Man's name? Jesus you say?" Well, at least it is Jewish. "Come on, Dad; I'll carry you the rest of the way."

"Hello, Sir. Mr. Jesus, this is my dad. Can you do anything for him? I'm sorry, but I must say that I am a little skeptical. I can't even talk right, but I would appreciate You fixing my dad. Yes, it is a beautiful day; and from what I have seen, it looks like a lot of people are having even better days now, thanks to You. But honestly, Sir, if you could heal him now . . . he is getting sort of heavy . . . but he can't stand up . . . do what? He already has been healed? I should put him down? You hear that, Dad? Let's try it out, okay? You're standing on your own!" It is true, and You are the one to come.

I don't know what to think of this. I saw it with my own eyes, but I still am skeptical. Why? I have to try and absorb all that has transpired today. Jesus has gone on down the road. I find myself longing to hear more of what He has to say. I know what I have to do; I have to go fishing. I'll get my boat and go out to the middle of the lake and just sit there and meditate to try and figure this out. "Mom, I'm going fishing; take care of Dad will you? But I guess he doesn't need special care now, does he?" I haven't even thought about work, that's ok, my guys know what to do. Here's my boat; man, that looks good. I haven't been fishing in a long time. I don't even care if the fish bite or not; I prefer they don't. I have to think this thing over. I really don't want to rely on people telling me what He said, but I have a job to do. I can't just up and leave my parents, or can I? Dad is running around like a chicken with his head cut off. Mom is so happy because of Dad's healing. This would be a great time to take a leave of absence. Dad knows the business as well as I do. I think I will ask him what I should do. I respect his opinion more than anyone else's opinion.

"Hi, Dad, may I ask you your opinion about something? Thanks, I would like to follow the Man that healed you for a while. What do you mean? I know His name. It's Jesus. You're right; I feel as though I'm not worthy to even speak His name. I stand in awe of His greatness; just thinking about Him makes me want to pray to Him. You won't mind? Oh, thanks, Dad." It is settled; I will follow Jesus for a little while. I feel so giddy. I am finally going to get to have my training in the Torah.

I have been traveling with Jesus now for several days, I think I have learned more in these few days than I ever did while studying under the priest in school. Jesus makes it so plain in a lot of areas, but so, so hard in others. Jesus takes the ones that are following Him steadily over to the side and teaches us deeper subjects, in ways I can't understand. But He says it will all come to us later. I can't count the people that he heals on a daily basis. Oh no, He is calling me over to speak to me; I sure hope I haven't done anything wrong. "Hi Jesus, what's up? You have noticed me in the crowd? You can tell I am sincere in my faith in You? Thank you, Sir. I do believe, don't understand a lot of it, but I do believe in You. I just want to learn more and more. You're going to do what? You're going to change my name? To what? Didymus? I don't quite get it, Sir, but doesn't that mean *twin*? I see. You think Peter and I are alike? How? Peter and I both do have a burning desire to serve You, and we both would go to bat for You. That's true. We both are strong-willed, that's for sure."

We have traveled back into Jerusalem; this is my second trip here. Sometimes the people are friendly; other times they want to kill us. Things are pretty calm right now, as long as the Pharisees leave us alone. Jesus is calling some of us over to the side. Usually that means He has something important to say. He has allowed me to attend a lot of these meetings. "Hey, Jesus, what's up? You say your ministries are growing ever so large now?" There are so many things to take care of that He wants to appoint the twelve of us, that are attending this meeting, as apostles. We each will have authority over the disciples, and will be able to heal the lame, even make the blind to see. "Oh, Jesus, thank You for putting Your faith and trust in me. I will serve you faithfully."

Our first command is to go out over the countryside to all the towns around and preach the message. "You mean I can't take anything with me, no food, water, or even a change of clothes? Gotcha, a test of faith. No problem, when do we start? Oh I see, we should have been gone already; see you when we get back."

That was some outing I had; you just never knew what is going to happen from one day to the next. I will go into one town and be received with open arms and then the next town I can't get out fast enough. "I did get to experience the feeling you get when you are able to heal someone's sickness, or help someone stand for the first time in a long time, like when my dad was healed. How about the rest of you guys? Do you get a warm feeling when you help someone? Yeah, me too. When that man that was demon possessed came up to me, you could feel the wickedness in the air. By the time the demon left, I was sweating up a storm. How about you all? I didn't know demons were so strong. We wouldn't have been able to handle it without the help of Jesus."

Jesus is gathering us back up again; that means another assignment. Good, I love doing this. "Hey, Jesus, what's up? Okay, we have to find seventy faithful disciples and have them come to You; that shouldn't be too hard. There is a large crowd gathered around outside anyway. Okay, we will pray over it to be sure to find the right ones; because this is going to be important. That would be a great business move, You sending all seventy out to make a massive wave through all areas. You're giving them the power also? Great! They will tell everyone that You will be coming through their areas before long and give them an example of what is instore for them at that time.

The selected ones have been out for a couple of months now; some of them have started to drift back in, in fact, most all of them are back. They all look just like we did when we came back, big ol' grins on their face and full of tales.

We have been in and out of towns, countries, and cities, with great success; but some of the Pharisees are starting to get agitated. They come in and try to trick Jesus, but they leave looking like fools and don't like that. I always say, if you don't like it, don't ask it. As apostles, we sort of stand back when Jesus is teaching. We observe the crowd to see how well they are receiving the Gospel.

Here comes trouble; it looks like the Pharisees, and it is an actual Pharisee this time. A lot of times they send in the trainees to ask the questions. But I guess they are stirred up enough that they are coming themselves this time; this ought to be interesting. They have some temple guards with them and they are just pushing their way through the crowd. Strange, I can barely hear them; but when Jesus speaks, I have no problem. I think they just told Jesus to shut it down and not to preach anymore. Ouch, Jesus called them hypocrites. Look at their collars, they are turning beet red. More soldiers are a coming; this is big trouble. The Pharisees are hollering for Jesus to show Himself. I don't know what their problem is; he is standing right in front of them. Here he comes; this is so comical, them hollering and him walking right by them.

Another few months of travel, I sure hadn't planned on staying this long, but I am totally involved. Jesus says it is time to go back to Jerusalem. "Hey, guys, we all know it is going to be dangerous, but I feel that I took this on to go to the end. If it means we die, we die with Jesus. Right, Peter? To. The. End." I hear that they have already beheaded John the Baptist. Jesus said that this is just the beginning. He has told us to go into town and get a big room. We are going to have a meal. That sounds good; I wonder what we are going to have?

That was the worst meal I have ever eaten. The food was okay, but Jesus said that one of us was going to betray him. I believe in Jesus, but I can't fathom anyone of us doing him harm. And on top of that, He showed us that we are to eat unleavened bread as a symbol of His body and then to drink a sip of wine in remembrance of His blood that will be spilt. I don't understand what is happening with things right now. But Jesus seems to be highly concerned about things He says are about to go on. I guess we need to pray, and pray hard.

"I guess I need to tell you . . . this is so hard to do . . . but while you were gone . . . maybe I should say it this way . . . remember I told you that Jesus said one of us would betray him? Well, that someone was Iscariot. You remember him? He was the treasurer. We went up on a hillside to pray and that bum brought a bunch of soldiers with him. He kissed Jesus on the cheek and the soldiers carried him off. We all scattered for a while, but they . . . oh gosh, this is the first time I have told this to anyone . . . they crucified Jesus. They hung Him on a cross, stuck a mocking crown on His head, and called him the King of the Jews. Do you remember Him saying anything about rising out of the grave? Well, He did, or so the others have said. I don't think He did. How long has it been now? Eight days, you say? Well, I will have to see it for myself to believe it. Didn't you tell me that one of you turned Him in? If that is so, who is that twelfth person in the room? I don't think you would allow Judas in, so who is it?

Oh, come on. I know my Jesus; so who are You? If you are the Jesus I know, then you must have the scars from the cross on Your hands and feet. Yes, I see them. Can I touch them? You want me to poke my finger in your side? Okay, it isn't going to hurt, is it? Oh, Jesus, I bow to You. You have risen, and You are alive. Yes, I had some business to take care of with my parents. I missed it; I'm so sorry. What was that? You are only going to be here a few days? I will stick to Your side Jesus, pardon the pun."

Jesus has ascended into the heavens; the apostles have met, and decisions have been made. We have replaced Iscariot with a guy named Matthias. Now this evening we are going to cast lots as to

THE APOSTLES 1ST PERSON A NARRATIVE

where each one of us is going to go. It is my turn to draw lots. Let me see, What?! India?! No, no, no. I am not going to go to India. Look, I'm a Hebrew; what am I to do with the Indians? No, you can't force me into going; I will just go my own way. Sorry, I guess this is where we part company. I will still preach the gospel, just not in India.

I don't understand those guys trying to force me into going to India. I think no one else wanted to go there, so they acted like I drew that lot. Well, they don't fool me. I know, I'll go up to Palestine and preach for a little bit, and then head more north and west, kind of stay close to the sea's edge.

Look at all the construction going on here. Some of these buildings are beautiful. You can tell who hired an architect and who didn't. I better get my mind back on the Gospel and preaching it. Sort of hard though, first Jesus dying, and then the apostles trying to pull the wool over my eyes.

"Hi, guys. How's it going? Not too good, you say? Nothing is fitting like it should. You wants some help? This is my trade, building buildings. I would be glad to do it.

Who is that group of guys over there? Looks like they are looking for someone. You don't say; they going to force someone to build for them. Me being Jewish, they wouldn't want me. Hello, gentlemen, yes, I am an architecture worker. Hey, wait a minute! Get your hands off me! I'll go wherever you're going, just get your hands off! Where are you going? No, no, no, I am not going to go to India! You can't make me! Please, no! Do I have to stay in the dungeon?!"

We have been out to sea for 3-4 days; I am still in the brig, and I think I've gotten myself in a pickle. Who said that? I'm the only one down here; there it goes again. "Who's there? Jesus? What are You doing here? Oh, no, You say the apostles did not set me up, that You directed the lot to fall on me? I have done them and You wrong. Jesus, will You please forgive me? You are going to protect me? Thank you, Jesus."

I guess they are going to take me up to see the king today; they say he isn't anything like the bullies that I met. I will soon find out. "Yes, sir, King, I do architectural work. You say you want me to build you a palace? Okay, what is my pay? Oh, my life? Gotcha. What am I to use as materials? Marble? Where am to get marble? Okay, you say that is no problem; whatever I need to do the job, you will get it? I always had to scrimp around to find enough materials. At least that is good. You give me how big, and I will build it."

I have been working on the palace now, I really can't say how long, but I have been able to spread the Gospel to many folks. They, the workers I'm talking about, seem to be genuinely interested in what I have to say. I have been going outside the city and teaching and preaching to the people. It is so pretty here, a lot different than back home. The mountains are so majestic. They are so tall; there is snow year round on them. The grass is green; the trees look like they came out of a scroll. There are all kinds of trees, banana trees, coconut trees, and such; a guy isn't going to go hungry here. Did you know there are seven major rivers in India? There are several glaciers that feed the rivers. The most important thing, there are all kinds of fish for great fishing. Whoohoo! I think I will stop talking and go out on the boat to try and get some supper. I really don't trust these boats around here. All they are is four to five poles tied together, the ends kind of go up but not much. I went out the other day and it was rather scary. But my fear isn't going to stop me, even if I have to fish off the bank.

A lot of the workers on the palace have been talking to their families about the Gospel. They all want to hear more about this Jesus. That is so good to hear; not only them, but a lot of the locals

THE APOSTLES 1ST PERSON A NARRATIVE

love listening to me teach. Most everyone in the area studies under the Buddhist religion. The priests are a lot like the Pharisees; they don't like me preaching. The only difference is the people don't pay them much mind. Here come the soldiers from the king. I wonder what I've done now; I thought I was doing a good job for him. "Hi, guys, he wants to see me? Okay, let's see what's up."

This is sort of strange; these soldiers aren't pushing me and trying to man handle me. They are actually smiling and cutting up with each other. I just hope the king is in a good mood. I sit here worried about this so much I don't realize I am at the palace door already. "You wanted to see me, sir? Well, thank you, sir; I am glad you are pleased with it. Yes, the rest of the process is time consuming work; nothing that is technical. A lot of rubbing on the blocks to make them smooth. Thank you, sir, I try to do the best job possible. No, sir, it hasn't seemed like I was a prisoner. In fact, I have rather enjoyed my time here. Really, sir? I am being relieved of my duties? I am free to go anywhere I want? Thank you, sir. I truly hope you enjoy living in the new palace."

Now what am I going to do? I guess I have all the time in the world to preach the Gospel. Should I stay here and preach, or should I go on? I think I will stay a little longer here, so I can help the new converts gain more knowledge. Then I will start heading up north.

I have reached the city of Malabar. It is a medium-sized town, a lot of travelers here. All kinds of goods are being sold. People seem to be friendly, of course, there are a few soreheads. What is so neat is the governor is interested in the Gospel. His name is Nambuthiri. He has invited me over to his house so I can tell all his family. "Sir, it is late in the evening, if you want to get baptized we can do it in the morning. You don't want to wait? Okay, let's go to the river. Wow, it is not only you and your wife but all your children and your servants too? May God be with us tonight." There were over forty people in his family, plus servants baptized. It is morning now, and as I look out on the banks, what do I see? People all over the bank, there must be over four hundred coming to be baptized. God is so good.

I am being told by a soldier that the King wants to see me; I need to go see him. Maybe he wants to be baptized too. Here comes a group of the priests from the temple. "Yes, sir, I am the one who is proclaiming Jesus is the way. You like what I am saying? That's strange, usually people want me dead. Jesus is working, so I will preach to them. You say a lot of people want to hear me? There is a place I can preach from and everyone can hear? That sounds reasonable. You are going to send 5 soldiers with me up on the hill? They will be keeping people from getting to close and accidentally hitting me, thus knocking me off? They will be standing at attention with their spears sharpened and ready for any trouble? Okay. Hello, friends and my new brothers. It is so good to see you. I hope you can hear me. I would like to . . . Ugh . . . they speared me . . . I'm coming home my Lord . . ."

APOSTLE
MATTHEW

"**HELLO, MY NAME** is Levi. I am the son of Alpheus. I am 31 years old and a tax collector. I am married and have four children. I collect taxes here in Capernaum for the government. I am a Jew from Palestine which is where I was born. Capernaum is a town on the north side of the Sea of Galilee. The population is around 1,500. The weather is a subtropical ninety to ninety-five degrees.

"Most all 'chief' collectors are Romans, but the collectors who are out in the public are of Jewish descent. I have a good life because I am on the main road leading in and out of Capernaum. I tax all items that come into town which are mostly new goods that have been shipped in on the Sea of Galilee. I also collect taxes on any animals that people have. I collect 10% on goods and 5% on animals. I should say, that's what the government gets. (You see, I make my living by what I collect over that amount; and I must say, I make a very good living.) My name even means "to take." As you might expect, I don't have that many friends, other than my fellow tax collectors. It is a known fact that tax collectors, myself included, like to have parties and invite a lot of upper-crust people, rich people, political people. You see, these people will always come with some sort of gift, mostly money. The reason being is they will try to buy our friendship, so they won't be taxed so heavily. The more parties, the more money we can get. Sneaky, huh?

GEORGE A REGISTER

"I am very good at figures and budgets, and keeping a journal of whose paid and who hasn't. Anything that deals with numbers or people, that's my thing. I can speak Hebrew, Greek, and Aramaic. I can also read, not too many Jews can say that.

"I am making a lot of extra money as of now because of all the activity. Meaning there are a lot of extra people in town and I charge for each person. I charge different people different taxes. If you look like you have money, I will charge a bunch. If you look poor, I charge less. (Don't go telling anybody this, okay?)

"I have several buddies at my table. It's a long table, so people don't have to stand in line too long. We can also keep an eye on everyone because a lot of people will try and skip around us. If we catch them, we will charge enormous sums of money.

"As I said earlier, there are a lot of extra people in town. Nothing special going on, but it seems like a lot of excitement is in the air. There is some scuttlebutt going on in some of the surrounding towns about some dude is going around playing doctor or something like that. I know that these priests around here are starting to get, what you might call, 'irritated' at this guy. I think He is stealing some of their business. Being a tax collector, I don't do the 'religious thing' so much. I do know the laws and Moses' Commandments, but I don't practice them. I have seen the Pharisees gathering together a lot lately, because I heard this dude is, or has, come to Capernaum. From what I have heard, there are a bunch of people following after Him. I guess I would too if someone in my family was sick. I don't know how He does it, but He has, what they call, 'healed' a lot of people. But you know, if He comes here and those people follow Him, I am going to make a lot of money. Let's see, what would a tax be on someone being healed? Hmmm . . . I hate to say this but . . . "I'm going to be rich!" I'm just dreaming. Why would He come here to Capernaum? A small Podunk town of 1,500 citizens. There are Bethsaida and Cana just a few miles down the road, and both of them are a lot bigger. Wait a minute . . . What's all that commotion going on down the street? You know what? I believe it is Him. Look at all those people! I think I can go get me a new pair of mules. I'm going to be rich, rolling in money!"

This dude I'm looking at, if that is Him, doesn't look like a king, doctor, or even a leader. But people are sure hanging onto Him. Well, I don't care if He is something special. He is going to have to pay His taxes. Doesn't look like He has any money. So, maybe He will go to one of the other collectors, and I can get some of the people that look a little more prosperous.

That guy looks like He doesn't have a care in the world. He is looking for something or maybe someone to pay His taxes, haha. Oh rats, looks like He is coming to my station. Well, it shouldn't take long to pass Him on through. "Good afternoon, Sir, what do you have to declare? Sir, are you okay? Why do you keep staring at me?" Those eyes, it's as if He is looking right into me. "Sir, answer me . . . now!" I think I'm going to have to call the soldiers over if He doesn't answer me.

I can't seem to move; I'm beginning to have a very strange feeling all over my body. I think I had better stand up and stretch; I might be having a heart attack or something. I am opening my mouth and no sound is coming out; this has got to be a heart attack. He just keeps staring at me; this is beginning to be very unnerving to me. Oh, no, I can't stand. Hey, guys! Can't you see I'm in trouble over here? All my fellow tax collectors are too busy working with all the other people to notice I'm in trouble; the only One paying any attention to me is that dude who is just staring at me. What can I do?

Wait a minute . . . I'm not feeling any pain, so I must not be having a heart attack. If I said how I felt it would be great. I just can't move. What is this? I am feeling this cool breeze-like sensation all over. It's like this Man has taken over my whole body. What's bad about that is I am kind of willing to let Him. He is still staring at me, but now I can see love, compassion, strength, and kindness. His eyes are telling me that He cares for me. That He is concerned about me. Most of all, He believes in me. What a great feeling! It's almost like taking a bath in nice, hot water and just soaking it all up. What is He saying? He is looking straight into my eyes and saying, "Follow Me." I can't figure this out, but I want to follow Him. I don't care if I lose all this business. I need to go with Him. I'll check out if I can move. Glory be to God! I can stand! I feel so giddy! I think that I will follow Him for a little while. See where He is going and what He is up to.

This feeling I have is so encompassing. I am beginning to believe what people are saying about Him that He is a great prophet. Do you know that some people are even calling Him the Messiah? I think I have an idea that will let me find out a little bit more about Him.

"Sir...uh...Jesus...I think that is what they are calling You. It is getting towards the evening, and I know that you must be getting a little tired, probably a little hungry too. So, why don't we go over to my house, and I will get my wife to fix us some supper and then we can talk. I even have a better idea. Let me send some of my children to invite my work buddies, or maybe I should say my 'former' working buddies, over so they can hear what You are telling me. I'm real sure they would be happy to hear about how we are to love one another. Besides, I have to tell my wife that I am going to go with You. After we finish eating and partying, You can spend the night here. I have plenty of room. Supper will be soon. Please, Jesus, tell me more and tell me why You selected me.

"All right, here come my friends. I told you they would come. Now let's start eating. I don't know if you realize this or not, but I am a vegetarian. I am not against eating meat, but I don't eat it myself. Man, oh man, my household has put out a great spread. With my belly full and a good night's rest, we can be ready to go in the morning."

What is all this? Look at all those people coming towards my house. They don't look like they are mad. I wonder what they want. Jesus has noticed all the people too. He is smiling big time. I guess maybe I need to run them off; but Jesus is motioning me to sit back down. He stands up to His feet and goes to the doorway. The whole town is outside. I guess they all have heard about the miracles Jesus performed on those people today. They have brought all their sick to see if He will help them and He does. All night Jesus has been healing different people. Then he tells them about God's love for all. It is all that I can do to keep my eyes open.

Wow, what a night! So many people, so much healing of the sick going on. The kindness that Jesus is showing. It's unbelievable how He shows this kind of love for all. You want to know something neat? He doesn't call me Levi anymore; He calls me Matthaeus, which means "Gift of Jehovah." Wow, me, little ol' me, a gift from God! That makes me feel so good. I must say though, some of these people, He calls them His disciples, don't want to accept me because I am a tax man. But that's okay, because Jesus wants me and told me to follow Him. So I am packing a few things to follow. Jesus seems to keep a few of us real close. The reason for this is He's always trying to teach us about what His duties are and what prophesies He is fulfilling while here. I haven't got a clue what He means by that. He did say we are going to Jerusalem. That is about ninety miles from my place. That is a long dusty dirt road we are going to have to walk. But none of us that are close to Jesus are upset about going.

Well, we made it to Jerusalem, what a walk. Jesus made good use of the time, by telling us about what is going to happen. How His message won't be accepted by all. Matter of fact, He was telling us how His own hometown basically will run Him out.

Some of the disciples were telling me about a lot of the miracles Jesus has been performing. After seeing and hearing about these things, how could a person not believe in Him?

I completely forgot that this is Passover time. That explains all these people being here. Doesn't say much about my religious activities, does it? Man, this water tastes good and that pool over there sure looks inviting. What is this? Jesus is heading over to someone. Oh my, you ought to see this poor man's hand. It is completely withered away. The man is looking at Jesus with eyes that seem to scream out with pain. Jesus healed the man; I'm sure glad, as he was in such pain. They say that people that are lame come to this pool to get relief from their pains. Another man, whose unable to walk, and has been lying there in the same place for thirty-eight years. Jesus walked right up to him and asked, "You want to be healed?" The man told Jesus he had no one to put him in the pool. Jesus said, "Get up, take your bed, and walk." You know what? He did! Wow, is all I can say.

Those stinking Pharisees are still trying to cause trouble. I even heard that they want to kill Jesus. Why? Why would they want to do this? Can't they see that He is a special man? I guess this is too distracting to Jesus. So we are going to start back towards Galilee. A lot of people are following us. Jesus, being the kind of person He is, is healing all of them.

THE APOSTLES 1ST PERSON A NARRATIVE

We have come back to Capernaum now; it was good to see my wife and kids. Time seems to be of the utmost importance right now. Jesus taught His faithful followers a lot of information on this last trip. I just got word that Jesus wants to see me on top of the hill just outside of town. I'm sure He wants to plot out our next tour. I had better get with it. I don't want to keep Jesus waiting, you know. I've never met anyone who has such a warm and loving spirit about Him. "Hi, Jesus, You wanted to see me? I see a few of Your close disciples are here. You say that our ministry is going to change a little? You are going to appoint Your 'apostles'? Oh, Lord Jesus . . . I don't deserve to be blessed like this. Whatever it takes, I'll try my best to carry out Your commands."

After a long discussion and a lot of praying, Jesus comes down the mountain, sits on a big rock, and starts to give one of the most beautiful sermons. If I only had that type of speaking ability. . .

Well, we are off to tour through Galilee. Things are a little, maybe I should say a lot, different on this trip. The twelve of us that have been chosen are able to heal and cast out demons and spread the Gospel. This is somewhat of a relief to Jesus. Or I should say, that's how I look at it. Jesus is gathering us up now. He says we need to get on board a ship, so we can go over to the Decapolis area and spread the Gospel there. On the way over, a big storm comes up. We almost sink, because the waves are so high. Doesn't bother Jesus any. He is sound asleep in front of the boat. Some of the apostles wake Him up; they want to see if He can do something about it. Well, guess what? Jesus kind of scolds us all. He says we don't have enough faith. So He looks out to the storm, tells it to settle down, and it does. This Man, or maybe I should say this Messiah, has dominion over even the weather. Oh, God, thank You for bringing Jesus into my life.

GEORGE A REGISTER

Well, we have been preaching in all ten cities of the Decapolis. Jesus says it's time to go back across the sea back home. So we head back home, and no sooner have we arrived, when a great crowd begins to form.

All of a sudden, a government worker, I think he is a ruler of some sort, come over and bows down to Jesus. I have never seen anything like it. This guy is used to everyone else bowing down to him. But he knows Jesus can help him. His daughter has passed away, and he wants Jesus to bring her back. So what does Jesus do? He tells Jairus to show Him the way to his house. Of course there is a big group of people wailing, gnashing, and just flatout grieving at Jairus's house. Wouldn't you know it? Jesus brings the girl back from the dead! I'm simply amazed at Jesus' ability. Looks like we are going back out on another missions trip. No telling where we are going. Jesus is in charge, so I don't need to know. While we are here at home, I replenish some of my money so we won't be strapped down with that worry. I have used a lot of my own money to finance our little trips. But please, don't tell the others. I try to be discreet about this. I have plenty of money so I need to share anonymously.

We have come to where Jesus was raised. These people are a little on the naïve side. They say Jesus was a man that was raised here by a carpenter. Nothing special about Him. Even though Jesus has performed miracles here, they still reject him. You can see the sorrow on Jesus' face. He told us it is time to leave. I think Jesus is wanting to be alone. He tells us to go all over the country and preach the Word. So we all leave Him and go to different towns preaching and teaching

THE APOSTLES 1ST PERSON A NARRATIVE

to any and all that will listen. Sometimes we stay together and other times we go to separate towns. We are all in agreement that it is time for us to go back to C-town.

Jesus shows back up a few days later and says that we are to all go get in a boat. We are going to Bethsaida. We all kind of keep to ourselves and start to pray. Jesus is always praying. He tells us to pray, and if possible to get alone so we can relax and talk to God without any interruptions.

Being up on the side of this hill, a nice cool breeze is blowing around us. That is, as cool as it can be at this time of the year. As usual, a great crowd begins to develop at the bottom of the hill. Not counting the women and children, I would dare say there are over 5,000 people here. All these people at this time are hungry for the Gospel. Most of them have traveled a long distance to listen to what Jesus has to say. They all are physically hungry also. There is no way we have enough money to feed all of these people. Then, Jesus pulls out another miracle. Not only does He feed them all, but He has baskets of food left over. Oh, why can't I just believe in Him? I feel so ashamed of myself.

After feeding everyone and preaching another great message, Jesus tells us to get in the boat and head on back. He will catch up later. So off we go. As we are traveling across the sea, a strange site comes up in the distance. I swear it looks like a ghost appears out of nowhere. I rub my eyes and look again. It is a little closer. Now all the apostles are able to see it. Oh my, oh my, it looks just like Jesus. It is Jesus! And He is walking out to the boat! He is walking on the water out to the boat! When He gets a little bit closer, He asks what we are looking at. All of us are marveling at this when one of the apostles, I think it is Peter, wants to try it. So Jesus says, "Come on out." Peter does and is doing pretty good until he loses focus. The poor boy almost drowns. Jesus is now scolding Peter for not having enough faith.

We then go on down south a little and land in the area of Gennesaret. This is flat country. A lot of people are here to meet us when we arrive. Jesus heals many of them, and we all spread the Word to every person that will listen. Jesus now says it is time to go back to C-town. But before we leave though, those stinking Pharisees show up. They once again traveled all the way from Jerusalem just to agitate Jesus. Once again Jesus answers them and sends them on their way. Jesus has us walk alongside the sea until we come upon the side of a mountain. Here He sits down and starts speaking to the large crowd that is gathering around Him. Once again He wants to feed these people; I bet there are over 4,000 people here.

After feeding and speaking to all these people, Jesus begins another journey. This time though, we go to the Caesarea Philippi district. Now let me tell you, that is a hike and a half. Jesus' mood is starting to change a little. He is beginning to speak with a lot of urgency. As we are walking along, Jesus turns around and asks us, "Who do people say that the Son of Man is?" We all give different answers. But then He asks us, "But who do you say I am?"

Peter speaks up and says, "You are the Christ." A very strange thing happens then, He tells us not to tell anyone this. I just don't get it.

Jesus gathers the twelve of us together and starts to explain that it is time to go to Jerusalem and suffer many things. Well, now that is kind of unexpected! He even tells us that He will die but will rise three days later. This really sets Peter off; he has always been a little on the hot-headed side anyway, but he takes Jesus to the side and speaks to Him. I don't know what he is saying, but boy, does Jesus jump all over him. Jesus even tells Satan to get out while He is looking straight at Peter. Jesus, for the last few days, has been speaking to us in a manner that has opened our eyes to some of the truths from His sermons.

On our way back home, we have to go through Capernaum to get to Jerusalem. Jesus pulls Simon, James, and John away to the top of a mountain. They aren't gone very long but when they get back, their whole attitudes have changed. They won't say what went on there, but they will tell us later.

We have been staying at home in C-town for just a little while. But Jesus hasn't stopped giving lesson after lesson on things that are happening right now and things that will happen later.

All this time we have been walking towards Jerusalem. As we are walking along, Jesus stops and turns around. Then He reminds us that the Sabbath is only two days away. Once again He says, "The Son of Man will be delivered up to be crucified." This, my friends, is not the happiest moment in my life. Jesus just sent a few of the other disciples to prepare a room for us to have a banquet in.

With all the people in town, I really am surprised that they actually found us a place. As the apostles are eating, Jesus drops another bombshell on us. He says that one of us is going to betray Him! I honestly can't think of anyone that would want to hurt Jesus. With a very stern voice He says, "Woe to that man who betrays the Son of God." We all sit around and sing some hymns, but everyone is sort of in a sorrowful mood. Jesus then tells us that we need to go out to this place called the Mount of Olives. Then He drops yet another bombshell on us. He says that we all will fall away from Him tonight. Then He says, "Let's go," so we do. We went straight out to that garden, all of us following . . . Wait a minute, there are only eleven of us. Who's missing? It is Judas. He must be counting the money from today.

Jesus tells us to stay while He and a couple of the others go on up to pray. While they are praying, I notice a lot of lights coming up. My first thought is that the people have found out that Jesus is up here and are wanting Him to heal some more folks. Wait a minute . . . that's not a crowd of people. That is a group of soldiers coming up here. What do they want? This is a public place. I think I recognize the one leading them. Yes, that's Judas with them. When they approach us, they stop. By this time, Jesus has come back down. As Jesus stands still, I can see His eyes looking at Judas. It is that same penetrating look that He gave me when He first called me. Only this time, it is filled with hurt. Then Jesus tells Judas to do what He has to do. Judas goes up and kisses Jesus on the cheek. That's when all the commotion starts. The soldiers grab hold of Jesus and start to drag Him off. You can count on Peter and his hot head. All of us are hiding in the bushes, but I think I see Peter chopping off a soldier's ear. Jesus quickly gets everyone to settle down and then bends down, picks up that ear, and heals the soldier.

Well, I guess Jesus was right; every one of us have fled to safety, even hot-headed Peter. Why did I run away? This Man, if you can call Him a Man, has done nothing wrong. He has healed hundreds of people, has brought joy to thousands, and has taught us so much.

I can do a lot more if I don't get caught. I can spread the Gospel all over town. Who am I kidding? I'm scared to death of jail time. My faith is smaller than a mustard seed just like He said. My heart is so heavy right now. I think I'll go see if I can find out what is happening to Jesus now. Oh, my God . . . they are beating Him. People around here are on a rampage. They are calling out for Jesus to be crucified; I have to get out of here. If they catch me, they might do the same to me.

THE APOSTLES 1ST PERSON A NARRATIVE

I guess I must have passed out or been in a tizzy, because I have missed a lot. The people seem to have settled down a lot. Oh, no, I now know why. They crucified Jesus! They killed Jesus!!!! I have to get back home and see my wife and kids. I'll find some of the others and tell them I'm leaving. Ah, there is one of the disciples now. He seems to be awfully happy considering Jesus has just been killed. Good, he sees me and is coming over. Matthew, Matthew, Jesus is alive! If I think I am in bad shape, this guy is delusional! He tells me the others are going to meet. So we all get back together; each one of us tell of our actions and how we all feel like we have let Jesus down. But Simon Peter tells us we are to stay in Jerusalem until further word.

About this time, Jesus appears to us. My heart is about to jump out of my chest! A very weird thing happens; He wants something to eat. After He eats, a strange but fulfilling feeling comes over me. It must be coming over the others too, because all of us have this look on our faces. All the things that Jesus had been trying to teach us become so clear. I guess you would say that our minds have been opened.

Then Jesus goes with us almost all the way to Bethany. There He starts praying and blesses each one of us. Then the most beautiful sight I have ever seen happens. Jesus starts to rise. He just keeps going until He is out of sight. I can't help myself; I fall to my knees and begin to praise Jesus and ask for forgiveness.

We all get back together, SImon Peter stands up and says that we need to replace Judas. So all of us agree that it should be a man named Matthias. That's not going to be too hard to remember because everyone is calling me Matthew.

We have been meeting together now with the other chosen ones and discussing what, how, and where we should start teaching this message about Jesus and how He can give us everlasting life.

I really think that someone should start writing down the acts of love that Jesus did. You know, maybe preserve some of the miracles. I have been writing down a lot of them, but some of them happened before I came along. I think Peter and Andrew could help me there. Also, some of the other miracles were done when we were doing missions in other places. We all have come to be a big family, so I think they will all help me.

Well, a lot of the apostles have started out on their journeys. They have been so good to help me with recalling things that happened while Jesus was here. I have decided that, with the others' blessings, I will stay here in Jerusalem. I am still gathering information about the miracles and people seem to be opening up somewhat about the Gospel and life everlasting.

I have been preaching and teaching in Jerusalem now for around fifteen years. I have been hearing good things from other disciples about the spreading of the Gospel. I believe I will now go out on a little journey of my own.

I have started out now on my way to a country named Persia. I have been well received here and have been able to preach in many little towns. But I must get back to my family in Jerusalem for a bit. My children are all grown now, so it is just my wife and me.

I enjoyed that trip so much I think I'll try it again. This time though I believe I'll go to Ethiopia. These people aren't as friendly as those in Persia were, so I think I'll go onto the country of Parthia.

THE APOSTLES 1ST PERSON A NARRATIVE

I have been on these trips now for five years, or thereabout. These people in this country are worse than the last country. Matter of fact, they are getting very hostile. I see some soldiers coming this way; I better go. It has been good meeting you.

APOSTLE
JAMES ALPHAEUS

"**I HOPE THIS** isn't going to be a lengthy stay for you; I don't like people. I would rather you stay back from me. I will answer a few questions from you, what do you want to know?

"What kind of work do I do? Right off the bat you want to start prying into my business? If you must know, I really don't have a career job; matter of fact, I don't have any job. I find work from fishing to shepherding to sweeping floors. I even tried carpentry for a while. My mother's cousin is married to a carpenter. I worked for him a while, but the kids were getting the good jobs. One even had the same name as me. I must say though, the one they named Jesus could build anything. I was always getting into fights with the other kids; Jesus said he didn't have time to worry about me, which was rather indecent of Him, I think. Don't get me wrong, I had some good times with them too. I am a few years older than they are, so I played a little rough with them. Joseph would chew me out, and I would leave mad.

"I was born in the Naphtali region, close to Capernaum. I have traveled all over; like I said, I have trouble keeping a job. My mother told me that my fiery temper was going to get me hurt or even killed.

I just can't help myself; I don't like people. If you disagree with me, I get mad as a wet hornet. Mom hoped that I would grow out of it.

"Hey, there is one thing I know; that is the Torah. I have spent hours reading it over and over. Reading it has a soothing effect on me. I like to talk with the priests and ask questions. I catch them quite often making things up and trying to get people to believe it. Most of them are whiny butts. I doubt if one of them could whip his way out of a parchment bag. Of course they don't have to; the soldiers protect them. Well, la-di-da!

"I am going to go over to the shore line and rest a while. The fishing boats with their crews, take up most of the beach, but over on the farside is a strip where no one goes.

"Have you seen my Torah? I thought I had it right here. Oh well, I can picture it in my mind. Of course, if you want to challenge me, I would be more than happy to engage. Oh, there's my Torah! It was in the back of my tunic."

What is going on over by the river? It looks like a pretty big crowd. That makes me want to go the other way. I don't know who it is, but he sure does have a booming voice. He is a good half-mile away from me, and I can still hear him. What is it he is saying? Something about repenting? You bring those people my way, and I'll show you repenting. You know what? Maybe I need to jump right in the middle of the people and show this freak up. That will shut him up. I'm afraid that would cause me problems. I am very nervous around people; I would be the freak if I were to do that. Maybe I should just go to the beach and cool it. I might even go swimming.

That guy is still preaching; he has been at it for several hours now. If I stay on the outskirt of the people, I think I can still hear him. People seem to be hanging onto every word. Look at him; he is in the water now. What is he doing? Baptizing people . . . he is baptizing people! Just who does he think he is?! I can feel the blood rushing to my head; I'm about to explode. Okay, I need to back off.

I think I am claustrophobic. I guess I might need to go to a doctor, but that costs money, and I am sort of short on that.

Well, I am going to go over to where that guy was yesterday and look around on the ground. People drop a lot of money and don't know they did till they get home. Hope no one beats me to it. I'll be! That guy is still there, and he is still preaching. "Hey, you! Who is that man? His name is John? Not a very royal name, is it? What does he charge to visit with him? He doesn't charge? Maybe if I can get to the front, I won't start getting sick." Here I go. "Step aside, please. Step aside; let me through." Ah, I made it. This is much better, As long as I don't turn around, I'll be okay. He is preaching, not only to repent, but that there is another Man coming soon.

The people being baptized are starting to flock around me; I don't know how much more I can take. John has stopped baptizing. He is coming out of the water and looking down the road. Someone is coming, and I think He has a bigger crowd than John does. That guy looks like Someone I ought to know. It is my second cousin, Jesus! "Wow, He sure has a following! You know anything about Him?" I haven't seen Him in years; He is all grown up and is walking straight up to John. John said that this is the One he has been talking about. When Jesus got up to John, He said He wants John to baptize Him; now John is throwing a hissy fit. John says that Jesus is supposed to baptize him not him baptize Jesus. But Jesus has His mind made up.

Now that Jesus is baptized, I guess He figures it is time to continue on. People have Him completely surrounded, but it doesn't seem to bother Him. I would be freaking out. What is He up to now? People are coming from everywhere with sick ones. What is this? He just touched that person, and he jumped up. I know I saw him a few minutes ago, and he couldn't even stand up. Now he is running, jumping, dancing, and shouting. He isn't the only one; it seems like Jesus is pulling this healing business off one right after another. People are starting to spread out a little bit; something is

THE APOSTLES 1ST PERSON A NARRATIVE

going on over in the far corner. I see it now. A person, I can't tell if it is a female or a male, is really acting weird. A couple of people standing close to me are talking with each other, saying the guy is demon possessed. He won't go near Jesus; every time Jesus takes a step toward him, the guy backs up. Listen, Jesus is saying something to him. The guy is foaming at the mouth, shaking all over, flying up into the air, and slamming back down to earth. I have never seen anything like this in my life. All of a sudden there is a loud scream and the man passes out. When he wakes up, the demon is gone, and the guy is normal. Where does this Jesus get His power from?

This has been going on for several hours now; Jesus hasn't even taken a break. There was a disturbance for a short time when a few Pharisees tried to stop Him, but He continued on. Looks like Jesus is finished now, since He is starting to walk off. Looks like He is going to walk right by me; He isn't going right by me but coming right at me! "Hello, Jesus, haven't seen You in many a year. Oh, my health is good, not going hungry. No, I still don't have a steady job. How come You remember that? Yes, Sir, I still get mad real easy and can't stand to be around people. You want me to go with You? Why would I want to do a dumb thing like that? You will help me with my attitude problem? What if I think the problem is people like You trying to get into my business. I'm sorry, You see, I get so mad so quick. You still want me to go with You? I see. You know? I do feel a lot calmer now." Maybe this will be a good deal for me, at least I will have plenty of food.

I have been following Jesus around now for a while, and as He said my tantrums have slowed down a whole lot. Matter of fact, now that I am thinking about it, I haven't had a fit in weeks. I am even able to stand in a crowd, can't say I enjoy it, but I can do it. There are a bunch that follow Him like I do, and they have been nothing but friendly to me. I have sat back and watched as Jesus performs these miracles, and it makes me feel so good. After the people settle back down from being cured, the others will talk with them and explain what this is all about. I haven't seen a one that has refused to accept Jesus. Jesus has asked me if I will help the others with the ministry. I'm just not ready yet; give me a little bit longer.

I was so blessed today; you see Jesus made, I think it was twelve of us, what He called "apostles." We are going to be able to help with some of the duties that are a little more than just talking to people. He says He is going to allow us to heal people and cast out the demons, although we have to be real careful doing that. Jesus didn't hurry me along; He let me get used to being with the people. I have overcome most of my fears and am able to be in crowds now without panicking. I still tend to hang back a lot, but that is just my nature.

Jesus gathered us together yesterday to give out some assignments. He told us that we were to go out and preach to the Jews, telling them about the wonders that He can and does do. I don't think you know how nervous I am; I've never done this. I sit back and watch; I don't join in. Jesus told me that I am capable of doing this and that He won't let anything happen to me. So I am going to do something I have never done before in my life, I am going to trust someone; and that person is Jesus. We aren't to take anything with us, like food, clothing, water, or anything. Hey, that ought to be easy for me, as I have done that all my life.

Wow, that was an experience! I went out there and talked to people, and they talked back to me. I had a lot of people get excited about Jesus coming. The big thing was Jesus giving us the power to heal people. The first one I did knocked me on my backside. I am about to say something I have never said before. I had fun! As we all came back in and reported to Jesus, a big smile came across His face.

THE APOSTLES 1ST PERSON A NARRATIVE

We had a great time going out, but Jesus said it is time for some of the disciples to go out. We are rounding up seventy of His faithful disciples. They have the same job we had, only they are going to go out to invite Gentiles too. No wonder He needs seventy of them! The chosen ones will be able to heal and cast demons also. So as we pray over the disciples, we will send them out, two by two.

A lot of things are happening right now. Jesus has been arrested; He was turned in by one of us, and I think it was the Judean. Jesus didn't resist arrest; He said this was going to happen. Jesus has always eluded the soldiers before, but it was like He needed it to happen this way. When they arrested Him, I ran away. You know me; I hate trouble. I cause a lot of trouble, but I hate to be in it.

Here comes one of the disciples. He must have some news. "Hi, Coburn, what is going on? They are taking him to be crucified?! They can't do that! Why doesn't He get Himself out of this mess?" Oh my, I'm starting to get sick; I feel like I am ready to explode. Surely He will get out of this.

Here comes Coburn again. They crucified him; they actually crucified him! I have to go someplace quiet and think. "Get out of my way! Move it!" I said, "Move it!" I have to get a hold of myself; I can do it, I know I can do it. "Shut up; I don't need your advice." Why did I do that? They haven't done anything to me. "Oh, God, help me; I don't want to slip back to my former self, please." I just need to be alone.

The group has asked me to join them. I don't know how they even found me, but they ask me to come and be a part of them. And this is after me being so ugly to them. You know what happened? Jesus came back to life. Yes, it is true; and I saw Him with my own two eyes. He has been appearing to a lot of the disciples; He even ate a meal with us. That was pretty neat; but Jesus said He doesn't have much time left with us but said another would come and be with us.

Jesus has left us now, and we kind of feel lost, or least I do. Peter is trying to keep everything together, but it is a big job, not so much with the apostles, but the disciples are starting to scatter. There aren't nearly as many as we had before, but I can't blame them too much. Jesus did ask us if we would stay in Jerusalem until the replacement came. Speaking of which, we held a meeting and selected Matthias to replace the traitor.

Now we are all together and a strange feeling is coming over us. All of a sudden, you can feel Jesus with us, only it isn't Jesus. It is like a cloud or something. After it disappeared, we went outside; now this is going to sound strange, but we could understand everybody. Now that may not sound too strange to you, but there are people from all over the world in town. I could speak a little of two languages before, but now I can understand every one of them. Let me check this out. "You, sir, can you understand me?" Did you hear that?! He understood! He is from Egypt, and I don't speak Egyptian. This will really help in spreading the Gospel. Bring it on!

Peter has sent one of the disciples over; he must have something he wants to say to us. "Hey, Pete, you enjoying the all-encompassing language ability? You say it is going to come in handy for our next journey? What journey? We are going to draw lots to see who goes where? We will take some of the disciples with us to help?" Peter says some of us may never come back! I can't wait to see where I'm going! It's my turn. Where is it?! Egypt!!!

At least I will have company on the first part of my journey. You see, Simon also received Egypt; of course, we will be in different parts but not too far from each other. I am going to get off with him at Alexandra. Then I will go out into the Nile region. I believe Jesus came through there for a short time. So this isn't going to be totally new to them, which will make it easier.

We have come into port in Alexandria now. "Look how big it is, Simon! They tell me there is another port on the other side. Sand is all you see; the desert just keeps on going. Simon, I am going to go towards the river villages; I guess we should pray before I take off." I am heading to Tanis. That is still by the sea yet is on a tributary of the Nile. Tanis used to be the capital of Egypt. They had everything there; but there were too many battles I guess, so they moved the capital to Carthage and then Alexandria.

I have been teaching here now for a few weeks; people are very hungry for the Gospel. So I believe I am going to leave a few men to keep the work alive. I must be moving on; I am now going over to Goshen.

I made it; that sun coming down is pure hot. But as promised, Jesus took care of me. Wow, do you know where you are? If you remember when I first met you, I said I loved to read the Torah. You are standing right in the middle of history. Joseph was brought here as a slave. Abraham and Sarah came through here escaping the famine. I remember Jesus telling how His family came to Goshen to escape Herod. That makes this almost sacred ground. A lot of Jews are living here, but I must say they aren't as friendly as you would think they would be. I must be moving again; now I am going to Abu Rawash.

Look over there; it is a pyramid. The pharaohs used them for their burial grounds. I must say, going down the Nile like this, there is no shortage of water; and the banana trees are full of fruit. The grass is always green, the cattle are fat, and so are some of the people.

GEORGE A REGISTER

The further I go on the Nile, the more people reject God's Word. So far they are just rejecting the Word and not getting hostile. So I have been able to leave at least one, if not two, disciples in each town. I believe it is about time for me to go back towards Alexandria and then on to Jerusalem. I must say, I have really enjoyed this journey. But I have to get back and report. I think I will go back the same way I came; that way I can check on my brothers and the progress they are making. Besides, I want to see Goshen again. I loved that town and area surrounding it.

Seems like the brothers are doing okay; they said the priests are getting rather mad because of our preaching. I think it has to do with us taking away some of their flock. Not that they care about the people, so much as, the money they won't be getting. They are self-centered just like the priesthood in Jerusalem.

I am back in Alexandria and waiting on a boat to go back to J-town. I haven't been able to contact any of my disciples that I left here; I wonder what has happened to them. There is a group of sailors talking over in the corner; I think I will eavesdrop on their conversation, sounds like they were talking about Simon and his group. I'll just sort of sit back and listen. Oh my, I hope it isn't true what they are saying. They said a man was preaching about some dude named Jesus, so the priests had him arrested, then beaten to within an inch of his life, and then thrown with his gang on a boat back to Jerusalem. That has to be Simon; I sure hope he is okay. They also said that a few men here in Alexandria have been rounded up and sent off with the others which explains why I couldn't find anyone. Looks like my ship has come in; the sooner I get out of here the better I am going to like it.

I have arrived back in Jerusalem; that is one of the longest trips I have been on. I couldn't get Simon off of my mind; I was having it so easy going up and down the Nile. All that time, my brother Simon was being manhandled by the locals. I think we should cool it on the preaching business until the priests start relaxing a bit. I have to go find Simon; I've never had a friend like Simon. He has been there for me everytime I've needed him; and when he needed me, I let him down. I have to find him.

There are a few of the disciples standing over there. "Hey, brothers, have you seen Simon? He is over at Peter's place resting? Thank you! Hi, Peter, yes, I am fine; I didn't have any trouble at all. How is my friend? Hi, Simon, man, you look like you've been run over by a stampede of camels. Yeah, it's good to see you too. I guess you will stay home now and start the healing process. You gotta be kidding me! You're leaving in the morning?! But you're still mending from your wounds. I understand, there are a lot of people needing to hear the Gospel. You and Thaddeus are going to go out together for a while? That is nice, but I think I am going to stay here for the time being. I need to get my thoughts unscrambled. You be careful, especially with those wounds."

I have been lying around taking it easy now for several weeks; it is starting to bother me a lot. All my fellow apostles are out preaching and teaching, and I am here doing nothing. You know what it is, don't you? I am scared. All the others are putting their lives in danger while I sit back all comfy and well-fed. I hide every time one of the soldiers walks by; I even hide when one of the apostles gets back in town. I can't muster up enough courage to face them. I can't live like this anymore. I am going over to see Peter.

"Peter, may I speak with you? I think you know I haven't been doing my share of spreading the Gospel. I have put myself back the way I used to be, crabby with everyone, even those who like me. I have prayed and prayed about what to do; but I didn't like the answers, so I dismissed them. But I can't sleep knowing my friends are out there risking their lives, and I am just goofing off. I guess what I'm saying is, please forgive me; and let me go on a journey. I promise I won't shirk my duties."

God, through Peter, has given me an opportunity to show my love for the Lord. Peter said I should stay in Jerusalem and witness to the locals. I could also go out into the surrounding towns and preach. It feels so good to be sharing the Gospel with the people once again. I have been back now for a couple of weeks, my confidence is peaking once again; so I think it is time to tackle the temple. I know the priests are very narrow-minded and get upset when we preach about Jesus. They not only had Jesus crucified, but they also had one of the disciples named Steven stoned; and not too long ago, one of the Zebedee boys, James, was beheaded. But their intolerance will not stop me, I am going to preach and teach until I die, which might be tomorrow or longer, depending on how mad they get.

Look at all the people! It is going to be a great day. As soon as I climb these steps, there is a platform; I can witness from there. You would think I might be a little nervous doing this, but I have Jesus with me and have never felt better in my life. "Gentlemen, businessmen, and travelers, listen to what the Lord has spoken. There is One Who cares for you; One Who wants you to be His family. Please come and let me show you His love for you!"

Well, that didn't take long; here comes the Pharisees strutting their stuff. "Fancy meeting you here, gentlemen. What took you so long? I have been preaching for two hours. What do you mean I can't speak here? I will challenge you on your presumption. This is the Lord's house, and the Lord has given me the right to speak.

THE APOSTLES 1ST PERSON A NARRATIVE

No, sir, I will not stop, and I will not leave this platform. You have no authority to ban me. Now, you leave and let me continue teaching these people the truth; something you have failed to do."

Did you see that? The faces of those priests were beet red; nobody but nobody has ever spoken to them that way. I guess I had better watch my back; no telling what those cripes will try to do. Matter of fact, here they come already. "Gentlemen, if you've come to try and stop me from spreading the Gospel, you can save your voice. You know, I think I am going to open your eyes. You and your buds are nothing but a bunch of hypocrites. You bend the laws to what you want to tell the people to do; and if there isn't a law, you make one. Now, get out of my house!!! Go intimidate someone else!" WHOOHOO! That felt so good! My temper came into play for good this time. I know they are going back to plot against me, but I am going to teach until they kill me or run me out of town. God, you are so good.

I have reached the platform once again; I have an unusually large crowd today. I don't recognize hardly any of them; it is like a whole new town. "Gentlemen, businessmen . . ." Why are they booing already? It is like they aren't going to let me preach; I think I see a trend going on. The Pharisees are hiring people to heckle me, that way no one can hear the message. I think I hear people behind me; it is the Pharisees, and they are smiling. I believe they may be up to no good. Good, the soldiers are coming out; they will quiet the crowd. "Wait a minute! Why are you manhandling me?! What do you mean I have been trying to cause a revolt against the government?!" The crowd is starting to get worked up into a frenzy. The soldiers are dragging me away down the steps; they must be big shots I guess, because there are only two of them. Usually several will escort someone around. I don't know where they are taking me, looks like towards the end of town, but I don't remember a jail at the end of town. Look out! The crowd has just stormed the soldiers and knocked them out away from me. I really don't think that is a good thing. "I am glad to see all of you surrounding me. Let me tell you about the One they call Jesus." Ouch! Someone just threw a stone at me; I see, they are going to stone me to death. Stone me if you wish, but I am going to tell about Jesus until my last words. "Jesus..."

APOSTLE THADDEUS

"WELL, GOOD AFTERNOON to you, I'm glad you have stopped by to see me. I would like to show you around some. This is basically my hometown. It has had several names, but we call it Caesarea Philippi. In earlier days the Greeks called it Paneas. Isn't this a beautiful place? Did you know that the Jordan River has its beginning here? Look right over there, where the cliffs are. See the water coming out of the mountain? That is a spring. You can't hardly see it but there is a cave back behind that temple. It is pretty much blocked off due to an earthquake a few years ago. They tell me the water came gushing out of the cave, causing a waterfall effect. A lot of pagan idol worshiping went on there. All the walls inside the cave were lined up with all kinds of temples. After the earthquake they built that temple you see over there. They also built a big patio on the front so they could have their pagan dances and some of the sacrifices, some which were human. The quake blocked a lot of the flow of the spring, but as you can see it comes up just outside of that temple. Look on a little farther and you will see Mt. Herman. That is about 20 miles from here. The rest of the country is low rolling hills and valleys. Very rich fertile land makes for big crops, which in turn means more money.

"As I said at first, I was born here. My father, his name is Cleopas

Alpheus, is a very strong man and a very hard worker. He has been a farmer all of his life. That is why I have taken up the family business I guess. It was good enough for my father, so it is good enough for me. We raise a lot of different crops; barley and wheat are the main crops. We have a couple of orchards also, some olive trees and some fig trees. We also have a grapevine or two.

"So you see, we do keep rather busy trying to take care of everything. Between my older brother and me, we work together a lot, doing most of the chores around here. We have to shear the sheep twice a year. We have quite a flock of sheep. My brother James does most of the shearing because I am kind of a meek type of guy. Okay, so I am a scaredy-cat. I wouldn't hurt a fly, and a lot of times the shears cut the sheep. The thought of that makes me shiver all over, so James does it.

"My dad's brother is a carpenter, so he made us some trenches so that it is easier to control the sheep. It is kind of funny to watch sometimes. We lead the first sheep into the trenches and the rest of the group just stands there in line waiting for their turn. Craziest thing I ever saw. Now that I'm getting older, I can't seem to find it in my heart to hurt anything, whether it is an animal, bug, or human. My dad says I'm too kind-hearted.

"We go up to see my uncle a lot. He lives up around Nazareth. Him and his wife, Mary, lived in Egypt for a while, but they came back to live in Nazareth. They have a couple of kids. One is named James, just like my brother, and the other one is Jesus. Jesus is real handy with a saw and chisel. You should see some of the toys He has made. I guess Uncle Joseph taught Him well.

"Hey guys, I hate to leave you, but I have to get ready. You see, I'm getting married here in a little while. I have to get over to Cana; that's where my beautiful bride is from. If you all want to tag along, you are more than welcome; it is just that I won't be able to pay you much attention. But come on along."

THE APOSTLES 1ST PERSON A NARRATIVE

The day I have been waiting for all my life. My wedding day. Look at all those flowers laid out on both sides of the room. All those people, I didn't know we knew that many people. Look over there, it's Dad and Mom. Boy, they sure have put on a feast for us.

Oh my, I sure wasn't looking for Uncle Joseph and Aunt Mary to be here. And look, there is Jesus too. I hear He is teaching what they call the "Gospel." I personally have been sort of following another cousin of mine. His name is John; a lot of people call him John the Baptist. He sure does make a lot of sense. He keeps telling us there is Someone coming who is greater than him. I know that when Jesus is around John acts differently. Over there, you see them? It's Simon and Andrew. Oh, my God, the most beautiful women in the world just walked in. My near future wife. Isn't she pretty? That long flowing gown of pure white silk. The honey-sweet fragrance of the perfume she is wearing. The veil covering her face. The ceremony is starting. I can't help myself. I am so nervous. My hands are shaking, and it is all I can do to put one foot in front of the other . . .

Well, I made it through the ceremony; I didn't even stumble. Now being the good people of Galilee we are, it is time to partake in the festive food sitting on the tables. My dad furnished the lamb for the occasion. We also supplied the wine. My wife's folks supplied all the sweets, the breads, and the flowers.

What a party we are having! My wife and I are dancing the night away. I just looked over at my parents. Something must be wrong. Mom is worried. I can see it on her face, and she is talking mighty fast to my dad. Maybe I should go over and see what is wrong? "Hi, Mom, something wrong? Whoa, it will be okay, Mom. If we run out, we run out. I know, but what can we do? Here comes Jesus, maybe He can think of something. Hi, Jesus, Aunt Mary, hope you all are having a good time. Yeah, we are running out of wine; worse things have happened. You two go on and have fun, okay?" What are Aunt Mary and Jesus talking about over there? Jesus just sent out some men to fetch water. Maybe He thinks people won't notice they are drinking water and not wine. The guys are coming back; man, they have several barrels of water. Looks like they just drew it up from the well. What is Jesus doing? He is laying His hand on the barrels and praying. Mom looked in the barrels and started crying. What now? Everybody is standing around the barrels with their mouths wide open. Let me see what it is. Oh, my God, it is wine, not water! Jesus has turned the water into wine, not cheap wine either! This wine tastes so good, almost like it has aged for years. Let the party keep going. "Thank you, Jesus! I don't know how You did that, but I am grateful to You. What is this that You are spreading across the country? My mom has told me stories about Aunt Mary and Uncle Joseph and how Your birth was different. They say You came from God Himself and that You came to save people from their sins. I can believe that after witnessing what You just did. You have left my dad speechless and that is hard to do. I think You are going to have a few more followers after this, including my father."

Well, the party lasted for several days but has now come to an end. My wife's dad left us the dowry, looks like it is pretty good sized. It will help us as we take to following Jesus. As I thought, my dad is following Jesus also, along with my mom; my whole family is going with us. Ever since word got out about the wine thing at the wedding more and more people are following Jesus. I would say over seventy-five to eighty people are walking along with us. I wish I could say they all were people that believed in Him. But some are people looking for a handout; or worse, some are the Pharisees, who like to strut their knowledge, or maybe lack thereof, always trying to trick Jesus with dumb questions.

It looks like we have arrived in Capernaum. I have relatives here. They are fisherman. I think our job on the farm is rough, but those fishermen work daylight to dark. People are flocking around Jesus. Between Him and John the Baptist seems like the whole town is out. What I thought was neat is that Jesus went over to John and had John baptize Him. Wow, I think this is the point now where I know Jesus is the Messiah. I can't count the number of people Jesus has healed. I think people are coming out of the woodwork. Looks like Jesus is trying to move further on down the road. We have stopped in front of our relative's place of business. Simon is there, so is James (not my brother), John, and Andrew. "Hi, fellas, long time no see. I guess it has only been a few days; you was at the wedding right? I see Jesus is coming over to talk to you, so I'll just go on a little further down the road and wait for Jesus to come that way."

Hey, here comes Jesus. Of course that means a bucketload of people are with Him. Wait a minute, isn't that Simon and Andrew? And look over there; that's James and John. What are they doing with Jesus? I bet I know; Simon and that rowdy bunch are cursing up a storm at Jesus. They never did like Jesus when we was growing up. Jesus always outsmarted them and made them look silly. As they get a little closer I can see Jesus talking with them. What's amazing is Simon and all them are listening to what Jesus is saying. "Hi, guys, what is going on? You're kidding me. You all are going to follow Jesus? I never thought I would see the day when Simon and Andrew would mellow out like that. I'm sure glad they did though. If things keep going on, my whole family is going to be traveling with us. All except my brother James; he hasn't accepted Jesus yet. I'm sure he will make up his mind soon.

So many people are hurting; I have lost count as to how many people Jesus has healed. After they have been healed, several of us talk with them and show them the way to eternal life. When they accept it, it makes my body tingle all over. It's my nature, okay?! Hey look, it's my brother; thank God He has decided to follow Jesus. That makes my whole family followers now.

When we enter a town such as big C-town, getting somewhere takes a while. I don't think I have ever seen Jesus turn down a crowd yet. A lot of people are in town paying their taxes. Actually, it looks like Jesus is going over to pay His taxes; I don't know why because He hasn't made anything to pay taxes on. He is over talking to this guy named Levi. Levi is very well-known for being ruthless going after money. Look, Levi is getting up and following Jesus. There are a few of us that are close to Jesus. I hate to say this, but these disciples are hot over Jesus bringing a tax collector into the fold. It doesn't bother Jesus though; He just put his arm around Levi and welcomed him into the fold. Jesus renamed Levi, calling him Matthew. Then He did something the Pharisees about died over; we all went to Matthew's house and had supper. Those worthless Pharisees was like a nest of stirred up bees.

Are you all getting tired yet? I sure am. We've been up and down the coast line and the mountains, people gathering every place we have been. Jesus even fed thousands of followers, just from a little boy's basket. It was an amazing sight. But Jesus' mood is changing a little every day; I'm sensitive about things like that. Simon came by yesterday and said that Jesus wanted to talk to a few of us up on the hillside. Something about assignments for us. I'll be back as soon as possible.

I hope you all got a good rest, because Jesus has just assigned

THE APOSTLES 1ST PERSON A NARRATIVE

twelve of us to special work. Jesus said we were going to be called His apostles. Each one of us has a job to do; mine is kind of what I have been doing all along, tending to the new believers. Simon was put in charge of, let's say, operations. The one they call Matthew now is in charge of counting up the treasury, what little there is. Another whose name is like mine, they call him Judas, carries the treasury and dispenses it.

Now that we have been given jobs to do, Jesus wants us to go out to different towns and preach the gospel. The unusual thing is that we aren't to take anything with us, not even a change of clothes. Oh, well, I have to trust in Jesus; and He said to go, so I go. You ready? Let's hit the road.

Jesus is spending more and more time trying to teach us what we are supposed to do when He leaves us. I don't like the way He keeps telling us that His life is about over. You know what else He told us? He said that one of us, I'm talking about the twelve of us, is going to betray Him. I guess that upset Judas so much that he got up and left. Jesus took a piece of bread and broke it and told us to eat it, that that represented His body. Then He took a cup of wine, raised it, and told us to drink it as it represented His blood that would be poured out for our sins. I don't understand, but I guess I'll figure it out sooner or later.

I'm thinking maybe after we finish this meal, most of us will go get some shuteye. Wait a minute, Jesus wants us to go up on Mt. Olivet to pray; and I guess that is okay. We can make camp there and sleep when we get through praying. Have you been looking at Jesus? His shoulders are slumped down like a heavy burden is upon him. His face looks like He is in agony from pain as though he has been beaten. I think I will pray a little harder for Jesus; maybe that will relieve some of the stress.

What has happened to Judas? He might have gone to put up some of the offering. No, I guess not; here he comes. Man, doesn't he know Jesus was wanting to be with just us? Look at all those soldiers coming. I guess Judas thought there might be some trouble tonight. The Pharisees have been giving us a lot of trouble lately. Jesus is going out to meet them. I can't hear what they have said to each other. Oh, no, what is this? The soldiers have grabbed Jesus. Simon is attacking one of the soldiers; he has a knife out. Oh my, he just cut that guy's ear off! I can't look. Why are they dragging Jesus away like that? "John, James, Bart, Andrew, what's happening?" Looks like big-time trouble brewing. I think I am going to gather all my family up and take them back down to the farm. I believe they will be safe there. I will then come back to see if there is anything I can do. There has been trouble before but this time it seems to be more intense. All the guys are taking cover and then disappearing. I did see Jesus put that man's ear back on. He is so compassionate.

"Thanks for helping me get the family back to the farm. They didn't want to go did they? We need to get back to C-town and find out if the trouble has settled down. Simon and Andrew will know.

"Hi, Mr. Zebedee, how are you? Is Simon or any of the guys here? They're not? As far as you know they are in Jerusalem? Okay, I guess we need to get back to Jerusalem and find them boys. Are you as scared about going back to Jerusalem as I am? The Pharisees have stirred the pot big time. Someone needs to step up and help Jesus; after all, think about what He has done for us.

THE APOSTLES 1ST PERSON A NARRATIVE

I just heard that both the Pharisees and the Sadducees are making false statements about Jesus. I also heard that they aren't allowing any outsiders to testify for Him. I think they are charioting Him. You know, running over Him, plowing Him under. Finally, I see Simon. I guess I need to call him Peter now, since Jesus gave him that new name. Oh good, he sees me. "Hi, Peter, what's up? You really think they will crucify Jesus? On what grounds? I see. I guess you're right; they don't need any grounds, just do it. You have something for me? It is a piece of cloth, a towel. Okay, I'll wait to find out what to do with it . . ."

It is a sad day for us. Those idiots actually convinced the Romans to crucify Jesus. What is going to happen to all us that put so much faith in Him? Here comes one of the disciples now. I wonder what he wants. Did you hear what he just called me? Judas. "Please don't call me that ever again. Judas may be my first name, but I don't want to be associated with that bum. My name is Thaddeus. So please call me that from now on; thank you. What is it you need? Okay, I will go meet with them in that upper room; see you there."

It is good to see all of the apostles here. Looks like Peter is taking charge; I believe he can keep us somewhat organized. Peter thinks we need to appoint someone to take the bum's place; I can't even say his name. I did hear that he committed suicide. You know, I have a lot of compassion for people, but I just can't find any for him. Enough about him. I can feel Jesus' presence in this room. I remember He said that He would send another to help us; the room is now filled with this smoke-like substance. A strange feeling is coming over me. It is a good feeling. That cloud is changing us to a certain way. Listen . . . you hear that? All these disciples are speaking in different languages. Even me, I can speak Hebrew and Greek, but I am able to speak Aramaic now too. Although all of us are speaking different languages, we can still understand each other. Strangest thing I have ever been a part of. You remember Jesus said to go out into the world? I guess if we have to go out everywhere we need to be able to speak to them, right?

Peter has blessed me, as you can see, by accompanying me on my mission. He has assigned me the territory of Armenia, but we have to go through Syria first. I wish I could speak as confidently as Peter. He told me to put my trust in God and I would be able to. I remember Peter telling of a vision he had. Some of the other guys might have told you about it, but as a Jew I found it pretty life- changing. You know, the vision of all meats being clean to eat. (Of course it didn't mean as much to me as it did the others with me being a vegetarian, you know.) Peter is always doing God's work. Reminds me of Jesus when He was on the earth.

We have come upon a crossroads, and Peter said this is where we part company. He has to go to some of the churches that have been started up north. He's one to always be giving encouragement to people. Love that guy. Just before he left, he told me about that towel. You see, there is a governor over in Edessa; his name is Abgarus. He lives and governs in the city of Metropolis in Osroene. I guess he has been ill for some time. He had heard of the miracles that Jesus had been doing, so he sent his messenger to find Jesus. But before he could get back to his master, those bums crucified Jesus. But before they had Him crucified, Jesus had given Peter a towel that He had washed his face with. Jesus told Peter to send someone, preferably me, along with the servant to give the towel to Abgarus; and it would help his illness. I guess that is why I got the assignment to go to Armenia. So blessed. It is so hard to say goodbye to my brothers that are following Peter in his journeys. But God's work needs to be done, so onward soldiers of Christ!

Wow, my family and I are closing in on the city of Edessa; man, this is a monster of a town. I think, or I guess, the population to be around 500,000. There are people from all over the country with so many different dialects; I'm really happy we were given the ability to be understood by the people no matter where they come from. Most of the natives here speak Hebrew.

Well, I am going to go find something to eat, and then I need to find the governor. Here comes Ananias, you remember him? He is the one who wanted us to come to Edessa. "Hi, brother, what's happening? Oh no, you say the governor is starting to fade pretty fast now? Let us skip this eating and go see the man. I sure hope we get there before he passes. I guess if he does, Jesus can help us bring him back. But let's not talk that way.

"Hello, Governor Abgarus, it is good to finally meet you. I am so sorry you are feeling bad. But Jesus said that He would heal You. Jesus sent this towel for you. Oh, my God! Look, look at it! On the towel . . . it is the image of Jesus on the towel! Governor, let us pray . . . What are you doing? You have been healed. Get up from that bed. Glory! Glory! Thank you, Jesus! Let's have a party! Look at the smiles on your family's faces!"

God has been so good to us. The governor and his family have accepted Jesus and have declared that all people are to worship Him. This sure makes my missions work easy. I think I need to go out into the countryside for a while to spread the Gospel . . .

This country is so hilly, more like mountains that hills. It is so rough that most of the different state-like governments have trouble going from one place to another. I stand in amazement at the history that comes with this country. "Hey, Simon. I'm sorry, I haven't introduced you to Simon. He is another one of us that Jesus called apostles. Anyway, Simon, did you know that it is highly believed that mountain over there ... can you see it? That is Mount Ararat, which is where the ark that Noah built is supposed to be. I'm not going to try and climb to the top to see if it is or not. Do you think it is time for us to start going towards Syria? I would like to do some preaching in Beirut. They say that place is in great need of the Gospel. Simon, we will leave the first of next week, if that is okay with you."

"Well, Simon, we have made it to Beirut. That was quite the journey. Look at all these false gods everywhere. It's enough to make you sick. What do you think about sending our families back home while we preach here? I sense trouble will be coming our way. Might as well do it now so they don't have to unpack and then pack right back up. I sure will miss them; they have been such great help in our ministry. We will be sure and send a large group of the disciples with them for protection ..."

Can you believe it has been many years since Jesus was crucified? I have heard through word of mouth that a few of us have been crucified also. What year is this now? I think it is about 65 right? Look out; here comes the magi. They think they own everything ... "No, we will not stop spreading the Gospel to the people. You have no right to throw us in prison. What do you mean you aren't taking us to prison? Simon, I think we had better start praying hard; it's not looking to good right now ... Why are you taking us out the back way? Get on my knees? Why? Those guys are bringing their swords out. Simon, thank you for being a good friend. Praise Go ..."

APOSTLE SIMON

"HELLO. I AM to understand that you will be following me around, if just in spirit. But before I let you do this, I must find out, do you believe in the fact that there is only one true God? If you don't, I will not allow you to be with me. For you see, I am a stickler for the Torah; and the Torah teaches there is only one God.

"That being said, I guess you would like to know where I was born. That would be in Cana. My family isn't rich by any means, but they aren't poor by any means either. My father is into several different business ventures; I, myself, am a tanner by trade. I know that isn't the sweetest smelling business to be in. I have to do my business down by the sea; I need the saltwater to help me work the hides. Also the smell needs to be blown away from the work area, and the winds off the sea help. It is a sort of crazy thing; I don't have that many Jewish friends because of the dead animals, although I never have the animal just its hide. Not too many people live around the workplace. I have to haul my water to the site; although there is a salt well real close to me, it just doesn't supply enough water for me to use. Needless to say, I have to have a bath every day.

"When work is slow I like to go down to the temple and have lively debates with the priests. Most of them are willing to debate with me; they think that just because I haven't studied under any priesthood, that I am easy pickins. After about an hour of discussion most remember they have something else to do. Some of the Jews will stand back away so that they won't be unclean for being close to me; they just don't understand my business, but that is okay. They don't understand the Torah either. I am getting rather bored with these priests; they don't even make good arguments anymore. If it sounds like I am bragging on myself, let me put your mind at ease, I am.

"I'm not going to get much work done in the next few days. It seems a friend of mine is getting married, and I have been invited; actually I am to be a part of the wedding celebration. I am going to be married soon. But for now, I am going to concentrate on my buddy. I hear that a lot of people from Capernaum will be there. I wonder if the priests from C-town will be there? That sure would give me some fresh minds to pick. I think when I get married I will perform the ceremony myself. Is that being a little conceited on my part? Tell me where I'm wrong. There I go again, debating everything. Sorry.

"Hey, wasn't that a great wedding? Did you notice I behaved myself? I didn't have a single debate with anyone. I think that is the first time ever. I am sure it was because of a strange thing that happened after the wedding. I noticed that the wine was being dished out very sparingly. All of a sudden they brought out several flasks and filled every glass full to almost running over, and I must say that wine was the best I have ever drank. My father would hold parties, and he would buy good wine to start with but that wine was never as good as this was. I bet it must have cost an arm and a leg. Hi Thad, great time, you have a great married life. By the way, what is the name of the wine?

"You know, that was some story about where that wine came from. I have to go home and think about it. Did you hear what they said? This Man from Nazareth prayed over the barrels of water and turned it into wine. There have been instances in the Torah about God's people getting water out of a rock and blocking water from flowing and such but never this type of thing. I am going to have to check this out."

Cana is a beautiful place to live. It sits on top of a hill overlooking a valley, and if you look hard enough you can actually see the Mediterranean Sea. If you look the other way, you can see the Sea of Galilee. A small river flows through the valley, but you have to be careful when digging a well because saltwater springs are everywhere.

Nevermind all of this; I want to find out who and where this Man is that turned the water into wine. Someone told me His name is Jesus. He travels all over. Give me enough time, and I will find Him; or He will find me. "Hand me that brush; will you?"

I heard some great news this morning; that guy Jesus is coming back this way. If He gets here, I will question Him on that trick He did. "Look down the road; I think that is Him. I sure hope He knows the Torah. I could use a good debate about now." Look at all the people that are following Him. I might not be able to get close to Him. I am a pretty big fella, so I ought to be able to bully myself right on in. I have to keep my eyes on the ground or I'll step into some animal leftovers, if you get my drift. "Look out; I'm coming through. Get out of my way. Umph. Hey, You didn't move. Oh my, it is You; the One they call Jesus. How did You get over here so fast? I have been pushing and shoving and You just walked over with no problem. Well, hi to You. How did You know my name? Jesus, isn't that Your name? Are You any good with the Torah? Great! You say You know a little bit about it? How about a debate? Don't be too sure about that; I haven't ever been beat. You haven't either? Well, You're fixing to be. Yes, I am cocky, but I can back it up. Tell me about this stuff You are preaching. Where does it come from?"

Well, guys, I hope you didn't witness that pounding; I just got whooped. That guy is good, I must hear more of what He is saying. I know He has my respect now. I guess He does with a lot of people; they all flock around Him. When His group goes down the road, a big dust cloud forms. Oh, man, He is coming back over to see me. What does He want? Maybe He wants to rub more salt in my wounds before He leaves town. "Hello, Jesus, can I help you? No one has ever come over to me and given me a compliment. Thank you. You want me to come follow You? I know I could learn a lot from You, but I don't know if I am worthy of it. You want me to be up close to You so You can teach me? I have this business here, but I will never get another opportunity like this. Okay, I'll go. What did You call me? Simon the Zealot? I don't belong to that organization. I see, You think that I am zealous in my beliefs? That I can't be easily swayed? Thank You, Sir."

I have been following Jesus now for some time. The more I see of the miracles that He performs on the sick and lame, it just makes me stronger and stronger in my devotion to Him. To be able to see people walk away after being bedridden for all their lives, it sends goosebumps over my entire body. I think the favorite miracle of mine is when a demon is sent out of a person. You can see the relief in the eyes of the person. He becomes happy again and praises God for his healing. But not everybody is happy about the cures, some of the magicians use these people to make money; they make them do weird things, like hitting each other, tearing each other's clothes off, biting others, etc. But you don't hear the recipient complain. Now the magicians will have to find different ways to make money.

We have walked all over Galilee and most of Judea. I was so happy the other day; Jesus called me and eleven others over to the side and said that we were going to be His apostles. I asked for clarification on what the duties of an "apostle" was. He went into detail as to what we are to do, but you know what the best thing is? All of us received the ability to heal and cast out demons. He said that since we have been so faithful to Him, He wants us to go out into the countryside and towns to preach the Gospel. There is a catch though, we are not to take anything with us, no extra clothing or food, just what we have on our backs. We are not to argue with or try to change anyone's mind. They either accept or we go on. Jesus told me this isn't a test; it is prep work.

Wow, that was so much fun. My heart is full for the love of the people that have come to know Jesus. You know, I never went hungry, nor did I have to sleep on the ground any. Food and drink were always plentiful. Jesus said they would be. My hardest thing was trying not to argue. I don't know if you have noticed or not, but I love to argue. I would rather call it debating though. I found that people will listen to me better if I first allow them to speak their mind and share their beliefs with me; this allows me to share mine with them. If a miracle has been performed, they listen even more closely.

"Are you ready to go hunting? Not animals. People. Jesus just gave us instructions to go find some people that are faithful to Him, are following Him, and are giving their all to Him. I think it will be easy to do. There are hundreds that follow us as we go from town to town. He said that seventy would be the number to come forward. I know several myself that are faithful. There are a bunch like that. One named Tim, he is sort of young, but he is dedicated to Jesus. How about that doctor? Isn't his name Luke?"

Jesus sent the seventy out to spread the Gospel but mostly to let people know that Jesus will be coming their way. What is nice is that the seventy have been given powers to heal, just like we were given. The only difference is they can go to the Gentiles where we couldn't.

Some of the seventy are returning now; it has been a couple of months. Look at their faces; they are full of the Spirit. I bet we'll have a lot to talk about tonight as we sit around the campfire.

The atmosphere is changing around here, have you noticed it? The priest are getting more and more agitated. Jesus has been revealing them to be what they really are, crooks. They are to guide people to worship God, but they are trying to have people worship them. They have brought shame on the temple, they have brought shame down on the position of priesthood. People don't look at them as Godly men, they look at them as money hackers. Sorry, I'm getting on a soapbox. They don't like being exposed for the truth, so they have been generating hate amongst people. They say that if you believe in this Jesus, you are against the authority of the priesthood. Remember yesterday? They came and made Jesus see the high priest, and that didn't turn out the way they wanted it to. Jesus made the high priest look like a schoolboy.

Jesus has gathered us together for a meal; He says there is something important to talk about. He sure is talking strange; He is saying something about He has a very short time left here on the earth. You don't think He has a sickness, do you? If He does, we as apostles will heal Him. Now, did you hear that right? Jesus says one of us is going to betray Him. I'm just like the other apostles; I don't buy that at all. I think it made Iscariot so mad he just up and left. I thought after the meal we would all lie down and get some sleep, but Jesus said we needed to go out on the hill and do some praying. After talking the way He did, I tend to agree with Him.

Once again, Jesus knew what He was talking about. Judas Iscariot betrayed Him. When he left the other night, he wasn't mad; he was in the process of turning Jesus over to the priests. I am ashamed to say this, but I ran like a scared rabbit when the soldiers came and arrested Jesus. As they hauled Him off, we all scattered, except for Peter and John. Peter followed for a little while and then left Him. John stayed with Him to the end. Those jerks from the priesthood got Jesus crucified. I just don't understand what has happened. I am going to go back home for a little while and see if I can make sense out of this.

Why didn't Jesus do like He had done before? Just walk right through them. Or maybe reappear somewhere else. But to do nothing to protect Himself, I don't understand. What am I going to do? People in town know I have been following Jesus, so they are going to make fun of me. I can't even debate anyone, because they will bring up the fact that Jesus couldn't even protect Himself, let alone anyone else. What am I going to do? I am just sick over this. Here comes one of the disciples that followed Jesus. Looks like it is John Mark; he was as loyal to Jesus as I was. "You say that Peter is wanting to get us all together? Why should I make that journey? You're kidding me! Someone stole Jesus' body? I hadn't heard! Yes, I remember Jesus saying that Peter was the most capable one of us to lead.

"Hello, brothers in Christ, where is Peter? Isn't he the one wanting to meet? Have they found the body yet? You're kidding! Who saw him? The women of the group? Oh, brother! You know you can't believe what a women tells you. John and Peter saw him after that?

Hey, Pete, they say you saw Jesus. Do what? Turn around to see Him myself? Oh, my God, it is You! But how? Things are clear now; You said all of this would happen. We just didn't grasp it. Now You are going to open our eyes to Your teachings? Please forgive me for not believing in You and for running away from You. You are going to leave but another called the Holy Spirit will come?"

"Are you ready to take a boat ride? We all, that is the apostles, have been given our assignments, actually we had to draw lots, as to where we were going to do our ministry. You and I are going to Egypt. Let's get on the boat before it leaves us. We should be in Alexandria in a few days. This is a pretty nice boat, big. I sure hope the winds blow well, so it won't take us too long. What is nice about going different places is that no matter what language they speak, I can understand it, and they can understand me. That is part of the Holy Spirit working in us."

I know Jesus had something to do with me going to Egypt; I am dark-skinned and so are they. Looks like we are about to pull into the port of Alexandria. It is hot here. I think my skin will burn if left exposed too long.

People are very friendly to me. The only problem I am going to have is figuring out which way to approach them. They have so many different gods. Each one does or protects a certain element, like a sun god, a rain god, an I-stubbed-my-toe god, and so on, but at least most of the people will listen. There are a lot of people here; the population is around 300,000 people. I really don't know how many slaves there are; they don't count them in their census. It is pretty around here, if you like sand. The Nile is running just outside of town. Everything is lush and green with big palm trees and vineyards all over. Cattle look like they have been well fed. There are the prettiest flowers in all the people's yards. There are some mountains off in the distance, and looking out east, south, and north, is the desert. They say the weather is nice most all year round. If that is true, I might have to stay awhile, haha. Enough of this wasting time. I did see a temple down on the other side of town, let's head that way.

"You know, if you get to thinking about it, our Jewish ancestors may have walked through this area. They were in captivity for many years; I don't know, but it could have happened. I heard, I can't back it up, but I heard that Joseph, when in captivity, helped build the Great Pyramid down in Giza. Just saying.

"The word is getting out, my friend. Here comes a group of people that look like they may need to receive some of the Holy Spirit. I see several have been infected with demons; I might be here awhile. All right, demons, listen to me. Stop with the hissing; that doesn't scare me a bit. You, stop with the making that poor soul shake; and you over there, stop with the foaming of the mouth. I tell you, leave these people now. In the name of Jesus, I command you to get out. Do not enter anyone else; get out of town. Stop! Do not approach me! You cannot touch me; I am protected by my Savior, and your enemy, Jesus Christ. Dear Jesus, please help me expel this group of demons; make them disappear. Okay, demons, leave now; or you will be destroyed forever. I command you in the name of Jesus."

I am so weak now, dispelling the demons has taken a lot out of me. But I have no times to rest; I must help and teach the others. All the people that came ran away when the demons started to cause those folks to foam at the mouth. I must find them and help them. I just heard that most of the people came down the Nile to see me. That means I need to travel up the Nile to their homes. More boat time.

Looks like we have arrived in Carthage. This is a totally different environment. Look at this port; it is separated into two ports. The one I am in here looks to be a commercial port, a busy one at that. A lot of the ships in port are carrying silver; others are full of tin. They use that to make bronze, and they use the bronze to make idols and statues of all kinds. They even have plows that are made out of iron. Let's look at the other ports. Oh my, look at the navy ships. Hundred or more, I forgot they told me it was a navy port. As I have been walking along, it just doesn't seem like the people are as friendly as they were in Alexandria. I guess everyone needs the Gospel, so let's get to that temple we saw earlier. I don't know for sure, but I think here comes trouble. The priests are coming, and they don't look like a welcoming party. "Yes, I am he. I am sorry but I cannot do as you propose me to do. I must spread the Gospel to all people. Ouch! What was that for?! You hit me with a whip, and I haven't done anything wrong! I tell you now, no matter what you do to me, I will not stop preaching the Gospel. You have heard word from Alexandria about my preaching? Then you must know I am a peaceful man. Ouch! You hit me again! Ouch! Don't I even get a trial to give my side? Your god said to banish me? Don't you mean your priests told you that?"

I must have been hit on the head. Ow, I have a lot of gashes on my back. I think I have been kicked in the ribs. Where am I? I am going to try and raise my head a little, no way. I am either swaying, like nauseated, or I'm on a boat. Okay, I'm going to try and raise my head . . . Oooooooh that hurts, but I did it. I think I'm in a dungeon; it sure smells like it. I have to lay my head back down. Ouch, someone just kicked me in the side. What is going on? We are back in Alexandria? I am trying to get up, but I can't walk. Oh, come on, please don't push. "Well, sir, if I'm not under arrest, what am I doing in the dungeon?"

THE APOSTLES 1ST PERSON A NARRATIVE

I was very fortunate that I didn't have any broken bones from that beating I took back in Carthage. I am going back towards Jerusalem I believe. I feel like the disciples that were left in Alexandria can take care of the brothers. My parents are getting old too, so I would like to see them.

Ah, good old Jerusalem. It sure does feel good to be back; most of the brothers are still out in the fields. But it is good to see so many new believers; God has been good. Well, I'll be, look who just showed up. "Brother Peter, how are you? Yes, it was a little rough towards the end. You ought to see my back; there are a few gashes that aren't healed yet, but I'm okay. I'd love to have a home cooked meal, thank you. I was headed back home to see my parents. Am I needed elsewhere? Yes, sir, I'll go that way; Persia isn't that far. Is Brother Jude, or I should say Thaddeus, doing a good job? That's great to hear. That is a pretty big area to cover. I'll start out tomorrow, okay?" Well, I guess I'm not going to go see my folks, too much work to do.

Seems like all I do is travel from one place to the other. But a brother needs help, and I'm the one chosen to help him. The last anyone heard, Thad was in a town called Persepolis. That isn't too far into the country, at least, and is a good starting place. What a town! Everything is helter-skelter; no sign of semblance anywhere. No wonder he needs help. Look up there; isn't that Thad? "Hey Thad!" Yep, that is him. I shouldn't have yelled like that; he is in the middle of a speech. Listen to him. He sure doesn't sound like the shy, timid Thad I first met.

"Hey, Thad, you sounding pretty good up there. I came to help, if you want it. Yes, they are scars from my last assignment, but they will be okay. How about you? They threw you in jail for a while, did they? Isn't it good that we suffer just a little bit like Jesus? Yes, I heard about James.

The ultimate sacrifice. What do you want me to do? Stay here with you or go on to another town? I agree. We will reach more people if we separate. I will leave a few of the disciples that are with me if you need them. Okay, they will go with me then."

I'm going to work my way up towards the north. I might even go all the way up to Armenia. This country is a little bit hard to get around in. If the people in Armenia are as friendly as the people in Kapan are, this is going to be enjoyable. People here are starving for some good news, and I am here to give it to them.

I guess I need to continue on up into Armenia; everyone needs to hear. I am in a town called Vardenis, gorgeous town. What makes this town is the lake; I believe they call it Sevan. The lake is big enough to have commercial fishing boats. There are sandy beaches around the lake, all kinds of seafood eateries. The people in this town are pretty diverse; many come here for vacationing. I will preach at the temple; most of the people won't stop and listen, as they're too busy having fun. I have been able to reach a few, and that is good. I am going to leave a couple of the disciples here to spread the Word.

I have reached the town of Alaverdi; this is at the top of Armenia. I am preaching here and going up the road a couple of miles and preaching in Georgia. I think you can see the difference in the attitude of the people up here. They are always seemingly agitated, and it doesn't take much to set them off. They don't like to debate anything; it is their way or nothing. From what I hear, I can't blame them too much. They get used to one ruler; and then someone else comes along and captures them, and they start all over. "I don't know about you, but I think we are about to be in trouble. A group of soldiers are coming. Ouch! Okay, okay, I am going. What is this all about? You are the soldiers from the temple priests? I see. Ouch!" I just got my wounds healed up from the last time. As with the other apostles, I could command the angels to stop this. But if Jesus was okay with being beaten, I must be too. I hear a lot of pounding going on. I wonder what they are building?

THE APOSTLES 1ST PERSON A NARRATIVE

This has been going on now for several days. I think it is about time for the soldiers to come in and give me my daily beating. It's okay. I don't feel anything anymore. I have been able to witness to the other prisoners and a few of the guards. Of course they can't see how I can talk about Jesus when He won't protect me from them. "Jesus, please open their eyes. I do not ask for me; I ask for them."

Once again it is about time for my whipping. I have noticed the pounding has stopped. And it is a little later than usual for their visit. Maybe they have had enough. No such thing, here they come. I don't know, but their attitude is different today. Maybe they have been told not to listen to me. "Take it easy, I haven't stood for several days, you know? Where are we going?" Maybe to set me free, haha. What kind of contraption is that? Is that what you've been building? You want me to get between those poles? There's not much room in there. I never saw anything like this before. What is the slit down the middle on both sides? You tying my hands up over my head? I can't even move, you are about to pull my shoulders out of their sockets. Now you're spreading my feet? I think I'm not going to like this. What is that? A saw? You are condemning me to death by sawing me in half???

Here they come; those slits were for the saw to travel down in. I feel the saw on my head now. Oh, I feel the scrapping. "I love you, Je...sus..."

APOSTLE
JUDAS ISCARIOT

"IS THIS GOING to be another attempt by the Galileans to discredit me? They are always trying to cause me trouble, like everytime I get a job they will steal from the owner and tell him they saw me do it.

"I am a Judean by birth, and I am very proud of it. I was born in a little town called Kerioth; it isn't too far from Jerusalem. When I was a wee little lad my parents moved me to Jericho. I have been at odds with my dad ever since. Jericho is right in Galilee, and I hate those nerds with a purple passion. I guess I shouldn't be that way, they make me a pretty good living. My dad is into various types of businesses, so I have been acquainted with all the other businessmen around the country. Those connections have helped send me to the upper schools. I am able to think things through, thus I can make the right decisions when required. As most kids were, I was carted off to the temple every time my parents went. My folks are Sadducees. My dad is very rude to people; I really don't understand how he stays in business with the way he treats some of the other people. I guess that is where I get my attitude. I am not that bad unless I am dealing with the Galileans. Did you know those dumb people think there are spirits, and that when you die there is an afterlife? When you die, they stick you in the ground, if you're lucky; and soon you are forgotten, and it's all over."

THE APOSTLES 1ST PERSON A NARRATIVE

I am going down to the lake to speak with a man about his business of fish drying. It isn't a very big company, but he has several small boats, a great supply of nets, and a drying facility. I need to buy this guy out; I have interest in another company, and this one has to go. If I can buy this one I will dismantle it and sell off a lot of extra parts to customers. I have tried before but he wanted too much money for it. Behind the scenes I have been undercutting him, so his business isn't doing too good. This means I ought to get it pretty cheap. Hard to sell a business that's losing money.

Man, this is a beautiful day. The sun is shining bright, and there is a slight breeze coming off the lake. I think after I talk with the gentleman about his business, I will go down to the shore and go swimming. I might even sun a little bit. What is all that commotion over there? Looks like one of those men who likes to get on his soapbox and tell everybody how wrong they are. I believe I will go over and have a listen to him. Sometimes it is a lot of fun to heckle the poor guys speaking. And then there are times when they actually make sense. The only problem is I am going to have to mix in with a bunch of Galileans. But I can run down to the lake and wash it off of me afterwards. Now isn't that mean of me?

This guy has a lot bigger crowd than most speakers; he must be well known. "Hey, you, who is this guy? Why are you laughing at me? Don't be laughing at me; you hear me? I'll knock a hole in your head; now stop it. I just want to know who he is. Okay, okay, I take it the man is well-known around here. But I'm not from around here, so please tell me. John the Baptist? I still haven't ever heard of him. What is he selling? Oh I see, preaching that bunk about the afterlife . . ." I've never believed in that stuff, but you know what? I could hear this guy out, and see what he has to say. That way I can ponder over his words. I can't see how anyone can accept such nonsense. I have to admit though I have never studied any of it; I have always just gone along with what my parents believe. Amazing since I have never followed after anything else of theirs . . . oh, well . . . I have to get back to business. I wonder where that gentleman is? Aw, there he is. "Hi, sir, remember me? I have returned to ask you to sell your business one more time. Well, sir, that might have been good a few months ago, but you have been losing money lately. I am offering you half your asking price, and that is being generous. Sure, you can think about it, but I need to know by tomorrow."

The only reason I didn't go ahead and push him is because they tell me this John guy is still going to be here tomorrow, and I want to hear him again. I heard just a little bit today, and what I did hear was sort of intriguing. I know I am better than these other scumbags around here. I am better educated, have more in the bank than most of the ones here, and have you seen how they live? Terrible, how can they sleep in all that filth? But what do you expect out of a lowly Galileans.

"Good morning, that John guy is at it already; I can hear that booming voice all the way up here at the inn. I have to get ready, so excuse me." It is another beautiful day. What is he doing now? He is in the water, I think they call that "baptizing." There must be over a hundred people lined up to have him dunk them. What does he do, hypnotize them? He is preaching again. Now is my chance to shred his speech to pieces. What is this "repent" business? I would like to know who it is that is coming, that one he calls the Messiah. I believe that comes out of that . . . What do they call it? Oh, yes, the Torah. He is saying a lot of things that I don't know, or understand. I can't believe I haven't looked this stuff up before. I might just see if I can get an audience with him. Matter of fact, he is walking this way. Maybe if I just kind of step in when he passes, I can ask him some questions. "Good afternoon, sir, would you mind me asking a couple questions? Where did you come up with this theory you preach? No, sir, I am a Judean. Yes, sir, my folks are Sadducees. Yes, that is Jewish. Then I should be aware of the Torah? I am aware of it, but I've never studied it. As a matter of fact, I don't ever remember even opening it.

I would love to have you teach me a little bit about the Torah. Right now? I had better get back home and report to my parents. Where are you going to be tomorrow? If I can get away, I will come listen to you some more." I plum forgot to go back by to check on the fish drying place. Oh, well, I'll get back to it soon.

"No, sir, but dad, he wants too much money for it. No, I didn't stop by yesterday; I got tied up in some other activity. I would rather not say at this time. Yes, sir, I know you pay me to work. Ok, if you must know, I spent the time listening to a man declare that a Messiah is coming, and he was preaching about the afterlife. I didn't say I believed him; I just said I was listening to him. What possibly could you have against me listening to him? You telling me that if I have anything else to do with this man that you are going to kick me out of the house, and fire me, your own son? I like what I am hearing, and what he has been preaching has just come true. He said that rough times would be ahead, and I just stepped into them. Thank you, Dad, for teaching me the business ways; but maybe you should have taught me about the Godly things. Goodbye."

I have been following John around now for several weeks. I have learned a lot, which is amazing considering I am so much smarter than him. I mean come on, he has no education at all. He says that the Lord has given him the knowledge to preach. I am beginning to believe him. Everywhere we go, there is a crowd that gathers, and he baptizes all who want it. I haven't done so just yet. I'm not quite ready yet. The other day he got real excited because this other Man came to him. That guy had a bigger crowd, but He wanted to be baptized. Come to find out John said that was Jesus, the Messiah he had been preaching about. I don't know what to think about that. I'll ask John tonight.

This is a quaint little town; I think they call it Tarichea. Right by the edge of the lake. I guess I should try to get a job here at the fish factory, but I can't seem to pull myself away from this John. "Hey, look over there, it is that Jesus guy." What a site, Jesus is on one side of the Jordan with His crowd and John is here on this side. Both are baptizing like crazy, although Jesus isn't, but He has some other guys doing it for Him. John keeps pushing everyone towards this Jesus guy. I don't think that is a very good business move, but he keeps saying that this is the Messiah. I just don't know. I must say, this Jesus' crowd seems to be better organized, maybe even a little better educated, just an observation.

Looks like a man from Jesus' camp is coming over to visit. I can't tell from here, but I think maybe he might have some education. Of course it isn't as much as mine. Looks like John and him are having a deep conversation. Both of them are getting up, they must want to go where it is a bit more private. They both are smiling, so I guess all is okay. I don't know what is going on, but it looks like they are coming over to visit with me. Maybe John thinks it is time for me to get baptized. "Hello, John. So your name is Nathaniel Bartholomew? Most people call you Bartholomew, or Bart for short? I have become a believer in John. John you want me to go with Bart to Jesus' camp? You think he can teach me deeper things? Well, at least John recognizes that I am smarter than most. I will go, sir, but I think I will be back. Shall we shove off, Bart?"

THE APOSTLES 1ST PERSON A NARRATIVE

"Hello, so you are this Jesus that John has been talking about. It is nice to meet you. Yes, I am a Judean, is my accent still that strong? I haven't lived in Judea for years. You say it isn't the accent, but you can read my heart? How did you know I hated all Galileans? I haven't told anybody here about that. Well, it is true, I am smarter than all of you. Someone must have told You about me. You want to challenge me on some business moves? Jesus, I will take you up on that, that is my forte. You name it, Sir ... I never thought about that happening, which would have cost a fortune. Okay, You got me on that one; You just got lucky. Okay, I'm listening, but I am smarter than the rest of these people. You agree with me on being brighter than most of the ones here? I hear a "but" in that ... Yes, Sir, I probably do need to show a little more compassion, but I have troubles with those people. Yes, Sir, I can give you my time, considering I have no place to go. You are going to help me overcome my prejudice of people, and not to think of myself so highly? Good luck with that one."

I have been introduced to all the guys that surround Jesus all the time. I am going to have to keep my eyes on them at all times; you see, every blasted one of them are Galileans. You can't trust any of them. Peter is coming over. If he thinks I am going to let him lord it over me, he has another think a comin'. If I am correct, which I am most always, Peter's real name was Simon. But Jesus renamed him Peter; that means "Rock." Ha! He is strong looking, fairly tall, but a rock? I don't think so. "Hi, Peter, what you know? Yes, sir (gag me), I was a businessman. I have handled large sums of money before.

You want me to be the treasurer?" Wow, that would be a simple task. How much money could this group have? They are all broke. Everyone has a job to do. I don't even have to count the money because everything is turned into Matthew. Matthew counts it and then he brings it to me to keep. I may not like these Galileans, but I am an honest man, as far as money is concerned. I understand that Matthew, who by the way Jesus renamed from Levi, was a tax collector. I bet people hated him as much as I hate Galileans. He has some pretty nice looking threads on, so he must have had some money. Nice looking wife too. You know, these guys aren't the brightest people. I am new here, and they are trusting me with all their money. That is the worst business move of the century.

Everybody has been kind to me, not a one of them has made a smart remark or told me to go skip rocks; it makes me kind of uneasy. I feel like they will let the anvil down on my head when I least expect it. I have been noticing that all twelve of us have been put in three groups. Let's see if I remember all their names . . . The first group consists of Peter, Andrew, James, and John. The second group is Philip, Bartholomew, Thaddaeus, and Thomas. The third group is Matthew, James Alphaeus, Simon, and me. These small groups do a lot of praying together. I haven't figured out what each man's job is, but we all have a duty. What always seemed like it was just a scrambled lot of people, is actually pretty well-organized. I believe Bart has the duty of having everything organized as far as these little journeys are concerned that is. Him and this guy named Philip work real good together. Philip makes the plans out, and Bart puts them all together. I could do a lot better job than they are doing, but what can you expect out of Galileans?

I have been so busy I haven't even been noticing Jesus. We started out on a journey, but we didn't get very far before people began to gather around Jesus. What is He up to? All these sick people, how can He stand to be around them? What's happening to the ones that are sick? They seem to disappear. The only ones coming back by are the ones that are healthy. I need to get up closer where I can see what is going on. Just in time. That man over there, he is on a bed, probably being carried by his sons. Jesus is going over to them. Wow, Jesus just touched the guy and he jumped up out of that bed! He is dancing around, praising Jesus! That was a pretty neat trick. I wonder how He did that. How much money did Jesus pay him to act that way? I don't think He paid him anything; I have the money and no one asked for any of it. I think I will try to get Bart over here and ask him what all this is about.

"I guess you know Bart came over yesterday evening and explained what Jesus was doing. From what I have been witnessing, I must say, I believe He is who He says He is. I never have seen anything like it before. But, I am a businessman; this guy has talent, whether it is from God, or some other source. He does it freely, and that bothers me. Just think how much money we could rake in. I can't stand to watch the money go down the drain."

Jesus has called all of us together, so I best go see what is going on, someone will probably need a little cash. Jesus is telling us that He wants us to go out and preach the Gospel ourselves. "Uh, Jesus I think I had better stay back here and protect You." Ouch, ouch, ouch, those words hurt. "Yes, Sir, I believe in You. Yes, Sir, I understand; I'll go out and witness. Do what? No one is to take any extra clothing, food, or water? Nothing is to be taken? You're kidding. We are going to be able to heal people and cast out demons, just like what You have been doing? I guess I had best be going, everyone else has already left. What am I to do with the money sack while I am gone? No one will bother it? There's a lot of trust needed with that. Okay, okay, I will stop prolonging this. Goodbye."

Wow, that was an experience. I actually was able to perform some of the healings that I have seen Jesus do. He said I would be able to; I just didn't believe him. "Hey, Bart, how about that; wasn't that fun? Did you get to heal anyone? I didn't have any of the demons but plenty of sick people. Yes, sir, I realize it wasn't me, but I think we ought to charge for this. People would pay dearly. Yes, I know, Jesus said we are to give freely; but it is evident Jesus isn't a businessperson. His heart is as good as gold, but His business skills are lacking."

Everyone is sitting by the fire tonight and telling stories of what went on in their journeys. "Thank you. I will join you; I have a couple of stories to tell . . ."

That was a great evening. All the apostles treated me like one of their own, but I can't seem to shake this animosity towards Galileans. I see so much waste and I can't stand waste, whether it be money or time. But I did have a good time talking with the guys about their adventures. I know I would never say anything to the guys, or to Jesus about my feelings, but they are strong, maybe to the point of being ingrained.

Looks like we have a bigger crowd today than yesterday, I didn't know so many people were sick or lame. I guess if you're sick or can't walk, you stay at home. If you need to go out and about when sick, you stick to yourself. Maybe that is my problem. I am sick in the head, and I didn't even know I was ill. Imagine that.

Man, here comes one; that guy is as skinny as a twig. Yuck, he is foaming at the mouth. He is trying to get away from the people that are holding him. If a guy don't want to be healed, then we should let him be. Jesus is walking over to him; I'd run the other way. Let me see what is going to happen. Jesus is staring right at him; some deep voice is coming out of the man. "Bart, what's going on? A demon?! I'm watching. Wow, you see that?!" The man must have flew in the air ten feet. Bart said I needed to pray over him along with Jesus. There he goes on the ground, spinning like a top; unearthly sounds are coming out of the guy. Jesus has had enough of this so called demon; Jesus told him to get out. I never have seen such a contortion of the body. I really don't see how that man survived. But all of a sudden there was a loud screeching sound and then the man fell to the ground. When he opened his eyes, he began to cry; he was free of that demon. This Jesus is the real thing.

Jesus has told us to go out and find seventy people who are loyal to Him. There are a lot of people but I don't know about the loyal part. I haven't exactly been loyal. I would never hurt the guys, but I am so conflicted in my heart. I haven't been paying too much attention to people since I look at the monetary side of everything. So I asked Bart if he would help me in this task.

We have the seventy people in a circle now. I can't believe this, Jesus is enlisting all of these people to go out and tell about this good news. That in itself wouldn't be bad; what makes it bad is, He is giving them the power to heal, just like He did us. If everyone is going to be able to do the miracles, then there won't be any money left. As soon as this session is over, I am going to speak with Jesus and His lack of business skills. I love the guy to pieces but I really don't know how much more of this mismanagement I can handle.

"Look, here are all the people coming back; look at their faces, all smiles. Let's go over and see what they have to say . . ." Wow, they went a long ways out there. All they were doing is preparing the small villages for Jesus' arrival. That part was a good business move on Jesus' part, about the first one He has made, as far as I am concerned.

Here, as of late, the priests from over at the temple are giving us a lot of trouble. They act like they are better than everyone else. I don't know where they get off thinking that. A Sadducee is much better, and a lot smarter in my opinion. At any rate, they have brought us into the temple to tell us not to preach this Gospel stuff. I guess they don't want people to have hope. Hasn't done them any good. Jesus just keeps on going. Most of the time they send the ones still in training to do the heckling. When the real ones come I don't know why Jesus won't pay them off; that is all they want. You can buy them off for next to nothing. Once again, bad management by Jesus, or I guess it could be said, bad advice from the apostles.

Do you know Jesus fed over 5,000 people the other day? Think of the cost of that. I don't know where the money came from; the men didn't come to me and ask for it. I wonder if they are holding some back on me. There is Bart. He seems to be a friend; I'll ask him about it. "You mean a little boy had a couple of fish and some bread, and Jesus just put it in a basket and all the guys went around feeding everyone?" Oh, boy, more poor management. I'm telling you, I can't take much more. All the gold in the world could be ours, if Jesus would just let me handle the organization.

"Did you see that? He is riding into Jerusalem on the back of a donkey. A donkey!" This is rather humiliating to watch even. People throwing palm branch down for him to ride across, what's next? People are treating Him like a king, yet He gives everything away for free. Good grief.

THE APOSTLES 1ST PERSON A NARRATIVE

Thank goodness that little escapade is over. Jesus is going to have supper at a friend's house, and we are all invited. Not a bad house, a lot different than what we live in. Everybody worships Jesus; they think He hung the moon. I love Him too, but things are getting sickening. I mean, if anyone should be looked up to, it should be me. I am the highly educated one, sure some of the others have had a little education from the Pharisees but still...

Now what? That women is bringing a tub of water over to Jesus. She is washing His feet with her hair. Yuck! That is gross! It wasn't so bad when Jesus washed all of our feet. But to have a women wash You, what's this world coming to? What is she doing now? She has a bottle of rosebud oil. That stuff is like one hundred dollars an ounce. Nooooo, I can't believe what I am seeing! She just poured the whole bottle on His feet. There must have been at least twenty ounces of oil in there. That was a total waste! I have to get out of here; I am about to explode. How could Jesus sit there and let that women waste all that oil? That just makes me so mad. These Galileans, how stupid are they? I am going to have to reconsider my position with them. Wasteful. Ugh...

Jesus is back to preaching the Gospel this morning. As for me, I am still reeling from the sight last night. While He is reaching out and healing the sick this morning, I am going to sit back and meditate for a while. I am seriously considering leaving. I have no idea where I will go, but I have to get away from here. Just what we need, here comes the Pharisees again. I don't know what Jesus just told them; whatever it was made their neck turn red. Look at Jesus, a picture of self-confidence. As he walks down the paths He walks straight up, good posture. So do all the apostles, except one, me.

The Pharisees have been trying to capture Jesus for some time, but whenever they get close, Jesus just disappears. I mean, He could be standing right in front of them, and they still couldn't see him. It is like He puts blinders on them. I wonder what they would pay me to lead them to Him. Strictly a business deal. They aren't going to do anything but put Him in jail a few days, and then let Him go. After all, the governor isn't going to sentence anyone that hasn't done anything wrong. I get a few dollars to live on and the Pharisees get their man. Now that, my friend, is a business deal. I still got it. It looks like it is time to rest again. I may just go down and talk, not tip my hand, but see what they would offer. I hope none of the brothers see me; they might get the wrong idea. Well, it wouldn't be wrong, but I would lose my surprise.

"Good evening, is there someone in charge that I might speak with? Thank you. Yes, sir, my name is Judas, and I have a proposition to offer you. I know how bad you would like to shut down this Jesus guy. I know how and when. I just want to know what it is worth to you. I have watched Him make fools out of you, so I know your heart. It is going to cost you 30 pieces of silver. Agreed, I will tell you when and where as soon as I am told where He is going to be. When you send the soldiers with me I will go up to Him and give Him a kiss on the cheek. Please, make it swift; and don't hurt the other guys, okay?

What have I done? My perfect scheme didn't turn out so good. I got carried away and let the cat out of the bag first thing. More than likely greed took over. I saw the evil in their eyes when I told them I would help. But what can they do? Just give Him a few whips on the back and send Him out of town. Here comes one of the brothers; what does he want? I am not in the mood for conversation. I have to act natural. "Hi, Mark what're you up to? Tonight? Okay, I'll be there. Jesus is having a meal tonight. I better go; don't want anyone suspicions.

This is a pretty nice meal. Jesus though isn't in one of his better moods; He isn't chipper. He is about to speak. As I look around the room, every jaw has dropped because of what He just said. He said one of us would betray Him. How did he know that? I haven't told a soul. Fortunately, everybody was so stunned they couldn't speak too much.

THE APOSTLES 1ST PERSON A NARRATIVE

I have to get out of here; I can't keep pretending. What have I done? These guys have been nothing but kind to me. I have let money blind me; greed is my king I guess. I know! I will go back and return the money. Well, not yet, let me think about it.

I found out that Jesus is going to go on the hill tonight to pray; He said He didn't want anyone but His apostles with Him. Perfect timing. I'll go tell the priests; they will be glad to get this over with, and so will I. They said the soldiers were all ready to go also; everything is falling into place.

There they are, just like I was told; and right in front of me, is Jesus. I don't know if I can do this . . . I feel a knife in my back, so I better do it. Here goes . . . "Hello, Jesus." He just looked at me with His sad eyes; I don't think I have ever seen Him with sad eyes. As I stand here, Jesus tells me to do what I have to do, so I kiss him on the cheek. I am pushed down; the soldiers grab Jesus and take off with Him. Oh, God, oh, God, what have I done? I need to leave. Maybe if I go see the priests, they will take their money back . . . "You, Pharisees, I implore you to take this silver back and release Jesus. I know what I have done; I don't need you to tell me. Please take the money back. This is blood money; here you pick it up. May you swallow your tongues!" Normally seeing all that money on the floor would make my mouth water, but I don't care now. I have made a major mistake. I can only hope that they just beat Him and let Him go.

Oh, my God, they have convicted Jesus on a trumped up charge, and they are going to crucify Him! They can't do that, but they are anyway. My stomach hurts; I'm going to vomit. I can't stand this. Maybe if I get out of town I will feel better. No, that won't help. What am I going to do? I feel like killing myself. Would that end my grief? I don't even know how to do that. There is a tree over on the other side of the road. I'll throw this rope over that lower branch. I haven't spoken to or heard about my parents since I started following John, so I can't go home. The only other friends I had were the apostles, and I've lost them now. The only man I could put total trust in was Jesus, and I have condemned Him. I haven't a penny to my name, so I can't catch a boat. I have nothing else to do but die; and quite frankly, I'm too chicken to kill myself. I could take this rope off my neck, stand up, and run off the side of this cliff. I know I would be too much of a scared rat for that. I might as well stand up and walk back into town. These rocks are sure loose. I better get this rope off my neck. "I'm . . . oh . . . oh, help . . . I'm falling . . . Get this rope . . ."

APOSTLE
MATTHIAS

"HI THERE, WHO are you? Zacchaeus is my name; I'm five years old. How old are you? I live here; where do you live? Silly, I wasn't born here; I was born in Bethlehem. Mommy and Daddy say I am from the tribe of Judah, whatever that means. Mommy and Daddy left me here to go to school. They said that I was to mind Mr. Simeon and do what he says to do, or they will give me a whipping. I haven't seen Mommy or Daddy for a long time, like maybe a hundred years. I like it here though; I get to do a lot of the things that other children don't get to do. Like when Mr. Simeon preaches, I get to hand him papers. I can't read, so I don't know what they say, silly. One of these days I will learn to read though. I remember when I first was left here, Mr. Simeon was doing a dead-a-tion . . . No, I can't say it . . . ded-i-ca-tion . . . Yeah, that is it, holding a baby. He called Him a King and raised Him up to the sky. I never had seen Mr. Simeon bow to a baby before, kind of cool. Well, I know you came to see Mr. Simeon, so I will go get him. Don't tell him I told you about that little Baby, okay?"

GEORGE A REGISTER

"I am fully grown now at fourteen; Mr. Simeon has taught me how to read and write. I can read about all the brave men through history, like King David, or how about Solomon, all the big tough people in the Torah. That King David was the best man, like he killed a lion with his bare hands, and then he went out and got himself a bear. The best part though is when he killed that Philly-sten . . . That isn't right; what was he? Oh, yeah, a Philistine. I mean, one shot, right between the ol' eyes. I will never be big and brave like that; as you can see, I'm not very tall. Mr. Simeon said I probably won't get much bigger; all the other kids make fun of me. I don't know how many times I have got into a fight. Every time though, Mr. Simeon makes me study more math and learn more languages. He is a nice old man, but I get so tired of being picked on. He won't let me take any lessons on how to protect myself; he says my temper is what gets in my way. You would get mad too if people was always making fun of you, wouldn't you? One of these days though, they will pay."

Well, I have grown up now; or maybe I should say, I have become a man. I am in my twenties now. I had to leave the temple; Mr. Simeon said I was causing too much trouble. I am going over to see if I can join the government and be a soldier. That was a waste of time; they just laughed at me and said I was too small. One of these days, bam! I think I will walk down the street; maybe I will throw a rock at a horse or a camel. You should see them jump! A lot of times they will buck high enough to throw the rider off. I have to run like you-know-what; those guys don't have a bit of humor in them. I have to find me a job. I think I will go to Rome, which is a lot bigger place; I ought to be able to find a job there. That will be a long trip; someone said it was 1,400 miles from here. Oh, well, what else do I have to do?

THE APOSTLES 1ST PERSON A NARRATIVE

Wow! Look at all these people; they are so thick you have to stir them with a stick. "Hey, you, sir, how many people live in this big city? You're kidding! 1.2 million?! Wow, that is a bunch of flesh in one spot. You say half of the people are slaves; the other half are rich? No middle class, you say? Are there any jobs to be had? I guess you are right; I never thought about it that way. You either have money, or you are a slave? I don't want to be a slave for sure. I think I will walk down Main Street and see what they offer." Look over there, a group of men; I think they call them tax collectors. I haven't found anybody that likes a tax collector. Wait a minute, you hear what I just said? Nobody likes a tax collector, but nobody will mess with a tax collector either. I wonder how I can become a tax collector. There is a man over there, who looks like he is in charge of the other ones, sitting taking money from people. Let's go find out. "Pardon me, sir. I would like to ask you about becoming a tax man. You say I have to know math and be able to count more than with your fingers and toes? I have to know how to write and read? Well, I'm your man; I can do all of that. I can understand you wanting to try me first; let me at 'em. How do I get paid? By whatever I over charge a person, that is what it boils down to, right? Yes, I am a Jew, but I won't let that stand in my way. I owe them a lot of heartache. Yes, sir, I will be here bright and early tomorrow morning ready to work. Thank you, sir."

This is pretty good; I like this, taking people's money. The boss man just came over and said that I was being too kind to people. Charge them more; make them bleed is what he said. Okay, watch me go. All these other collectors have guards around them; I don't have anyone. I think I will ask the boss. "Boss, why don't I have any guards to protect me? I see, I have to pay for my own protection? If I want a guard, then I must pay for him? I guess I will have to wing it until I make enough to pay for one. How much are they? Let them be tax free and their household? But I have to pay their taxes for them, which is a lot lower than if they had to pay for them. Sneaky, huh? I know I want two big ol' bruisers. Nobody is going to mess with me anymore."

I think I have got into the swing of things; I have two big boys, who call me "sir." I like that. Nobody has ever called me "sir." I even have me a nice room at the inn. I can afford meat everyday if I want it. If I need to have something, I will have it by the end of the day. I'll charge double out of everybody that day. I think I am getting a reputation amongst the others. I hear them talking among themselves about how hard I am on people. Good, I am paying people back for making fun of me; I told you I would make them pay. I am tired of this little room I have. I am going to go over and buy me a house. I guess I had better go see the boss first; he called for me a little while ago.

"Hi, Boss, what can I do for you? You're kidding! You want me to go over to Jericho? You are going to let me be the chief collector? How many people can I hire? As many as I want? Okay, when do you want me to go? That soon, huh? I am sure glad I didn't go buy that house awhile ago. I need to go pack, and say goodbye to the few friends that I have, true friends that is. There aren't very many. Most of the people that want to be friends are rich people wanting to get out of taxes. My motto is, "Grease my palm, and I'll give you a break.""

Well, now, I think I have had enough of that boat ride. I have arrived here in Jericho, 2,177 miles later. What a journey. The nuts on that boat where the straggliest guys I believe I have ever been around. You know what they remind me of? People after I sap all the taxes from them, hahaha. I didn't dare turn my back on them. They all knew what I was and where I was going. Some of them live in Jericho where I am headed to work. You can't trust anyone nowadays.

I think I will look around and see some of the sites. I'm not going to look too long; it is hot here. After all, we are in the desert. That hot wind comes in off the sand out in the plains and heats everything up, including my head.

I want to go over to Jerusalem and see Mr. Simeon, if he is still alive. I guess I should have kept in touch with him, but he would always start in on me. Oh, well, it's not but a little under seventeen miles over there. I am not going to go until it is dark though; there is a cool breeze at night which makes travel a lot easier. Of course, those pesky robbers are out at night too. But I brought my boys from Rome with me, so I don't think anybody will bother me. I think I will take my wagon, because it is uphill all the way.

Someone told me it is right at 3,500 feet higher in Jerusalem than it is in Jericho. It is a real deep valley going to Jericho. The only thing that keeps people here is the citrus and banana trees. I kept wondering how they find enough water to make the fruit. A guide I have hired took me to the edge of town and said to look at that mound in the distance. Sure enough, a barren hill, or mound, which ever you want to call it, was laying by itself. He told me that there was a bunch of springs that came out of that hill. The water from those springs feeds all the orchards and gardens in the area. I think I see potential for some tax revenue. That guide told me that there was a lake not too far, about six miles from here. He said I could go fishing if I wanted to. Do I look like a fool to you? I know there aren't any fish in the Dead Sea, I will remember him when he comes to pay his taxes.

GEORGE A REGISTER

Well, I have my tables set up now. I have them set on both ends of town, that way no one can sneak in or out on me. If they go any other direction they're going out into the desert and will die. No one has been collecting for some time so I must get my books out and start going house to house; they are going to be surprised. I am legally bound to charge each person one percent of their income, but I will charge them at least five percent. I have to live too, you know. My guys on the tables at the edges of town tax people one tenth of their grain. I tell them to charge at least three tenths of the grain. And then there is the wine; I am to charge one fifth of the wine, fruit, and olive oil. I charge two fifths. Hey, I have to pay my people out of my own pocket. I told you that before. Now I make a lot of money when I go around to these houses. I get to keep all the property taxes, sales taxes, and emergency taxes. I told you I was going to charge for the water taxes; and if they don't like it, they can move out. Oh, yeah, I'll charge moving taxes then. The government taxes are what keeps the roads up and cleans up the city which I think is a waste of money.

I think I have got into a pretty good groove on collecting these taxes. Most people cough up the money; they know they owe it. Some try to cheat me, but there is a tough penalty for lying to me. I followed behind one man the other day after he had just bought some wine at the inn. I asked him for his taxes, and he said he didn't have any money. I drug him off to jail; his wife came and paid the taxes. Some of the people don't have any money, so they have been living tax-free for several years. I took their homes and made them get out of town. They had to walk out, because I took their cows and camels. You cannot live for free in my town. Yep, it is my town now.

I am sitting under a tree here sipping on some fruit drink; I think

THE APOSTLES 1ST PERSON A NARRATIVE

it is some kind of citrus and banana. I am minding my own business, not bothering anyone, that doesn't happen very often. Look, here comes one of my big boys dragging some poor soul along. "What's going on, Tiger? He is giving you some lip about the taxes being charged? Don't I know you? Yes, I know you. You are one of those kids that kept making fun of me, aren't you? I don't care if you don't have any money. What did you do with it? You stole enough from me when we was kids. You and your buddies would beat me up, call me names, and just torment me every day. Well, it is my turn now. Why should I have mercy on you? I have waited for years to get even with you and your monsters. Tiger, take this bum to the dungeon. Put him at the back; I will see what the council wants to do with him. Seize his belongings as he won't be needing them for a long time." I know the council will let him out, but it is going to take me some time to turn the paper work in, maybe a year or two.

Ah, that felt good. I hope some more of them bums come over to my town. Look, here comes one of the politicians; I bet I know what he wants. "Hello, Arias. Tomorrow night? I will have to check my schedule. Thank you for inviting me. See you later." The bum is trying to make nice with me. He knows I am going to tax his campaign money. Some of the richer business owners are always throwing parties in my honor; all they want is a tax break. Some of them think I should relieve them of any taxes. Like that's going to happen. I have more money now than anyone else in town, and I intend on keeping it that way.

I have been at this tax business now for several years. I think that if there is a nickel to be had, I've got it. I don't know if I'm just getting older or what. I don't seem to have the zeal I use to have.

GEORGE A REGISTER

Everybody is scared of me. My only friends, or so-called friends, only like me because I take bribes from them. Even my guys are afraid to move just in case I am in a bad mood or something. Can't anyone like me just for me? I guess not. I guess I made my bed, and now I have to lay in it. Here comes a bunch of travelers. "What you have to declare? You're in the ministry service, you say? Where is your Pharisees to support you? You follow who? I see. You know, I think I know him from somewhere; I'll have to think on it. You know what? I believe you, so go. I will not charge you. Take it as a token of good cheer." What am I doing? I just passed up a bunch of money. Something strange here; I still think I know Him. I believe I will go over and listen to what these guys have to say.

That preacher man sure could put a spell on you. He made me think about myself when I was growing up in the temple. I remember Mr. Simeon talking about those same verses that the preacher quoted. Kind of funny, I still remember them. You would think I'd forget them, but after listening to Him I could recall several verses. Oh, well, I haven't got time for that. Here comes another victim, I mean taxpayer. "Hey, I know you. You're another one of those guys that made fun of me when I younger. Did you come to pay your taxes or beg? You have how many kids?! Who you married to? I think I remember her. She was a pretty one; you are very lucky to have her. Let us do business. I see, this is all you have to declare? Been a little on the slow side lately, you say? Is that the only donkey you have? You plow with him, and try to raise a garden to help feed your family? Looks a little old to me. I tell you what I'm going to do. You trade that old donkey in to me for this much younger mule, and every six months you bring me a portion of your crop. As long as you bring me this, I will let the taxes be low. Okay, no need to thank me. I have no idea why I'm doing this; be gone before I change my mind."

I hear that preacher man is going to come through here again. I am going to go over and listen one more time. I see He has arrived over on the south side of town. He is getting smarter; as long as He stays outside of town, He doesn't have to pay taxes. Man, I still think I know Him. I forgot to check on Him last time; I was too busy. Goodness, He sure does have a crowd around Him. I can't see a thing. Be quiet; listen to what He is saying. Something about how God loves everyone. And He can give us eternal life with Him in the heavens. I bet He doesn't love me. Wait a minute, He just said even the biggest sinners, which would be me. I like this guy, He is turning around and leaving now. I guess He is going back to Jerusalem. Too bad, that is a big following He has. I've got to shake this feeling; I know I have met Him somewhere. I bet I'll know before He comes back again, if He ever does.

Several weeks have passed since I last saw that preacher man. I am going to take a few days off and go to Jerusalem to listen to Him. While I am there I will go to the temple and talk to some of the priests there. Surely they will know who He is. "Come on, Tiger. We going for a ride; bring a couple body guards with you, just in case, you know." It doesn't seem as hot today, which is a good thing. I would have to hire some fan wavers to keep me cool if it was any hotter. Now where is that guy? There He is. Once again, I can't see Him, but I can hear Him. He's preaching that same message, you know, about God loving everyone. One of the other speakers said that God loved the world so much He is sending His only Son to save the world. Now that is love; you think He could love me that way? No, I am too wicked to be loved by a good person. "Come on, Tiger. Let's go on back home; I don't belong here. If He comes back through, I might listen to Him again.

I have been trying to treat people a little bit different lately. I know that I'm headed towards hell, but no one can help me. But I'm going to try and make other people have an easier time of it. I have even let some of the ones I have put in prison out. If only I could believe this guy. Oh, yes, I found out His name is Jesus. You remember when I was a little boy, Mr. Simeon said that a Baby was the King? Well, that is this guy. He sure has grown up to be so kind and loving. "What did you say, Tiger? He is coming this way. Oh, joy, I think I will go out and meet Him. He probably won't talk to me, but I can try. "What did you say? That is a good idea." I haven't been able to see Him, because I'm too short. But if I get up in a tree, I will be able to see and hear Him. Over there is a sycamore tree. That branch isn't too high, but it will give me a vantage point. Way to go, Zac. Here He comes, still preaching. He has such a pure voice. He doesn't have to scream or anything. Everyone can hear, and now I can see. He is almost underneath me; He is looking right at me. I hope He doesn't mind me being in this tree. What? He just called me by name. How did He know my name? He just told me to get down out of this tree. "You want to do what? But sir, Your kind think my house is unclean. I would be glad to feed You and Your people. Come on, I want to hear more of this. Tiger, run up ahead of me and tell the cooks to get ready for a feast. Jesus, will You tell me more about this kingdom that You are talking about?

"Jesus, oh, Jesus, I have been such a jerk all of my life. I have cheated many people just to make myself rich. Is there anything I can do to make up for this? I want to follow You and learn about this glory. Can I give all this up? Yes, I think I can. Matter of fact, I am going to give back to the people that I have cheated. I will give them back more than I have taken from them. Tiger, I want you to start rounding up all those people. You know who they are, all the prisoners; and give the other collectors a bonus. I am going to follow Jesus. He loves me, and I love God. I have a major problem though; everyone is going to know me by name. I can change it to something else. Let's see, how about John? No, too many Johns. What should I be called? Matthias? Not too many people are called that. It's a good name. From now on, I am Matthias."

THE APOSTLES 1ST PERSON A NARRATIVE

I never knew Jesus traveled so much. We go into a town, and the next thing you know, there are a bunch of people. Then a large crowd will start to form; you know why? He does all kinds of healings for people. People that have been bedridden all their lives, He will walk up to them and say, "Rise," and up they pop. The only problem we have is a group of Pharisees who try to disrupt Jesus when He is speaking. They ask some very sharp questions, but Jesus answers them without any hesitation. I remember some of the areas of the Torah where they are quoting from. Kind of nice to learn what all that means. We have been in some towns where the Pharisees get so upset that they will send soldiers to arrest Him. Weirdest thing though, the soldiers shove themselves through the crowd and when they get to the middle, they can't find Jesus. They look all over for Him, but they don't see him. And He is standing right in front of them; it's rather funny. It is like they have blinders on their eyes.

Jesus has a few men that He calls His apostles. I think there are around twelve of them. As we go up and down the countryside to the little towns, Jesus is always teaching. He calls people like me disciples. A lot of us travel the whole time with Him. I have learned so much from Him. I can't see how I missed so much; it is so clear now. I have made several friends in the group, and I am talking true friends. One guy I know is named John Mark; he is writing things down all the time, you know, like what Jesus taught that day or night. He will let me look at his notes a lot of the time; I like him a lot. There is a very young boy, I would call him (man if it makes you feel better); his name is Timothy.

Those twelve guys I told you about are nice to me too. I think they learned a lesson from the first time when we were sitting around a little campfire one night and some of them were telling about Matthew; he was a publican too, tax collector. Most of them was ready to walk off when he came into the fold, but Jesus straightened that out in a hurry. I guess that is why they didn't put up much of a hassle when they all came to my house.

Jesus has set up camp in Capernaum. This is close to most places; also there are homes here that belong to some of the apostles. I really don't know what is going on right now. Jesus has called all of the apostles to one side, away from the crowd that has already formed. That didn't take long; looks like the apostles are pairing up and walking out of town. "Jesus, is something wrong? Oh, good, I thought maybe trouble was a brewing." This is good for me. Now Jesus will be concentrating on the disciples more. I can't see how much more my mind can absorb; but if He is teaching, I am listening. I still don't see how Jesus can just keep on going all the time. If He isn't teaching, He is praying.

Oh, look, the apostles are coming back; that really wasn't too long of a time. They are in giving Jesus a report of their activities. I will say that every one of them have smiles on their faces. The apostles are starting to disperse now; this is good. They are choosing a few to go in and meet up with Jesus. Here comes one now; hope he has time to tell me about his journey. "Hi, brother, what's up? You say Jesus wants to see me?" Other than Him having a meal in my house, I didn't think He even knew I was still here. Let's go in and find out what He needs. There is a pretty big crowd in here. I would say there are at least seventy or more. Jesus is giving us compliments on our staying with Him as He traveled. It looks like He is looking right at me; I know, it just looks that way. Everyone feels the same way. He said He is going to give us a project to do; we are to go out to the cities and towns and tell them that Jesus is going to come there. And (this is a biggy) we will have the authority to heal people and cast out demons. Jesus told us to be careful about doing that because the demons are very powerful, and we are to be sure to cast them out in His name. And something else, we can go to the Gentiles. That is something the apostles weren't able to do. Let's get going. Time's a wastin'.

Now that was invigorating. We have been on the road now for I guess maybe three months, somewhere around there anyway. You know time flies when you are having fun. I have never felt so good and needed in my life. I never encountered any problems except when the Pharisees would send soldiers to run us out of town. I even was able to cast a demon out; by the time the demon left, I was sweating profusely and tired. I've never been that tired in my life. Jesus was right that it would be hard work, but it was well worth it.

I have been with Jesus now for a long time. I'm not sure how long, but we have been from one country to the other spreading the Gospel. The Pharisees are starting to get frustrated with Jesus. It is very apparent there are things that they don't want taught. They have made so many laws so that people can't possibly obey all of them; most of the laws are to benefit the Pharisees. Jesus seems to have stepped up the intensity of His preaching. You know, urgency is in His voice. He even is talking about His time on earth being almost over. He even said that one of the apostles would betray Him. I really can't see that happening, but anything is possible. "Have you seen this in Him? Maybe it is just me. Hi, Barabbas. You know, I was just sitting here talking to my friends about the very same thing. I believe something big is about to happen. There goes Jesus taking the apostles up on the hill again." Looks like they all are there, except the one they call Judas. I can't shake this feeling in my bones; there is some spiritual activity going on. I think I am just tired maybe; I am going to go over to the other side of town and lay down. I can get some rest and be ready for whatever Jesus has for us to do tomorrow. This feeling is still nagging at me.

A guy can't even get any sleep around here. People are abuzz over something; I better get over on the other side and see what we are doing. "Hey, you, what's all the commotion about? No, I haven't heard anything; I just got up from my night's rest. No!!! Not possible! Why would the people would let them arrest Jesus? Where were the apostles during all this time? I have to go find one of the apostles and get the facts. I know the Pharisees are upset, but to just come right out and have Jesus arrested? No way. There is one of the apostles now. Hey, Bart, tell me the scuttlebutt isn't true. Not looking too good right now, huh? I will go over and see if I can get him released. You say they aren't letting anyone in the area? They must be afraid of a riot, you know."

I hate not knowing what is going on; I can't find any of the apostles. People say they have scattered all over, and there is a rumor they are taking Jesus to the Roman governor. The Sadducees and the Pharisees both have made false testimonies about Jesus. Wait a minute, how can they condemn Jesus for preaching the Gospel? What is this world coming to?

I have heard that Peter and John are hanging around the palace to see what is happening or what is going to happen. John is closer that Peter because John knows a lot of those priests and soldiers. Here comes Peter now; I hope he has good news. "They have started beating Jesus and have a beam ready to fasten Jesus on? Are you saying they are going to crucify Jesus?" He has started up the road to Skull Hill carrying that beam. I am going to go see Him. Give him some encouragement just like He was always giving us love and encouragement. Here He comes now. Oh my, is that really Jesus?

THE APOSTLES 1ST PERSON A NARRATIVE

He has been beaten so badly that you can't even recognize Him. Oh, He just fell. I can't watch this anymore. It is too awful to look at. I think I'm going to be sick; excuse me. He did say His time on earth was short, but I thought He would just rise to the heavens like the apostle James said Jesus did awhile back when He met with Moses and Elijah.

Well, those hypocrite Pharisees have went and done it. They crucified Jesus. I heard that Jesus asked John to take care of His mother. The apostles have all gone this way and that way, but for the most part are still around the area. Some of the other disciples said that a lot of the apostles are meeting in secret. I don't know what I'm going to do now; I had devoted my entire life to serving Jesus. Now he is gone, and I have no place to go. I sure can't go back to Jericho and start tax collecting again. I can't stay here; the Pharisees will be looking for Jesus' followers. Peter's house is being watched day and night. I know, I'll do what Jesus would have done; I'll pray.

Look over there; it is the apostles, and they are smiling. I guess it didn't take them long to get over Jesus' death. I wish I had my guards; I would have them go over and whip the tar out of 'em. Oh, rats, here they come. "You guys seem to be mighty cheerful. Doesn't it bother you that Jesus has been crucified? Come on, guys, don't make the situation worse by pretending He is alive. You're serious? You saw Him? I do remember Him saying something about coming back after death. You saw Him? Yeah, I'll go with you and see Him." There is a crowd over there; I recognize a lot of them as His disciples. It is Jesus!!! I must get on my knees and worship Him! Guess what He is doing? He is still teaching. He said He wouldn't be here very long, but there was just a smidgen of work left to be done.

Jesus has been here a lot longer than I figured He would be. A few of us have been summoned outside of the city. Jesus said it was important. Jesus looks so majestic in His white robe; He looks so peaceful. Jesus is getting up to His feet and raising His arms now. Oh, my goodness, He is rising into the air saying, "Peace to you." Up into the clouds He has gone. All the apostles and disciples are standing around praising the Savior, dancing, and praying. I am going to go over to Peter and volunteer my services to him.

The apostles have a lot better attitudes now that Jesus has proved He is alive. Peter is leading us nowadays. Seems like there is more work to do now than when Jesus was with us (in body that is). The whole thing has to be restructured and new assignments have to be handed out. That is okay though, because that keeps our minds off the loss of our leader Jesus. Peter is good, but he isn't anything like Jesus. Here comes Peter now; looks like he is going to say something to us all. He just told us that the apostles are going to have a meeting and that all of us should hang around until they come out. I have been in some of those meetings; they aren't short. I am going to go over and get some bread to eat while they talk.

I don't know what they are talking about, but it must be serious. They have been in there for several hours now. If this keeps up, I will have to get my bedding out. All right, I see them coming out now. They want us to gather around. I sure hope they weren't voting on disbanding; I don't believe Jesus would like that. Okay, here it comes; Peter is about to speak. He is telling us that since one of us betrayed Jesus, then that one must be replaced. He said that great discussion has been going on and that they, with the help of the Holy Spirit, have chosen the one to replace the evil one. He says that everyone must get on their knees and pray hard. I am so jittery; I'm about to wet my pants. "Hey, James, do what? The apostles want me to come up front? Oh, I know, I am going to get to pray over the new one, whoever he is. Pardon, I don't think I heard you correctly. You, you have chosen me to be the new one? Oh, my Lord, I don't know if I am worthy of this. You're right; no one is worthy. I will do my duties to the best of my ability." Peter then went on to explain how they chose me. I'm still flabbergasted.

All the apostles are receiving their instructions as to what they are to do at this point of the program. Man, oh, man, we are being scattered all over but will still run into one another on occasion. Peter has asked me to stay in Judea for now and then figure where to go after that. I can understand this because of the newness of my ministry. Most everyone has heard of the Gospel in my area, but I needed to get the people to take the next step and accept Jesus as their Savior.

I have been out on the journey for several months now; I must go see Peter or whoever is left. I could go see James, Jesus' brother; I think he is in charge of the Jerusalem church. Oh, nevermind, I see Peter. "Peter, I have come to give an account of my travels. Thank you, sir. No one is going down south? Well, if you want me to go that way, then that is where I will go. Ethiopia? Uh, ok, never been there. I will get ready to make the boat trip."

I am here now. This is a lot different than up in Judea, the landscape I'm talking about. The mountains are a lot bigger here; some they say reach up to 14,000 feet. Looks like that area is lush and green which means it probably gets a lot of rain. The valleys are a different story. They look to be dry; nothing is growing. They look like the deserts around home. Well, I am going to start by going towards the interior of the country. If I remember correctly this country was named Cush in the Torah. The people aren't very friendly. I try to present the Gospel, and they just walk off. That is okay. I am to plant the seed, and Jesus is going to water it. I am going to try and work my way back toward the sea. No one is listening, so it doesn't take long in one spot. Here comes a group of men. "Good afternoon, men. Wait a minute. What are you doing? Let go of me. Where are you taking me?"

I have never been man-handled like this in my life. "Who are you? Well, here comes an official. Sir, what is the meaning of this? What do you mean I am to bow down to this guy? He is your god? Well, he is about the ugliest god I have ever seen. I'm not going to drink anything. Get away from me! Ugh, that tasted awful. What was it? Poison?! You gave me poison, why?! You're going to eat me?! Oh, boy! Jesus, help! What you doing now? Get that knife away from . . . Ahhhh! Oh, that hurts! You cut my stomach open! Now you're going to burn me with fire?! Dear Jesus, please take this away. Now what're you going to do? You're taking me to a cell? Death would be welcomed right now, but the Lord is keeping me safe. What did you say? You gave me enough poison to kill a camel, but I lived? You tore my stomach deep enough to kill any animal, but I am still here? So you're going to throw me into jail? You know what? I don't feel any pain."

I have been sitting in this cell for I guess thirty days or more. They haven't come to get me; maybe they are scared of me. Oh, boy, I shouldn't have said anything; here they come now. "I can walk fellas; no need to drag me. Ouch, the rocks are sharp. You are ready to eat me? Have any salt?" They didn't think that was funny. Here I go, tied up to this stake. Looks like they are going to gut me again. Who was that? "Andrew, is that you? You want me to come over there? I have a problem. I am chained up. What in the world? How did you do that? I'm coming over; did you see that? Those chains just dropped off as if someone cut them. Jesus did it, I know. Here comes Mister-Show-Off-God of theirs. I think his name is Amani, or something like that." Wow, you ought to see Andy giving that thug what for! He is on the ground writhing in pain. Andy just told him to leave and to never come back. He turned to me and asked me why I hadn't done that? That hurt but was true. He said we needed to go now, but the people have seen what our Jesus can do, and they want to know more. "If it is okay, I want to stay just a little longer. You can go on, but I want to take care of these people." After a long prayer, I have to say bye to Andrew. Boy, it was good to see him.

Many people have come to know Christ here in Ethiopia; I think it is time to go back to see the apostles at home. It is a long trip, but I can go back satisfied with the results. I hear that the people at home are still all stirred up. I know, I am going to just go out into Galilee and spread the Message further. At least I have friends not too far off. Here come my first Jews, "Hi, fellow countrymen, have you heard the good news that Jesus has given us? Ouch, what is it? Okay, you don't want to hear about it? No need treating me this way." Oh, boy, here I go again being dragged. Only this time it is by my own people taking me to the temple. "I know you; you're the High Priest Annas. I hear you don't like Christians. Come on, Annas, you know we aren't going to stop this preaching. Why waste your time telling us? I do have respect for the office of High Priest;

I just don't have any respect for you." I think I have made him mad. They are dragging me out of the city. "You pushed me down; I will stay on my knees and pray. Ouch, ouch! One minute, please. Those first two stones, would you please bury them with me? They show I was faithful to the end. Ouch! Oh, Jesus, would you make this swift?"

APOSTLE PAUL

THIS HAS SURE been a long and strenuous campaign. The zealots are pushing more and more. I think we must have imprisoned more than one hundred rebels. They are always trying to cause trouble between the Roman government and the Jews themselves. Over the past year, I can't even begin to tell you how many have been put in jail. Honestly, I can't tell that we have made any progress in squelching the uprising; I am going to rest for a while.

 I love being able to sit out here in the gazebo or swing in the hammock. I just close my eyes and think of more peaceful moments. Sometimes I think of myself as a child back in my hometown of Tarsus. My mom and dad are fairly wealthy Jews, and they are Roman citizens also. My grandfather, as well as his father before him, were given Roman citizenship. So this gave me citizenship also. But I am more proud of the fact that I am pure blood, coming from the tribe of Benjamin. As a boy I would go out and play with the neighborhood kids; we had a ball made out of goatskin and filled with straw. We would kick the fire out that ball and play all day sometimes, that is, until I reached the age of five. Then I had to start school, I was taught the philosophy of the Roman world. By the time I did all my studies, there wasn't much time for play.

 When I turned fourteen, my parents sent me to Jerusalem to

study under a man named Gamaliel. These studies were of the Torah and the Jewish traditions. Gamaliel was the most respected professor in the world, so Dad spent a fortune on my education. If it wasn't for my dad wanting me to study under Gamaliel, I could have stayed in Tarsus. I loved it there. They had everything in that city. A population of around 250,000 people. The universities in Tarsus were among the best in the world, they rivaled Athens or even Alexandria. But Dad wanted the best, so off I went. I will say, they moved to Jerusalem also. While studying, I learned how to wield a sword. I also learned a lot of military moves, which really wasn't part of my school work; I just did it in my spare time.

Here comes a messenger with a note, which usually meant the head Roman officer wants me for another assignment. So much for the rest. I have been given another round of zealot gathering. This time I have to go to Cadasa in the region of Galilee. I guess I will have to take the prisoners to Jerusalem; all the other jails are full. Our custom is that we will execute everyone if we haven't got space. If they are just suspected of uprising, we whip them forty times on the back and then send them out.

We have arrived in Cadasa and the air is thick with animosity. This group isn't even trying to hide; they are coming at us with clubs, swords, spears, and anything else to fight with. There is a glaze over their eyes; reasoning with them is going to be out of the question. I am the commander in charge, so I need to make a decision about if we fight or back off. That really is an easy decision. "Take no prisoners; kill them all. Charge!" It is a shame that these people try to fight with no idea as to how to fight. Looks like about thirty of the enemy, so this shouldn't take long. In a battle such as this, you make sure to hit in the heart area with your sword; this way they can't get back up and sneak up in back of you. Of course, in a big battle it is totally different.

As I said, it didn't take very long to squelch that little group of Jews. I had taken ten soldiers with me, but I could have got by with maybe five. No use taking chances though. We will go house-to-house now and see if there is any more opposition. The Roman government has given fairly loose rein with the Jews. If they keep up with this we may have to start reining in their activities . . .

I understand there is another group of people that are stirring up trouble. We thought everything would be over with when we crucified the leader. That guy swore that he was the Messiah, which was a big laugh. If he was the Messiah, why didn't He protect Himself? Here comes another messenger. I wonder what it is this time. Oh no, I have to go to Rome.

I truly enjoy coming to Rome as this is a place that appreciates philosophical debates. And the town is so beautiful, all the coliseums and the architecture of the government buildings are a sight to behold. Look over there, it is the hot springs; I'll be going there tonight. The town is clean from top to bottom. The who's who all either live here or vacation here. I think I will buy a home here in the city when I retire. I guess I had better move onto the court.

Pontius Pilate isn't one to be kept waiting. "Yes, sir, I am here to see the king. Yes, he is expecting me. Yes, I have been aware of the Pharisees getting their pants waded up. They don't like those Christ-followers cutting in on their territory. Yes, sir, I know they can't bring judgment on them without our permission. Isn't there a law that says they can give thirty-nine lashes but not forty? Even at that, they have to have permission. I am not a big fan of those people, but I can't see where they have broken any laws. I see, both the Sadducees and the Pharisees say they are plotting against the government? Yes, sir, you and I both know that is a ploy to get us to arrest the group. Well, thank you, sir, if you want me to gather them up into prison, then that is what I will do. Do I have permission to flog them? And if so, how many strokes can I give? I have free rein just terrorize all of them? This just might be fun. How many men do I have? That will be plenty; I don't really expect trouble out of any of them. I can spread them out to various towns and make this campaign go a lot faster. I must be present at all floggings done in the name of Rome? I am to be stationed in Jerusalem and work out of that area which is where most of the conflict is coming from? And where do I house all the prisoners? That is a great idea, sir. Capture them and then have them build their own prison? Do I flog the women and children? Are the women eligible to be raped? Good, because the men will need to have some way to vent frustration. Children up to thirteen years of age are not to be touched? If anyone gives trouble, they are to be flogged and then strung up to die? I believe I can handle all of this; I thank you for the task."

I have my army mounted and ready to go. The first place I am going to go is Naples. A lot of activity is going on there, and it will be a good training session for my troops. Here comes some of the Pharisees. "What can I do for you? You show me the people that follow this Jesus character, and I will do the rest. Sir, you are a priest; and I respect you for that, but do not tell me how to do my job. I have my orders, and they are not from you. So get out of the way when we start, understood? Men, follow the priests, and bring to me the prisoners. Priests, do you have a jail that will hold all here? I should have known you did. Men, bring the prisoners to the temple."

My men have ransacked every home where suspected enemy were. Looks like maybe a hundred men and women. "Take the men to the courtyard in the middle of the temple, tie them securely, and then come back here. Once you get back, strip the women and rape them, which is your reward for doing a great job. Afterwards, I will chose twenty of you to flog the men forty lashes. If they die, don't worry about it. The priest will clean up the mess and bury the dead."

I really thought the priest might look the other way when we raped the women, but they joined in with the soldiers. Not all, but some of them. It is time to move on. "Priests, leave the prisoners locked up for at least a year; and if you want, keep them longer. Let us go to Ephesus next; there's a pretty big following there they say.

"Ok, men, this is Ephesus. Bring the prisoners outside of the city when you capture them; then go back in. The Sadducees will help you locate the homes. If I remember correctly, there is a group of zealots in this town, so be careful. If they need to be killed on the spot, do not hesitate; run them through with the sword. Do not try and rape any of the women; wait until everyone has been taken captive. Put the children in a separate circle, and do not touch the children, clear?"

Wow, I think we must have rounded up over half the town. One of my soldiers came to me and said that a group of zealots had tried to interfere with the operation: they had to kill close to thirty men. Most of them they beheaded, so they have a lot of blood on them. I'm not real sure, but I think my men are having a little too much fun. "Look at all those men, four hundred maybe. I need fifty men to flog all these. First regiment, that is your lot this time. Forty lashes. I see a couple of women I think I might like to have my way with. Private, bring those two women over to me. Now go have fun with the rest of the women, and tell the others."

We are in Jerusalem now, so I need to set up a more permanent type of camp. The township has a large prison in which we can put the prisoners. I went through some towns that I know had those Christians in them, but I need to incarcerate the rebels I have first. After we get done with this group, I'll go back. I also hear that

Jerusalem has a large group of people following that Jesus guy. Oh, brother, here comes the Pharisees already. Look at them dragging some poor sucker by the neck. "What is it you priests want? I have just arrived, and here you are. What gives? This man is breaking the law by preaching what is contrary to your teachings and needs to be put to death? You, scumbag, what is your name? Well, Mr. Stephen, what do you have to say for yourself? So you admit your guilt? Okay, priests, I am not going to punish this man, you are. I give you permission to stone him till death. I will be there to witness the execution, for that is the law, but you are going to do the deed. Tie the rope to my horse; I will drag him outside the city.

"Are you ready? Start stoning. Ah, come on you wimp arms! Throw that stone like you meant it. A girl could out stone you. You're hitting his back; throw a little higher. What was that he just said? Forgive them; they don't know what they do? It is for sure they don't know how to stone someone. All right, enough, you have killed him; now throw him over the cliff to the garbage pile." That was rather amusing watching the priests. Why do the people keep preaching about this Jesus? Hasn't He been dead for over two years? I don't get it.

"Okay, it is time to gather some of the prisoners up; we don't need to keep them for the rest of their lives. I just need to give them a whipping and then release them. I got a better idea. Let's give them forty lashes and then drag them through town. When you reach the outskirts of the city, release them. If they give you any trouble stick them. Let them walk back to their hometown; that will give them time to think about what or who is in charge around here." They ought to be thankful we brought them here instead of going to Rome with them. If they were in Rome a lot of them would be thrown into the arena with hungry lions. Maybe we should open up the colosseum here in Jerusalem and execute them that way; it would be a lot of fun to watch.

THE APOSTLES 1ST PERSON A NARRATIVE

One of my soldiers has arrived from staying in Damascus with family. He said that this Jesus' group is growing and growing. They are about to take over. I am going to go over to the temple and talk with the High Priest. I know that these Jesus freaks are annoying, but they are Jews. So I need to act like the priests have given me the authority to capture and flog. The priests want me to bring the prisoners back to Jerusalem. I don't agree with that strategy. For one, I will have to feed the people. I am going to have to take more men with me; it just isn't a good idea. I'll see after I get there as to what will be the best strategy.

I have decided that I am going to take the minimum amount of soldiers with me. It is a long trip, a little over one hundred thirty-six miles one way. I have a few soldiers stationed in Damascus, so I ought to be good. I am taking all mounted soldiers, mainly because of the length of the trip. I want them to be refreshed when we arrive. As a matter of fact, I think we will camp outside the city overnight. I want this campaign to be short and sweet.

This is a long, boring journey. I don't have to be on guard fearing any road robbers, and the road is smoothed all the way. Not that much traffic right now and I am getting rather sleepy; I think I will take a little nap. We are only about twenty miles outside of Damascus; like I said, it has been a long, boring trip. "Whoa, what's wrong steed? Get back down; stop bucking. Ouch, you just threw me off." I hit the road pretty hard, but I can't feel any broken bones. Wait a minute. I can't see. I can't see! "Who is speaking to me? Jesus? Can't be, You are dead. You are breaking every Jewish law. Yes, Sir, I'll listen. Oh, please, give me sight. You say You are upholding God's Law, not the stripped down laws of the priests? Where is my horse?

Did it run away? My men, where are they? They can see, but they don't see you? I want my sight back. My men have been instructed to lead me into Damascus? Did they see that bright light? Good, I thought maybe I was the only one. I am to go in and pray, and you will come back to me later? All my men lost their horses? The bright light scared all of them off? Okay, men, guide me to town, and be careful with me."

I am to stay at a man named Judas' house. This is so upsetting, I can't seem to be able to eat or drink or anything. All I can think of is what Jesus told me. In a dream He told me a man named Ananias would come and give me my sight back. If that does happen, I will give praise to Jesus and help spread the Gospel.

It has been three days now; my entire outlook on life has changed. I am ashamed of my actions towards the Christians, I doubt if any of them will have anything to do with me. "There is someone at the front door. Go open it and see who it is. I really don't want any company right now. Who did you say? Send him in. Hurry. Send him to me. Yes, Jesus said a man named Ananias would stop by and give me sight. I remember Jesus saying that, and here you are. You are the one Jesus sent, right? Oh, thank You, Jesus. Thank You for being true to Your Word. Thank you, Ananias, for obeying Jesus' instructions. Yes, yes, in my prayers for the last three days I have been receiving instructions. I have been instructed to have you baptize me in the name of Jesus. Let us do this first; then I will eat, so I can get my strength back. I never realized how beautiful the world was. Darkness is a demoralizing place to be, but now I see the light. Thank You, Jesus. Ananias, let's go to the synagogue and shout in the Lord's name. I feel so full of the Holy Spirit. Nothing is going to stop me."

THE APOSTLES 1ST PERSON A NARRATIVE

I have been preaching in the synagogues now for several days; I feel so light-footed, almost to the point of being giddy. Here comes one of my brothers now. When I was introduced to some of the disciples at first, an air of uncertainty filled the room. I can't blame them. Oh my, he just told me there is a plot to try and kill me. He said that they have put men at the gates and in the streets to catch me and kill me. Here comes a group of my brothers; I would say they have come to help get me captured, but something is different. All right, they are hiding me. I must trust these guys. That is something I have never done before, but I know these men's heart. It is starting to get dark outside; I hear some of the brothers talking out by the door. "Yes, I am ready to leave, you going to lower me down from the wall? The Jews are waiting by the gates. Yes, the backside is out of sight of the gates. Brothers, let us pray before you start lowering me, okay?" I hadn't realized the wall was so uneven until I started going down, but I make it down. One of the brothers is at the bottom waiting for me. "You are going to go with me to Jerusalem? I appreciate that, it is a long trip."

I have to be very careful going into Jerusalem. Not everybody is friendly here, and of course, I am talking about my new brothers. It will take some work to convince them that I am a new man in love with the Lord. Sometimes I wish I had a funny side to myself. But I've never pulled a joke on anybody. Maybe if I smiled more . . .

Let us worry about things at hand instead of what could be. I have tried to get in contact with the apostles but none will meet with me. All right, here comes a brother now. "Hello, my name is Saul. You know who I am, and you are not afraid of me? What is your name, sir? Well, Barnabas, I am glad you have been to Damascus. You know the works I have been doing there? Yes, sir, I have been looking for the apostles, but they seem to have disappeared. You will take me to them? Oh, thank you, brother." Barnabas is trying to get the apostles to open their door; I guess they are too scared. Barnabas has told me to stand outside while he talks with the other brothers.

It has been well over an hour since he went in to speak to the men. I may have to go it alone. All right, the door is opening. I am invited in; that is progress. "Hello, brothers, I come in the name of Jesus."

I have studied the Torah all my life but have never understood it. But now with the Holy Spirit on me I can not only tell you about the Torah; I can explain it to you. I have been going to the synagogue and arguing with the priests ever since I have come back to Jerusalem. Every day they seem to get more and more agitated with my boldness. I have proved them wrong on every subject that has arisen. At one point they sent for the soldiers to come arrest me, but the brothers found out about it and helped me escaped the barbarians. The apostles said that it might be better if I was to go preach in my hometown of Tarsus. So here I go again on another journey, but at least it is for the Lord. I am being taken to Caesarea, from there I will catch a boat going to Tarsus. "I thank you, brothers; may we see each other again."

I have been serving the Lord alone in the Tarsus area for five years now. I have seen some good progress, and then I have seen some bad times. I have been preaching in the temples and using my talents in tent making. It is just enough to keep me from going hungry.

I had forgotten how beautiful the region of Cilicia was, gentle hills giving way to fertile plains. The river Cydnus runs swiftly along from the Tarsus mountains. Cleopatra came down that the river to meet up with Mark Antony. That was a big deal back in the olden days. They say her boat was covered in gold and silver. She rode that boat right into town. What a site that had to be.

THE APOSTLES 1ST PERSON A NARRATIVE

"Well, I'll be, look who is here. Brother Barnabas, it is so good to see you again. Let's go have supper and chat about what is going on. You say that more and more people in Antioch are coming to know the Lord? That is so good to hear. Do what? The brothers want me to come back to Antioch and help you? I will be more that glad to. It has become rather lonely here. I have a few good friends that have become believers, but it isn't the same as having the group of brothers that stand behind you."

Look at all the activity in and around this town. It is hustle and bustle all day long. No wonder Barnabas needed help. I haven't been here but a day or two, and I already have been able to bring a couple to know Jesus. Barnabas said that wasn't unusual. I believe that Antioch has around 500,000 inhabitants. Many of the disciples are holding Torah studies all over town. It just makes you feel good. Some of the people are giving us a new name; they call us Christians. Sounds good; I like it.

A prophet predicted that there is going to be a famine. Knowing the brothers are going to need supplies, some of the men of the faith asked if Barnabas and I would take the supplies to the brothers. So of course we went. We finally unloaded all the supplies and felt that we should be going back. I have found a man that is very knowledgeable; his name is John Mark. I believe he would be of great help to us in Antioch, so I am bringing him along.

I am having prayer time and the elders of the church have asked me and Barnabas come to see them. We just got back but I guess if we are needed someplace, then I need to go. "Hello, brothers, am I going on another journey? No, I hadn't heard. Herod is dead? Wow, did someone kill him, he get run over, or what? He got to acting as God, you say?

So God had worms start eating on him, while he was still alive? That would not be a pleasant way to go. The Holy Spirit is telling us we need to go to Seleucia and then over to Cyprus. Since we had brought John Mark to Antioch, we were allowed to take him with us.

We have been traveling for some time now and have reached Antioch Pisidia. The Gospel is reaching the far corners of the world. One of the disciples said that John Mark wanted to talk with us, so I sent for him. J.M. said he had some business that he had to attend to back in Jerusalem, so he was going to have to leave us. I hate to lose him, but sometimes things just can't be helped. I am being given the privilege of speaking in the synagogue to the entire town.

Many miles have been put on this body, and many more are to come. Barnabas and I have been in Iconium, but some of the Jews have stirred up a crowd of people. Barnabas and I slid out by the back gate; we headed towards Lystra. I thought we had got rid of the ones causing trouble in Iconium, but as soon as I started to preach in the synagogue, the group from Iconium and Antioch stirred up the people, and they started stoning me. I am about to go to sleep, but I thank You, Jesus, for allowing me to spread Your Message.

What is this? I am laying on the ground; a lot of my brothers are standing over me. What is going on? They thought I was dead; I thought I was dead. Those idiots just left me. Isn't Jesus great? Let us surprise our brothers and just walk right back into Lystra. "Hello, brothers, don't just stand there with your mouths wide open; let us celebrate our Lord and Savior. Barnabas and I are going to appoint some of you as leaders in the church, okay? As soon as this is done, Barnabas and I are going to head back towards Antioch in Syria."

THE APOSTLES 1ST PERSON A NARRATIVE

I have been in Antioch now for quite some time. I believe I need to go check on some of the congregations that have started in the cities I visited. I will go see if Barnabas wants to go. "Hi, Barnabas, how are you doing? I am going to go see how our brothers are. Would you care to come along? You think we should take John Mark? I'm sorry, but I don't want him to come. Remember, he left us right in the middle of our journey. I know it was family problems, but you need to put the Lord's work ahead of family. If you think he is okay, then you take him by yourself, but he isn't going with me. I will get Silas to help me; he is a good speaker."

Silas and I have arrived now in Lystra; we made a quick stop in Derbe. The brothers are making great strides. Especially one named Timothy, that guy is a ball of fire. "Silas, you think we should take Tim with us? I think he would make a great compliment to our tours. Yes, I know he is of Greek heritage. To satisfy the Jews, I will have to have him circumcised. I don't think that will be a problem. Great."

It is time to go and pray. The last few days a woman has been following us around proclaiming we are servants of God. That's okay, except she is shouting it and we can't give a decent message which is getting rather annoying. Here she comes again; I'm not going to put up with it anymore. I look straight into her eyes and say, "Demon, remove yourself from this women." I am amazed. The demon just left; it didn't make the women foam at the mouth or throw her on the ground but just left. Now maybe we can preach the message. "Who are you? Let go of me. Silas, are they bothering you? You own that women and you say I have taken your livelihood away from you?" I am now standing in front of the magistrate being accused of subversive activities.

I hadn't planned on spending a night in the jail, but it won't be the last time this happens I imagine. It is amazing that when they are flogging me it doesn't hurt as bad as it should. Jesus is taking a lot of the pain from me. I guess they must be through because they are untying us. The soldiers are about to pull my hair out. "I'm coming; there's no use dragging us." Man, they really must be mad at us; we have been put in the middle of the jail with no windows or air vents. It is pitch dark in here. Silas and I both have shackles on our legs. "Silas, you okay? Good, I believe it is time to pray, you agree? I hear other people in here. You other prisoners, let me tell you about my Lord and Savior..."

It must be getting close to midnight, I don't hear any sounds coming from above. What was that? I think we are having an earthquake, a big one I'm afraid. "Silas, I think my shackles have come off. How about you? We must stay here, all you other prisoners stand down." I haven't said that since I left the military, but it fit. Here comes the jailer. His light is showing that the door to the cell is wide open. He can't see us. "Hold on, sir. Don't kill yourself; we all are here." Here he comes in with his light shining on us. "Get up, sir, let us tell you about Jesus. Thank you for allowing us to stay at your house. A very good gesture. That ointment feels good on those sores from the beating. Thank you. We will hide here until daybreak. All of you want to be baptized? Praise the Lord.

"It is daylight now, so you must go to work. The magistrate said to release us and send us away. I think you need to tell the magistrate come tell us himself, because he is in deep trouble. Silas and I both are Roman citizens, and we did not get a fair trial. You go and tell him."

It seems like I have been on the road forever. I left Lydia and went to Thessalonica, and then I went down to Berea. They were a lot friendlier there than the Thessalonians were. Now I am in Athens. Silas and Tim were asked to stay for awhile in Berea. I miss them already, but they are to come meet me later. I am going to Corinth.

This is a neat little town; I like it. I must get over to the synagogue and start preaching. These Jews are very upbeat. There is a lot of discussion going on, but I can't seem to break through to them. I did meet a couple of believers, Aquila and his wife Priscilla. They have invited me to stay with them; they are tentmakers just like I was. Aquila gave me some work to help me survive.

I think I need to be going on, because there is too much animosity from the Jews. I will do this in the morning; right now I need sleep. Prayer time. "Jesus, be with me as I travel tomorrow. Do what? You don't want me to leave? Go stay with a man name Titius Justus; he lives next to the synagogue? I need to write a letter to the Thessalonians? But since Silas and Timothy have caught up with me, I am going to change my preaching and start preaching to the Gentile?"

I am back in Antioch, feels good. But I know I will have to go out once again because of all the work that needs to be done. Before I do go out, I need to write a few letters to my brothers. I'll write to Corinth again; then I need to write to Ephesus and Thessalonica. I will write a few encouraging words to Galatia and Philippi also.

Now I'm ready; I will head out to Macedonia and then go to Greece. So much work to do. I am blessed to have so many brothers that are well-versed in the Scriptures with me. Timothy is among them; what a fine young gentleman. A couple of Thessalonians, Aristarchus and Secundus, are following along. I must give a speech of encouragement to the brothers, but I am going to wait till midnight to start.

Look at all the brothers gathered to hear me and send me off with their love; it makes me warm all over. Even little ones are here with their fathers. It is midnight, so I will begin. Seems like the Holy

Spirit has taken over for me, I have run out of words. What is the commotion in the back? A little one has fallen out of the window. It is three stories up; how is he? Oh my, they say he is dead. Let me go down to him. I must put him in my arms. "Son, wake up!" When the boy jumped up, the brothers were astonished and began to shout praises to the Lord. I must go down to the port and catch my boat. I have to hurry. I have a long way to go, and I want to be in Jerusalem by Passover. This is going to be a sad journey, for I must tell everyone this is going to be the last time they will see me.

My normal procedure is to first go to the temple or synagogue and preach, but I feel I must find the other apostles. I need to give a report. One of the apostles is approaching. I see him clearly now; it is James. "Hello, James, so good to see you. Yes, I have a good report. You know where the others are, so I will follow you to them.

"Thank you all for inviting me in. How are you all doing? I had a wonderful time, a few bumps here and there, but our Savior always pulled us through. Yes, it is true; I was stoned and left for dead . . . Brothers, I feel the Holy Spirit leading me to preach in the temple; so if you don't mind, I will take a leave of absence for now. I will be back."

There was an issue about purification for a few days but I think it has been resolved. I speak not only to the Jews but also to the Gentiles. For the Lord said that He loves all mankind. "What is it you are trying to accuse me of? No, I have not defiled the temple; I did not take the Gentiles in. Why did you follow me all the way from Asia? You are hypocrites, always stirring up trouble. And for what am I being arrested? I don't think the tribune is aware as to what he is doing. He has bound me up, and that is a no-no to a Roman citizen. A centurion is getting ready to flog me. Sir, is it lawful now for a Roman citizen who has not been condemned to be flogged?" You should have seen his face when I asked this; he took off to talk with the tribune. Here they come back; that guy don't look so good. He said that I am going to be extradited to Caesarea, so the big wigs can deal with me. Good grief, I must be some bad dude. Look at all the soldiers, must be over two hundred, a lot of them riding horses. "A little overkill isn't it? I see. I didn't know this. The Asian Jews were going to ambush a small detail and kill me? Well, thank you, I didn't know I was going to have a horse too." I think the tribune is trying to make up for his mistake.

I am now in front of Felix; he is the governor. I might have a chance here. Felix is real familiar with the way. I guess we are waiting on the priests from Jerusalem to arrive. Felix said that I was to remain in custody, but not in prison. I could have freedom to move around but couldn't leave the house. I could even have friends over. The Jews are presenting their case against me, but I don't think the governor is buying all of it.

I heard that Agrippa was coming to town; I might have to go in front of him. I have no idea but I do know that he is not persuaded by a bunch of Jews. Here comes some soldiers now; I have been invited to stand before Agrippa and present my case. So I am going to give it all for my defense. I have to listen to the hypocrites give their falsehoods. I think I will take a nap. Boring.

The king and all his cabinet are getting up. They are leaving; I guess he has heard enough. Here comes the soldiers; they handle me with care this time. I thought maybe I was going to be set free but instead I was taken to the port. One of the soldiers told me I was going to be sent to Rome. I don't think that is a wise idea, but I must do as I'm told. After all, it is early winter, and the storms are so unpredictable this time of the year. Several prisoners have been loaded, but the centurion has made me comfortable, separate from the others.

GEORGE A REGISTER

We have been at sea now several days; the breeze is carrying a chill to it. A storm is starting to occur. The winds are throwing us back and forth and up and down; the winds are getting stronger and stronger. What makes it so bad is it is dark. You can't see your nose in front of your face. We do know there are rocks not too far off of the bow of the ship. "Look out!" One of the masts has just come crashing down. That was close. The soldiers are wanting to kill all of us that are prisoners. If we were to escape, they would be executed themselves. The centurion stopped them from doing that; I assured him that not a single life would be taken by the storm. About that time, we ran on some rocks and got stranded. I must give the centurion credit; he devised a plan. He first had the soldiers swim ashore; then he had us prisoners swim ashore. That way, no one escaped. Although it was rainy and cold some of the natives on the island brought firewood and welcomed all of us.

I wanted to help, so I am going after some firewood. There was plenty of it on the shore. I found a pile about right to handle, so I scooped it up. I was putting the wood on the fire when a snake came out of the pile and bit me. I shook the snake off of me, and it went into the fire. "What are you staring at? Yes, the snake bit me. No, I feel nothing from it. My arm isn't swelling." Gospel moment. I am sitting by the fire keeping warm and talking with a man name Publius; I think he is the chief around here. He just happened to mention that his father was running a fever and had dysentery real bad. I asked if I could see him; the chief said that it wasn't safe to see him as I would more than likely get the illness too. I am not concerned with myself but would like to help him. As I walked into the small hut, a man was laying on the ground shivering. I walked over to him and laid my hand on him, and speaking to Jesus I asked that he be healed from this affliction. Immediately he stopped shaking and sat up in his blanket. As soon as the other people on the island heard about this, let's just say, I was busy the rest of the day. I was able to spread the Gospel to the whole island.

THE APOSTLES 1ST PERSON A NARRATIVE

I didn't think we would ever get to Rome; our ship has been three months out to sea. But here we are; it feels good to put my feet on solid ground. I have been given the freedom to preach all over Rome. Everyone knows where I live, and they all come by to hear my teachings. I like to walk around while I teach, but these leg irons prohibit a lot of movement. I am tied to a soldier too and sometimes they are reluctant to let me go too far. You see, they have to walk with me. Most of them, they change every four hours, listen, but others act like knuckleheads and won't budge. When that happens, I call the centurion over and the soldier moves with me, amazing. I really have a lot of freedom but not complete freedom. My brothers come by and give me food. They also take care of the premises, and these houses always need some kind of repair. Other brothers will stop by and give me reports about their journeys, and how God has blessed them. I get itchy feet every time they give the report. I know I'm getting older, but I still have that yearning to travel.

It has been two years now that I have been under house arrest. My friend, Luke, who has stayed with me through thick and thin, has helped me so much. I have written several letters to the congregations in places like Ephesus, Colossae, and Philippi. While I was writing these letters, Luke wrote my adventures down.

I guess this is to be another beautiful day; I had a very restful night's sleep. I need to pray. I always do, you know, first thing every morning. Then after the good Lord gives me the message for that day, I eat my breakfast. I love this time of day; because it is cooler, and I'm energized to the max and ready to meet the believers. Many of these people have come from far away; they have heard about the message being presented and the healing that is carried on. Some of them are relatives of the soldiers that are chained to me; they get somebody to go tell them about it and they come. A lot of the soldiers will apologize to me for keeping me in chains. No need for that. I have been able to preach and teach to a lot of people that otherwise would not have heard about Jesus. It is time for the changing of the soldiers. What is this? A whole platoon is coming this morning? Most of the time, it is only a couple of guards. This morning, I would say, twenty or so, are coming. "Good morning, soldiers. Centurion, good to see you. Why so many this morning? You want me to go with you? Nero wants to see me? Oh my, that is never good. Maybe I will be able to see my Jesus today.

"Yes, sir, I am Saul, the one they call Paul of Tarsus. Yes, sir, we have met on several occasions. Yes, I have been detained under house arrest for two years. No, sir, I have not been found guilty of any crime. Thank you, sir, it will feel good not having these leg irons on. I must say I will miss some of the guards though. I hope they come around and say hello once in awhile."

I'm free! I'm free! Thank you, Lord Jesus! I'm free! I think the first thing I'll do is go speak with the brothers at their places. "Hey, Luke, look no leg irons. I'm free. Yes, it is time for a celebration. Most of the others are out in the field spreading the Word, but that is all right. I believe the good Lord is wanting me to adventure out. I'm going to go to some of the congregations I helped start. The brothers are in need of some encouragement. First, I'll go to Corinth and then on down to Ephesus." How great to be able to breath the fresh open air. Even the dust clouds caused by passing horsemen smells good. I'm still a little wobbly on my feet when I walk. The leg irons were heavy and I keep wanting to raise my legs way up. I don't think I could win a race right now. Of course, I couldn't have won a race before the leg irons. Wait a minute. A great heaviness has just come over me; it's like I'm in leg irons again. What is going on? I can't put one foot in front of the other. I need to pray.

"I'm sorry, Luke; I'm not to go to the congregations right now. I need to head back towards Rome, catch a boat, and head to Crete. There is a brother there that needs me. Once again, I tried to do what I wanted to do, but Jesus had other ideas for me.

"Hello, Brother Titus, it is good to see you again. Yes, being free has many advantages. Our Lord and Savior guided me here to see to your problem. You have not any elders in your congregations? Looks like everything is a shambles as far as organization is concerned. I will help as much as I can, but I'm not to stay very long. We shall go from town to town and appoint leaders in the organizations.

"I am sorry, Brother Titus, but I have to leave for another assignment in Nicopolis. I must leave immediately. Stay firm in the faith, brother; you are doing a great job."

I guess boat rides are better than walking, but I hate the rolling up and down. I should be in Nicopolis in a few days. I need pen and papyrus to write instructions for Titus to follow. I will send it back to him when I reach shore. One of my disciples will carry it. The Lord has commanded me to evangelize this country. So while I am here, I might as well preach over in the Acarnania region also.

The people here are friendly but not interested in the Gospel. Many of the priests from the local synagogues try to disrupt my preaching, but a lot of times they will ask questions. Some send the temple guards out to run us off. Never works though. I need to get back to Nicopolis; I have a meeting with a couple of brothers there.

"If you will look over your right shoulder you will see a group of guards coming our way. There are more than usual this time, which by now, you know means trouble. All we can do is pray." These aren't temple guards either. They are government guards. Here we go again with wrist irons this time. May I ask where we are headed? I have caused too much trouble here, so you are taking me back to Rome? I have heard Nero is on the warpath against Christians. All we want is to give everyone an opportunity to know the love and care that Jesus is ready to give. How long am I to stay in jail here in Nicopolis? I thought you said we were going to Rome?" I need more papyrus and another pen; I must write to Timothy again.

I have arrived in Rome once more, stuck in prison this time, buried in a far corner that way I have no contact with people. I can't preach or teach from here, but I can say that I have given it a good fight. Here come the guards. "Guys, careful, I have these leg irons on and can't move that fast. Does it make you feel better to drag me? Why're you going to beat me? Nero really has a mad on, doesn't he? Ouch! Whip me all you want; I can rest assured I will be with my Savior. How about you? Where are you going?

"You are breaking your own laws. You have bound me, and I am a Roman citizen, which, my friend, is against your law. You've torn my back to shreds, but I feel no pain. I have become numb to your punishments. Oh, now you are dragging me? You are dragging me behind your horse? Oh, Jesus, is it time for me to come to You?" Look at me. I'm a total mess. My back, legs, and shins are bleeding like crazy, but I feel nothing. "I have my eyes upon you, Lord. I see now. As a citizen, you can't crucify me, but you can behead me? I lay my head on this block in the name of Jes . . ."

CPSIA information can be obtained
at www.ICGtesting.com
Printed in the USA
LVOW04s0011200516
489119LV00001B/1/P